Children
of a
FIRELAND

Children
of a
FIRELAND

A NOVEL

———

GARY PAK

A LATITUDE 20 BOOK

University of Hawai'i Press
HONOLULU

To Merle

I would like to thank the staff at University of Hawai'i Press and
especially my editor, Masako Ikeda, for her unwavering support
and patience; the Van Gogh Club members for their great talk,
insights and swims; Rob Wilson for his brotherly watchfulness;
the Bamboo Ridge study group; and Kapi'olani Community
College and the Department of English, UHM.

And all my love and devotion to Mom and Pop; my life partner,
Merle; and BozuBoy, Hey Man!, and Boogie for their everlasting
gifts of pure love.

Library of Congress Cataloging-in-Publication Data

Pak, Gary
    Children of a fireland : a novel / Gary Pak.
        p. cm.
    ISBN 0-8248-2836-4 (pbk.)
    1. Hawaii—Fiction. I. Title.
    PS3566.A39C48 2004
    813'.54—dc22

                          2004047112

Designed by Trina Stahl
Printed by Versa Press

One

T HE LAST SHOWING at old Kānewai Theater was to a crowd
of two. The movie playing was George Lucas's *The
Empire Strikes Back*. Earlier in the week, the first showing of
the movie drew a crowd of twenty-three, and each night thereafter the crowd diminished by half. It didn't help that the
movie was showing after premiering seven years earlier in a
more posh theater one town over. And it didn't help the theater's turnstile that most of the young folks of the community
would rather hang out at the new bowling alley or the family
billiards parlor than at the theater to see the latest third-run
movie. And, anyway, when there was a new movie to see,
most of the residents would make the trip to Honolulu and
pay five dollars for admission, more than three times what
they would pay for a ticket at the Kānewai Theater. The downtown theaters were always air-conditioned and reasonably
clean, though one thing that the Kānewai Theater had over
its ultramodern rivals was its fresh popcorn. The old-timers
always made the point that you couldn't get better-tasting
popcorn than at the theater's concession, which made its own
popcorn from scratch using a popper purchased secondhand
from a renovated Savoy in Brooklyn. The uniquely good taste
of the popcorn came from the touch of sesame oil and pul-
verized Hawaiian salt that were used to flavor the butter. And
at fifty cents a bag, it was a bargain that was hard to pass up.

The old theater, the first on the windward side of the
island, had seen better days. The doors had initially opened to
the public in 1946. Those days the showings started on Thurs-

day and ran to Tuesday, with matinees on the weekends at noon and 4:00 P.M. People from miles around came to the theater on horses and in buggies; and, later, with the popularization of the automobile, in cars. The walls of the building were constructed with crushed-coral hollow tile and its roof was covered with corrugated iron sheeting that was painted a metallic avocado green; when it rained, the projectionist had to turn up the volume so that people could hear over the drumming from above.

The original owner of the theater was Casey Akana, the only son of a prominent Chinese-Hawaiian family in Kānewai who had owned several sizable properties in Kānewai before the big earthquake. He had left the islands in the late thirties and went to a small liberal arts college in upper state New York. Dropping out during his third year following an unfortunate relationship with the son of the college president, he bought a one-way train ticket to New York City and joined a small off-Broadway company, getting bit parts in a few productions but being mainly the company's all-purpose techie. After seven years of living hand-to-hand and being frustrated professionally—at best, the only acting parts he could get were that of Oriental servants and the like—he began yearning for the country living in Kānewai and the life of leisure and dignity that he had taken for granted, being the son of rich parents. He returned home for good right before the war ended. Back in Kānewai and immediately missing the social life of New York, he cajoled and finally won over his mother to manipulate his father into liquidating a large portion of the family's land holdings. With this small fortune, he built a theater on a small leftover parcel in the middle of the town. In three years he was forced to sell out because poor management had turned the theater into a disastrously losing business.

The theater was bought by Wah Lau Ching, the autocratic family head who owned one of the two grocery stores in Kānewai. One son, Hennesey, was the town drunk and dunce, denounced by the senior Ching as "unworthy to be part of my family" (translation from the Cantonese). Early one Sunday morning, while driving to Mass, Claudio Yoon saw him wading out on the mudflats, and that was the last time anyone in Kānewai ever saw him again. With the help of his other son Hiram, Mr. Ching began the renovation of the front of the theater, which Hiram finished after his father's death only three weeks into the project. Two small commercial store fronts were added; a carpet of deep carmine was laid in the lobby and aisles; and the exterior of the theater was repainted in a Kaiser pink, according to the wishes of Mr. Ching. One year and one day after his father's death, Hiram hired Paul Navarro to repaint the theater a light sienna. One of the store fronts became storage for the theater, and the other was rented to Mr. Pedro Rizon, a barber, who stayed in that location for forty-three years. Rizon gave the best scissors-cut this side of the Koʻolaus, and for twenty-seven years no one could find a better bargain than his fifty-cent haircut.

The last showing was announced in a one-by-two-inch ad in the local daily. Nobody in the community seemed to care, for the theater had lost its purpose, which was to provide *the* source of Hollywood entertainment in town, years before. For every household now had at least one television with a VCR and almost all subscribed to some form of cable TV service. And, if anyone wanted to see the latest movie, all that it took was a trip to Honolulu, an excellent excuse for a family to go holoholo.

Three months before the announcement, negotiations were fast being finalized by the Ching family with a fast-food corporation based in Carson City, Nevada—Mama Mason's Country Fried Chicken & Tacos. There were already three franchises in Honolulu and another on a neighbor island, and this would be the first one on the windward side. The Chings had given Mama Mason a twenty-five-year lease, which would give them a gross income of $3.6 million. The plans called for the tearing down of the ancient structure one month after the last showing and the start of construction shortly after. Everything seemed to be on schedule until the signs started coming up on the side of the theater, one week after the theater officially closed its doors.

No one knew who was spraypainting the graffiti, and everyone wanted to know. The signs started innocently enough. The first graffiti was a large red heart with the words "Richard 'n Cindy" inside. People smiled or laughed at the sign, for they knew that the names were for Richard Cordeiro and Cynthia Naelehu, who later became Cynthia Cordeiro. There followed others—"Katie 'n Norton," "Lance 'n Lily," "Harry 'n Amy"—who were all legitimately paired off. Everyone thought it was a big joke, someone playing a nostalgic prank using the side of the condemned theater, which had once been the social gathering spot for the entire community. But it became disturbing when other messages started showing up on the wall, like "Charley McKinley's father is not his real father," and "Bobby Kim 'n Sandy Wakashida" (who were both happily married, but not to each other), and "Matilda Nunes got pregnant in Row 37" (whose only child, Jason, was told that his father had died in Vietnam), and so on.

———

"I t'ink is da humbug boy doing all dis," said George Hayashida, referring to Kalani Humphrey, the community bad boy.

"How can?" his wife, Joyce, remarked. She cracked two eggs in the hot cast-iron frying pan. George liked his eggs with the yolks intact and the whites just turning solid around them. "He in jail."

"But den mus' be one of his friends coming 'round and putting up dose signs, making trouble. Maybe he wen go visit da bastard in jail and da bastard wen tell him put up dose kine stupid signs, fo' make trouble fo' everybody, like he always doing."

Joyce Hayashida shrugged her shoulders, though nodding her head in tentative agreement. No one could pass any fair judgment on Kalani Humphrey. He had earned his notoriety by ripping off almost every other household in the community. He had knocked up at least a half dozen maidens of the town. He even stole twenty dollars from his great-grand-father's coin purse when he was eight years old, though he didn't know that the old blind man was a relation. Nobody liked Kalani Humphrey, and whenever something went wrong in Kānewai, it seemed that somehow Kalani Humphrey was connected to it.

"But you know," Joyce Hayashida reflected, "he been in prison fo' t'ree years already. I dunno if he wen do 'em."

"If I say he did it, then he did it," George growled. He gave an extra stir to his coffee. "I know he did it. If he nevah do it, den wouldn't have no mo' stupid signs like on da side like dat."

Joyce shook her head, her lips pursed. It wasn't worth arguing with her husband. Let him think he always right, she thought. Then she broke the egg yolks and turned off the stove.

———————

WHEN HIRAM CHING and a representative of Trinity Corporation, the mother company of Mama Mason's Country Fried Chicken & Tacos, went to inspect the premises early one morning, they could not get in. A six-foot-high pile of garbage was pressed against the front glass doors from the inside. Hiram Ching went to the back to unlock the door, but this door, too, would not budge.

"Damn vandals," he quipped to Mr. Henderson, the representative of Trinity.

"Do you have problems like this all the time?" Henderson looked a bit worried.

"No—no—no—no," Hiram rattled off. "This the first time. Kānewai is one peaceful town. We cleaned up our act long time ago. All the bad elements either left town or in jail right now." For a moment he thought of Kalani Humphrey. He shook his head, thinking how stupid he had been to hire the Humphrey boy as an usher a few years back; the boy had scammed him by taking in kids for half the price and pocketing the rest of the money.

"Is there any other way into the building?" an irritated Henderson asked.

"Yeah-yeah. Let me think." Hiram tried the back door again, then sighed and led Henderson to the side of the building, where there were two windows, one for the women's restroom and the other for the men's.

"What's all this?" Henderson asked, referring to the graffiti-covered walls.

"Ahh . . . just some of the young punks around here. They don't have anything else to do."

"Do you have problems with graffiti? I thought you said you didn't have problems with vandals?"

"No, not really."

"Then what's all this?"

"Must be the work of outsiders coming in. This the only time we been getting this. Like I told you, this community is real quiet and peaceful."

The window to the women's restroom was ajar. Hiram placed an empty wooden box under the window of the men's restroom, which was locked shut, and stepped up on the box. He slipped one of his keys under the lower edge of the window and ran it to the middle to find the lock.

"What are you doing?" Henderson asked, looking at the other, open window.

"I'm going inside," Hiram answered, thinking to himself how stupid the haole was, though he didn't think it necessary to explain that it was improper to enter the building through the women's side.

"But . . ."

Before Henderson could verbalize his thought, the lock popped free. Hiram pried the window open with his fingertips, then wiggled his pear-shaped body through the opening and climbed in, balancing on a narrow ledge inside the window. Catching his breath for a few seconds, he stepped down from the ledge, misnegotiated a shadow as a foothold, and fell to the concrete floor. But it was a small fall, and no physical damage was done.

"Come inside," Hiram puffed, picking himself up from the floor and dusting off his jacket.

"Why don't you open the back door for me?"

Hiram muttered an "Okay," but not without feeling like a guinea pig. He shook off the remaining dust and dirt from his pants, picked up the pen and bits of paper notes that had fallen out of his shirt pocket, then proceeded to the auditorium. He passed the entrance to the women's restroom with a touch of apprehension, for though he never personally saw or experienced it, he was very aware of the many stories about a milk-white, faceless apparition that appeared behind the backs of women touching up their makeup in the mirror. It became a common practice for them to use the restroom in pairs. Hiram's hands became sweaty and his heart skipped a beat. No, there's no ghost here, he reasoned to himself, but that couldn't settle the skin crawling on the back of his neck.

In the semi-darkness, he felt his way along the hallway to the switch box and turned on the interior lights, then entered the auditorium, where his nostrils were smacked with the awful odor of cheap perfume. It was as if someone had dumped an entire bottle right in the middle of the room. He swore loudly at the vandals whom he was sure had broken into the theater and committed this foul-smelling play. Later in the afternoon, he told himself, he'd see Val Rodriguez, slip him a twenty, and ask him to visit the pool hall and find out who among the punks did it. Then he'd slip Val another twenty, and Val would know what to do with those bums. Hiram nodded and smiled in selfish glee as he visualized Val busting their heads.

But he stopped in the middle of an upbeat of an assuring nod. Slashed in bright red paint on the baseboard of the movie screen was a message in large, bold letters: "KALANI HUMPHREY WENT SLEEP WITH CLARISSA IN THE LADY'S BATHROOM."

For a moment, he actually had some doubts about his wife, but he shook off his uncertainty and cursed at the ridiculous fiction of the punks.

Henderson was pounding at the back door.

Hiram rushed to the janitor's closet and took out a bottle of cleaning fluid and raced back to the sign. But no matter how hard he scoured, the paint wouldn't rub off. Henderson was now pounding and shouting for Hiram to open up. Hiram hoofed it to the front office and brought back a fresh gallon of paint. Using an old mop, he sloshed the paint over the graffiti, then hid the paint and mop in the janitor's closet. He hurried to the back door, which had been latched from the inside, and let Henderson in.

"How come it took you so long?" Henderson asked, scanning the dim interior for clues.

"Oh, I had to do something."

"I hope you didn't start painting the interior," the representative of Trinity Corporation commented, noticing a splash of paint on Ching's right hand. "Smells like fresh paint in here."

Ching thought quickly, rubbing off some of the paint on his hand on a wall. "Ah—the stupid janitor—he was painting the wall and he never tell me about the wet paint." He laughed and before Henderson could pry more said, "Tell me, why you want to look inside the building for anyway?" He wished he had thought of the question earlier.

"Well," an observing Henderson began as they entered the auditorium, "my company thought that we might keep the existing structure if it was unique in design, but . . ." He turned to the stage and regarded the ratty drapery for a moment. "But from the looks of what I've seen so far, this building is just four tile walls and an old rusty roof. I think our best bet is to tear it down, rather than renovate an old junk building."

Ching nodded his head, then led the representative of Trinity on a short tour of the projection room.

———

THE GRAFFITI ON the outside walls continued, becoming progressively more scandalous.

"HARRY AND ELLA HAVE NOT DONE IT IN EIGHT AND A HALF YEARS."

"PAUL NAVARRO AND CASSIE CHUN USED TO MEET EVERY THURSDAY IN ROW FORTY-FOUR." (Thursday nights were Pat Navarro's night for blackjack with her friends; her husband was a member of the Thursday Night Jackpot Bowling League.)

"WHERE IS DICKEY BOY JR.?"

"I THINK I going down there and burn da friggin' building down," Richard Pimente said to his wife Jackie, setting down the Saturday morning paper on the breakfast table. He had browsed over the baseball box scores without paying attention to whether his favorite teams had won or not. "Is one real eye sore. All dat graffiti on da side wall."

"Why you so concerned about all that?" Jackie said. She stirred the cream into her third cup of coffee. "You never was before. Did you tell Darren and Micah that breakfast is ready?"

"Yeah, but is different now."

"What is different?"

"Because—because—" He reopened the newspaper, searching for a good excuse. "Because how da hell Ching going sell da property to da Mama Mason outfit if get all dis kine vandalism all over da building?"

"Ching already signed it over to the restaurant. And anyway, since when you started getting cozy with Ching? I thought you hated his guts. Eh, where are those kids? Playing Nintendo so early in the morning? Did you call them for breakfast?"

"No. But I jus' no can stand dat sneaky old pākē," said the former high-school star lineman. He shook his head, set the newspaper to the side, and sipped his coffee.

Years before marrying Ching, Clarissa Lee had been Richard Pimente's sweetheart, though Clarissa's parents disproved of him. And when Clarissa, the head song leader of the Wilson High School Warriors, had to leave school three months before graduating, Hiram Ching, twelve years her senior, agreed to marry her, but with the ironclad stipulation that the baby had to be put up for adoption.

The couple was silent for a minute, Richard going back to his newspaper and Jackie staring into space.

"Honey, who you think is putting up all those signs?" Jackie asked.

Richard put down his newspaper. "You asking me? I dunno. But I sure as hell would like to know. I string da buggah up so fast if I find out, faster den he can say 'I nevah do it.'"

—————

IT PAINED CLARISSA Ching to hear rumors about how bad her son was. She knew he wasn't born a bad egg. It just wasn't fair that everyone in the community had written him off even when he was just a little boy. And it pained her more that it had been impossible for her to take care of him when he needed it the most. She had seen how the Humphreys, that childless, elderly haole couple, schoolteachers for many years at Wilson High, were not suited to the raising of children. They were too strict; they refused to feed him when he was bad; and they punished him severely when he peed in his bed. Their abusive tendencies were so widely known that Father Rosehill from the Catholic parish had visited them at least twice, even though the Humphreys were Congregationalists, and pleaded them to be more tolerant of their son's hyperactivity. And through this all, Clarissa was unable to come to her son's rescue, for the agreement that had been made was the Humphreys would adopt the baby only if Clarissa never exposed herself as the boy's true mother. Though she hated the Humphreys and herself for making that promise, Clarissa was a woman of her word, and this hurt her terribly.

—————

"YOU KNOW, ALL dis is very, very strange," Matt Goo was saying to Freddie Tanaka at Freddie's service station, which was just a traffic light down from the theater. The two men were sitting on the removed back seat of a '69 Dodge Dart set in the front of the station. Freddie was listening with his short, hairy arms folded, the fingers of his right hand rubbing the left elbow. "You know, all dis business dey putting da blame on Kalani Humphrey. I tell you fo' one plain fact, da Humphrey boy is in jail. And one nada fact—"

"Try wait," Freddie Tanaka interrupted, unfolding his arms. "I get one customer." Freddie went out to the pumps and filled up the gas tank of a tourist car. Upon returning, he said, "What you was saying again?"

"I dunno. What I was saying?"

"About da Humphrey boy. You think he not da one who doing all dis."

"Yeah. I no think he doing all dis. How can? Fo' one, he in jail. And fo' one nada fact, how he know all dis stuff he putting up on da wall?"

Freddie nodded his head in agreement. He chased a fly off his arm. "Then who you think da buggah doing all dis, then?" Freddie asked.

Matt sipped a can of soda. "I dunno. Maybe is da ghost haunting da moviehouse."

Freddie switched his rubbing to the other elbow. "Could be," he said.

It was a well known fact that a ghost—or something— was or had been living in the theater. The old-timers pointed to the fact that the theater had been foolishly constructed next to an ancient Hawaiian pathway to a heiau. Some said that the ghost was the spirit of Casey Akana, coming back to haunt Hiram Ching, whose father had bankrupted him and thus forced him to sell the theater at a loss.

"If I was Ching," Matt said, "I wouldn't knock down da building."

"Why?"

"'Cause if I was him, I no like die."

"Whachu mean?"

Matt Goo shook his head slowly. "If he break down the

building, maybe da ghost might . . ." Matt didn't have to finish the sentence; Freddie was nodding his head in agreement. Then he got up with the arrival of another tourist car.

———————

IT WAS BECOMING a community habit—or rather, passion—to visit the theater's wall on a daily basis. It was becoming, for many of the residents, a kind of daily bulletin board of gossip. For every day—no miss—a new quip of scandal would be painted on the wall. It was becoming customary to drive by there, even if it was out of the way, to see the latest news of the unexpected. And it was becoming acerbically amusing for the others to witness what the backstabbing messages were doing to the marital stability of those individuals selected as targets, though deep down inside each and every resident who had not as yet been elected for representation was the fear that perhaps the next time around his or her name might grace the wall.

A small group from the bowling league became so concerned with the lambasting that they decided to organize a twenty-four-hour vigil at the theater. Their stated intention was to catch the vandals, because "all they want to do is make trouble fo' our town." Of course, the real reason behind the forming of the group was to contain any further disruption that would threaten the stability of their organization. One of their own, Paul Navarro, had been exposed. It would be only a matter of time, if this was allowed to continue, that the unstated purpose of the group for a significant minority of its members—that of providing an alibi for their extramarital activities—would be exposed.

So they organized an around-the-clock watch one weekend, divided into four-hour shifts, with the robust determination to nab the troublemaking sign-maker. Tiny Vierra, all 267 pounds of him, pulled the first evening shift on the Friday, from 6:00 to 10:00, sitting in the darkness of his parked pickup across the street from the wall. And everything went well during Claudio Yoon's 10:00 P.M. to 2:00 A.M. slot; the watch was as quiet as the man himself. (As a fine example of the group, Claudio was not the cheating type. To be exact, he had no one to cheat on.) And things were going routine for Henry Kila—up to the time he dozed off for a few minutes, an hour before the end of his shift. Quintin Lee arrived for his shift forty-five minutes early to talk story with his good friend, bringing along fast-food breakfast and coffee, and noticed Henry snoring and a freshly painted sign gleaming and dripping from the wall. Silently he read the sign, then began laughing loudly, then cursing after dropping one extra large coffee (he had bought four) on his foot. Henry was wakened by Quintin's painful, unholy deprecations to the gods of defecation and jumped to attention. The off-duty firefighter habitually grabbed for his pants and boots before realizing where he was.

"Whas so funny," a dopey Henry asked, scratching his head, "and whas wit' da racket? Gimme one coffee."

"I thought you was supposed to be watching da place?"

"So I wen nod out fo' couple minutes. So what?"

"Couple minutes?! Couple minutes is couple minutes, brah. Couple minutes was enough fo' dis. Look." Quintin pointed to the new sign and began laughing.

Henry read the sign out loud. "HIRAM CHING JAGS OFF IN HIS OFFICE WITH HIS DIRTY BOOKS." A smile came to Henry's chunky face and he laughed guardedly with Quintin. Then he was quiet. A concerned look came to his face, and he aspirated a sour "Shit."

"Whas dah mattah?" Quintin asked.

"Eh, brah. Dis sign gotta come down. Right now. Dis sign no mo' . . . taste."

"Hah? Whas wrong wit' dis?"

Henry shuffled his feet. He looked up at the sign, the whites of his eyes reddened and wide and begging with a simple innocence. "Stuff like dis . . . is private. No man in his right mind wants da world to know he whacking off on da side."

"But everybody jag off. Whas so secret 'bout dis?"

"Dis not moral, not in good taste."

Quintin looked hard at Henry, who was now regarding the sign with a strained expression, as if he was becoming more and more emotionally attached to it. Quintin was about to say something about the morality of Henry's extramarital activities since the birth of his third daughter, but decided against it. It wasn't the time and place to argue with a disturbed Henry Kila, who was known for his slow-burning fuse and a fist that could break burning bricks in half. "Yeah, maybe you right," Quintin conceded. "But what we going do?"

Henry silently went to the wall and touched the fresh paint with a fingertip, then sniffed the tainted finger. "Oil paint," he said to no one. "Who use oil-base in dis day and age?"

Quintin touched and smelled, too. "Smell like old paint."

"And da buggah use da same kine all over." Henry scanned the wall of graffiti.

"At least da buggah wen spell da names right." Quintin broke into a laughter that was quickly suppressed when Henry suggested what they must do. "What?" Quintin protested. "How da hell we going do dat? Da sun coming up already."

"Den we gotta work fast. Go call Dennis come down with da stepladder. And Val. Tell him bring some oil paint and brush. You go home and get what you get. Me . . . I stay down here and try cover up." Henry was already trying to smear the tacky paint with his hands, though the paint was already being absorbed into the pores of the wall.

Within a half hour, the gang was repainting the wall, covering all the graffiti. It took them an hour to paint over every bit. But somehow, the most recent message had already leaked out of their circle and had spread through the community grapevine, and a good laugh, as well as a singular degree of pathos, was had by most of the community.

Henry's spontaneous plan to vanquish all the graffiti didn't last too long. Approximately twenty-four hours later, during Dennis Umeda's shift, the sign-maker broke through Dennis's watchdog defense. So jolting to Dennis was the content of the message (now painted in black on white) that he thought he was going to have a heart attack. When he recovered from the shock and the heartburn, he limped off to the pay telephone across the street and called Watson Kamei, who was to relieve him. "Come down now," Dennis said tersely.

"But it only five o'clock," Watson whined, yawning in the phone. "I still get one hour mo'."

"Come down now," Dennis demanded, then hung up.

He waited at the phone booth until he saw Watson's monstrous black four-wheeler trundle to a stop next to his Toyota. Watson had his engine on for nearly a full minute, the headlights of the truck switched to high, lighting up the wall. Finally, he killed the engine and got out. Dennis called from the booth, and Watson crossed the street.

"Whas da meaning of dat?" Watson whispered. "Who did dat?"

"You . . . asking me?"

"You wen fall asleep, too?"

Dennis shook his head. Watson noticed the slight trembling of Dennis's hand, which was still clutching the hung receiver.

"Nah, all dis gotta be part of one big fucking joke," Watson said, smiling as wide as his sleep-stiffened cheeks could give.

Dennis nodded his head. "But what should we do?"

Watson stuffed his hands all the way in the pockets of his blue jeans, rubbing the sides of his testicles. "We gotta go paint 'em over. Das what we gotta do."

Dennis agreed. But before they could cross the street, a sleek white car whizzed by, slowing to check the bulletin board. Though it was moonless and the incandescent light from the streetlamp feeble, the message was brazened by the bleak whiteness of the freshly painted wall: "HIRAM CHING IS

TO DIE." The car stopped, its radiating brake lights gripping the mute, watching men, then sped away.

"Who—dat?" Watson gasped after realizing that he had momentarily stopped breathing. They crossed the street. "You saw who . . . was dat?"

"Was Clarissa Ching," Dennis said. Then he jumped in his car and drove off.

T W O

Hiram Ching died a week later. He was found slumped in a front row seat of the theater. There seemed to have been no foul play involved, though what was strange was that all the doors of the theater were locked from the inside. There was some speculation that Hiram had committed suicide, but the results of his autopsy confirmed that he had died of a massive heart attack. His funeral was well attended by the members of the community, and, as requested in his will, his gravestone was engraved with the epitaph, "I May Be Down Today, But Tomorrow IT Will Rise." The silent majority of the community believed the "IT" referred to the theater's curtains.

Strangely enough, no signs were painted on the wall of the theater. For exactly one week. The new sign sent shivers through every believing member of the community, for though it was directed at no one in particular, the message was meant for everyone. It read: "OTHERS MAY FALL." Soon after, a petition began circulating, calling for Clarissa Ching to expedite the demolition of the building. Though initial signs concerning the shady history of particular members of Kānewai town were malicious and embarrassing, they were also comical. And more important, they were harmless, in the sense of life and death. Now, many feared that the wall was cursed with prophecy, and nearly all the members of the community feared its vision of the future. Reading the graffiti now, as a God-fearing member of the community had suggested to another grandparent while waiting for their grandchildren in the car queue at the end of another school day, was like taking a walk, a step at a time, into the Valley of Death.

There was only one person who was not afraid of that incendiary wall, and that was Gabriel Ho'okano, the younger brother of the late Jacob Ho'okano, the hermit-kahuna of nearby Waiola Valley. He thought that all of the business about the theater was nonsense. In fact, he made the bold assertion that all the jokers who were getting all riled up about the signs on the wall were the very ones who were putting them up. "Dey complaining 'bout da smoke from dey own smokes," he told his common-law wife of forty-nine years, Mary Wahineokekaimalino, in his ever-raspy voice.

Mary nodded her head dutifully, then returned to the subject that she had asked—in her languid though urgent kind of way—Gabriel about three minutes before. "Did you t'row away today's newspepah?"

Gabriel had heard her the first time, but he didn't want to get into any hassle with her, at least not this early in the day. Earlier in the morning, he needed something to wrap up the shit that the neighborhood dogs had left the night before in the front yard, which he had been cleaning up every morning for as long as he could remember. Conveniently, he found the morning newspaper balanced like a seesaw on the edge of the bottom front step. He took a furtive look around, making sure Mary was still in the kitchen getting breakfast ready, then stripped the newspaper of its rubber band, spread the pages out like a mat, and wrapped into a tight ball all the shit that he had collected in his scooper. He never read the newspaper anymore, since Nixon and Watergate, which was around the time he retired from the federal shipyard. There was nothing in it that was worth reading, he believed, and he wasn't really sure why he and Mary kept on subscribing to it. Getting the daily newspaper on their doorstep was just one of those things, like an age-old habit that was hard to break. For the small money that he paid every month, he'd rather just have it keep coming. It was like keeping an old dog around even though it'd only eat and sleep and shit and very infrequently bark at a stranger. As he secured the parcel of shit with the rubber band, he told himself that he would tell Mary that the newspaper wasn't delivered. But later that morning, while relaxing on the porch and gazing into the yard and across the quiet dirt road that fronted the house, he forgot his excuse, and when Mary started asking him about the status of the newspaper, he tossed out a bit of the subject that had been of late clouding his mind, a weak attempt to change the subject.

"Get coupons in today's pepah," Mary continued. "I need them so I can go market this afternoon."

"You know, Kuʻuipo, Ching knocking down his old building actually going bring something good to dis town."

Mary nodded her head again. He probably used the newspaper to wrap the dog you-know-what again, she thought. But she decided not to press her accusation. She liked it when he called her "My Sweetheart"; it made her feel young again, all warm and itchy inside. Even if he one old man, sometimes he can get so romantic, her thoughts sang to her. She began reminiscing about the time they had gone to the beach on their thirtieth anniversary and had made love under a kamani tree. Oh, it was so lovely, even with the nuts falling on them while she giggled and he chuckled. She would wait patiently for the next time he beckoned her. Smiling, she looked at her lover and beamed with pleasure, though she wasn't listening to him, only to her warm thoughts. It didn't matter; sometimes he talked nonsense, sometimes not. At least he still called her Kuʻuipo. This is what mattered the most. And he had never called that to anyone else; this she knew as an asphyxiating truth.

"Dese crazy buggahs," Gabriel continued. "Dey scared of dey own shadow. And who would know 'bout all dis business get on da walls but da very ones who did it, right?" He looked over at Mary and when he got her smiling approval, he pointed to a spot across the street. "Look ovah there . . . try look. You see da spot dey wen miss."

Mary sat up, adjusted her glasses, but could not see—or understand—what Gabriel was referring to. "What you asking about?" she asked.

"There . . . ovah there. You no can see?"

"See what? I just see the grass and the abandon car."

"Das what I mean," Gabriel Ho'okano said, a satisfied smile coming to his face. "Da car. Da car da Humphrey boy wen dump. One '66 Ford Mustang."

"What the car got to do with the signs on the moviehouse wall?"

"Plenny. Da moviehouse is abandon, right? But now worth plenny money, and all going to Ching. Everybody jealous. So everybody like get in da act, like get one piece of cake. And if dey cannot get nothing, dey all going try make Ching get nothing, too. Everybody trying fo' bring everybody else down. Everybody no like see somebody else get up there in da world, you know what I mean? I know dis game by heart. Jus' like da 'a'ama crab pulling down da ada 'a'ama crab from crawling outta da bucket. If dis car ovah there all of a sudden become valuable property, eh, you going find everybody in town coming ovah here and try claim da car as his. Right? Now everybody trying put dey name on the moviehouse 'cause they like get 'em fo' themselves. But dey know dey going get shit. So instead, dey trying make Ching get all piss off, make him lose out. Da mainland company, dey going come here and see all dis trouble happening and dey going back outta da deal."

"Hiram Ching wen ma-ke, you know. One heart at—"

"Den Ching, he going get all piss off, maybe he going jus' kick back and maybe ma-ke, right on da spot."

"But he wen ma-ke already."

"What?"

"Hiram Ching . . . he wen ma-ke two days ago."

"You see, Mary. I was right . . . right?" He sat back in his chair and folded his arms over his chest. "How he wen ma-ke?"

"They said, and this is what Georgette told me, the ghost wen get him at the moviehouse."

Gabriel's eyes stared out over the vacant lot, unblinking, which made Mary uneasy.

"Gabe . . . you okay?"

"Yeah," he said softly.

"I going Georgette's house. I think I can get the coupons from her. What you like for dinner tonight? I going market right after I see Georgette."

Gabriel thought for a long moment, too long for Mary to wait. But as she rose from her seat to leave, her longtime lover stopped her with a request. "Go to da hardware store fo' me and buy me one gallon can paint. White enamel paint."

Three

FLORA GOTO DIDN'T want the old theater to go. She was the very last customer of the theater—actually, she and her husband, Matt, whom she had dragged away from his Thursday night football game. She began to cry fifteen minutes into the movie. By the time the movie ended, those dismal orangey wall lights officially glowing on for the last time, her tears were all used up. But she kept on crying anyway. Matt felt kind of foolish—they being the only ones in the audience—and gently but anxiously tugged at the sleeve of his wife's black silk jacket, which he brought back after a tour in Vietnam. Flora rose slowly from her seat, stroking the worn felt of the chair in front of her as if smoothing out the wrinkles on the clothes of a dear and dead, casket-lain relative. They lumbered into the lobby, and Flora stopped in front of the concession counter—the glass of the display case worn from the uncountable thousands of transactions—and asked Mildred Kahalekua for a bag of popcorn. Mildred told Flora that they had stopped making popcorn for two weeks already, but that there were a couple of boxes of chocolate nuggets that she could have manuahi. Flora thanked her old friend for the complimentary souvenirs, then the two started crying for no good reason—as Matt would have said but didn't since he was also feeling a bit sad, for no real good reason—and Mildred came out from behind the counter, and the two women embraced in their shivers and tears. Matt was feeling foolish watching them, so he went to the usher standing at the door, Henderson Kahalewai, Mildred's husband, and started talking about the football game that Matt had missed, which Henderson had caught snatches of on the portable TV in the projectionist's room, and never once did they dare talk or mention in the slightest about the scrubbed fate of the theater. Finally, when Flora and Mildred were finished, the Gotos left the lobby. Matt chided Flora, who was all out of tears and words and feelings, and they went home, where Matt rewound the videotaped recording of the game on the VCR, a Father's Day gift from his son, and then watched the game he had missed, even though Henderson had told him the score and that his favorite team, the '49ers, had been on the losing end.

When the unlawful graffiti first appeared, temporarily halting the demolition, Flora, of all people, became secretly elated. This was surprising, for she was the secretary to the most conservative circuit court judge in Honolulu; it had always been her longstanding conviction that the law was supreme and anyone breaking it should be punished without a hint of impunity. This sudden, strange reversal came in large part from a desperate hope that the interruption would prevent a nightmare that had been recurring for weeks from turning to a reality.

The nightmare was this: She enters the theater and sits in her favorite seat, halfway down the left aisle to row M and four seats over to the left. White light floods the screen, then there is a shot of the front of the theater. The theater is shaking, as if in the middle of an earthquake, and the roof collapses and the walls tumble inward, followed by a towering cloud of dust and debris. A trumpet, in brazen high squeals of "C," wails in the background. As the dust settles, as the trumpet's sound diminishes to a distant point, a gilded platform rises from the wreckage, pink satiny sheets flowing and flapping on all sides. On it, a naked couple. Kalani Humphrey thrusting into a writhing and gasping Clarissa Ching.

———

BEYOND GABRIEL HOʻOKANO'S backyard was a small pasture that contained Harriet O'Casey's three venerable cows, which spent all their days and nights eating and chewing their cud and wandering from one end of the field to the other. If one were able to get a bird's-eye view of the pasture, it would look like an irregular triangle: partly bordering the shortest side was Gabriel Hoʻokano's house lot; adjacent to the longest side was a hilly, dense forest of mango and guava trees, haole koa, and whatnot (the old-timers say that a heiau for a fishing deity was located somewhere in that mix, though no one had ever located it; scientists from the downtown museum and from the university had tried to excavate certain promising areas, but with no results); and running along the third side was an old Hawaiian graveyard. In the old days, the graveyard had been sectioned off by family, but as time passed on and with everyone in Kānewai marrying everyone else, the distinction between families became less and less discerning, to the point now where each crumbling gravestone represented a withered root of practically every family in Kānewai. There were some exceptions: for example, in one corner was buried Goro Fukushima, a Japanese gardener who at the turn of the century was executed on the old plantation by a mob of vindictive haoles; he had no known family. And there was the marker for Father Emile VanderHoeff, a well-respected priest from Belgium, who served at St. Mark's Church and drowned mysteriously in an irrigation ditch about a year after the Fukushima murder.

There were two ways to get to the graveyard. One was through a narrow dirt trail that ran the mauka line of the Hoʻokano property; it was the only way, too, to get to Harriet's pasture. The other way was to go farther down the road that fronted Gabriel Hoʻokano's house. The broken-up macadam road turned into a dirt one; the road split, the left fork heading toward the graveyard and the other leading to the back of the town's garbage dump.

Harriet O'Casey, who was a second cousin to Gabriel Hoʻokano, visited her cows daily, at about an hour before sunset. Her husband had been a patternmaker in the U.S. Navy during World War II and had died on the torpedoed *Indianapolis.* She never remarried and raised by herself two sons, Casey Jr. and Patrick, both practicing attorneys in Honolulu. Though she passed Gabriel's house every day (except when it rained) and though they both were related to each other through his mother's side and her father's side, Harriet never talked to Gabriel, probably because as children growing up in their great-grandmother's house Gabriel had always teased her about her large, pendulous ear lobes but perhaps more so for the fact that he had been living in sin for years. Regardless of her glacial profile, Gabriel was always happy to see her. He always greeted her, and when she breezed past him daily without a glance of recognition or a breath of acknowledgment, he'd mutter to Mary (or to himself if Mary was unavailable) his usual comment: "Still she no get ovah her husband ma-ke."

And there was good reason for Gabriel to think that she was not all there, for Harriet would spend the last drifting minutes of sunlight (and sometimes many more minutes into the seeping darkness of early evening) talking to her three cows, one of which she had named Casey, the other, Casey, and the third. It baffled Gabriel why Harriet did not choose to slaughter the cows when they were younger, more tender, and tastier; through a backroom window, he had often studied them moseying about and eating peacefully in the pasture, and would calculate how many tasty steaks he could make from each. But Harriet was fanatic about letting them live their lives without any worry of being ground into hamburger or roasted whole over a bed of evenly glowing kiawe charcoal. In fact, the cows were descendants of a father and a mother also let out to pasture by Harriet. She had let each parent cow die and rot in the pasture, and her two sons had to convince her each time to hire someone (Kalani Humphrey) to dig a pit in the far corner of the pasture (near to where Goro Fukushima was interred) to bury the carcasses, since they had been receiving three to twelve phone calls a day at their

Bishop Street offices from an irate Uncle Gabe complaining about the pilau smell.

———

Clarissa Ching's phone did not stop ringing for three days straight after the funeral of her husband. Concerned members of the community were alarmed about the slow progress of the theater's demolition by Trinity Corporation; they feared that the company was in the process of pulling out of the deal, thus jeopardizing—they adamantly maintained—Kānewai's anticipated economic gain. Clarissa gave them her guarded assurance that the company would not back out of the deal, though secretly she wished that her husband had not signed the contract in the first place. But when three weeks passed and there was still no sign of activity, some of the residents began to take things into their own hands. There was talk of having a kahuna brought to the theater to exorcise the evil spirit that was presumably creating all of the pilikia. Some didn't believe that a ghost was doing this; they were sure that it was the work of a flesh-and-blood person, someone from the community and most probably a young kid. Most people disregarded the theory that Kalani Humphrey was behind the graffiti, though some diehards would not let go of their insistence that everything bad in Kānewai had a link to that misfit boy. But regardless of theory, there was a general consensus that something had to be done. Someone with authority, a kahuna or a priest or whoever, had to be brought to the theater to bless it. After much talk, the women of the bowling league decided against a kahuna and voted to get Father David Fonseca, the young Catholic priest from St. Mark's Church, to perform the Holy Ritual of Exorcism.

"I wish I could help you" was the Father's tenuous answer. He explained that he was not versed in the protocols of exorcism, and besides, there just hadn't been that many evil spirits to do away with in the past fifty years or so.

"But you think you can jus' bless da place?" asked Cynthia Cordeiro.

"Yes, Father," added Sandy Kim. "If you could only bless the place. Make it holy again."

"I don't understand," Father Fonseca said, his eyes protruding with question. "Why is there so much attention being paid to this theater all of a sudden? I had the impression that the theater is going to be demolished."

Cindy and Sandy exchanged discomforting looks. "But you see, Father," Cindy said, "we like see that things go good for business in Kānewai."

The Father studied their faces, trying to understand the real intent of their motive.

"You see, Father, the place," Sandy said finally, "the theater . . . it kind of . . . haunted."

"Haunted? By a ghost?"

"Yes . . .by ghost."

"And if we don't do something about it," Cindy added, "then something going happen to us."

"I see." He looked to the wall behind them at a framed photograph of his grandmother, who had passed on for several years now, draped with a fragrant but dried puakenikeni lei. He returned to their worried faces. "But what's going to happen? And to whom exactly?"

"The ghost taking revenge on us."

"All of you? Revenge? What kind of revenge are you talking about?"

"Well, I really don't know," Sandy said.

"You see, Father, we don't know what we did to offend the ghost, but the ghost fo' sure thinks we did something bad for it to do what it's doing."

"And what *is* it doing?" The Father felt a gloom that had suddenly weighed the air. He sat back in his chair and took in a deep breath. "Whatever it is that's bothering you, I'm here to help," he said. "Feel . . . that this is a confession that you are giving me."

"It's not that we feel guilty about it," Sandy said, "because we really don't know what is going on ourselves. But we know this: that this ghost is an evil spirit and it's trying to kill us all."

Father Fonseca regarded with mild suspicion the faces of the two faithful members of the congregation. Were they holding back something from him?

"Father, I know it must be hard for you to believe this," Cindy said, "but remember Hiram Ching dying so suddenly in the theater?"

The Father nodded gravely.

"Well, the ghost is the one who did that," Cindy continued.

"What . . . exactly did the . . . ghost do?"

"Kill him," Sandy whispered.

Father Fonseca raised his eyebrows. "The coroner report said that he died from heart failure. Hiram had a bad heart. He was a sick man. I visited him the last time he was in the hospital."

"But how can you account for the fact that the inside of the theater was all locked up?" Cindy pleaded.

"Well, there must be a reason. There's a solution for everything, you know. Well, look. Perhaps he went in and was afraid that someone might sneak in and rob him or something like that. Perhaps he went in to collect the proceeds from the night before."

"But the last showing was weeks before," Cindy said.

"All right. Well, maybe he left the proceeds from the previous weeks in his office. And so after entering the building he may have locked all the exits and entrances to prevent any robbery from occurring. And then he got his heart attack."

"And did you hear about the sign that was painted on the outside of the theater just before he died?" Sandy asked.

The Father lowered his eyes knowingly. "Yes, that does seem strange," he said. "Ah . . . can I get you both more tea?"

Thanking him, the women declined the offer.

"That does seem beyond the norm," the priest said. He cleared his throat, then added, "But though Hiram was a very good member of the community, I am not without the understanding that Hiram had a few enemies. I know for a fact that he was undergoing a lot of stress, which could have led to his bad physical state."

"But who's going be next?" Sandy said. "Me, or her, or—or whoever?"

"I don't understand."

"The other sign on the wall, right after Hiram's funeral," Sandy said. Cindy looked at her friend and nodded her head in agreement. "It said if we don't do something now, somebody else going to die."

"I'm not aware of that sign."

The two women lowered their eyes. Sandy informed the Father of the sign's message.

"And Father," Cindy added, "if you not going bless the theater, somebody else going die."

A chill entered the Father's body and spread to his limbs. He took a sip of the lukewarm tea. The eyes of the women focused on his shaking hand. Setting the cup down and patting his wet lips with a napkin, he cleared his throat again and nodded his head. "All right, if you want me to bless the theater, then I will go this afternoon."

When the women left his office, the priest sat at his desk in silence, thinking about what had been asked of him. And he began to think of his old friend, classmate, and teammate, Kalani Humphrey, and though he was still fond of Kalani, he also had a strong hunch that it was his old friend, whom he hadn't talked to or seen for at least three years, that was responsible for the signs and the death of Hiram Ching. Kalani had confessed to him, at the district courthouse just before his sentencing to prison for burglary, that he would get even with Ching, even if it took him the rest of his life . . . or his life. He had asked him why.

"Because I no like . . . that slimy bastard . . . touching my mother," Kalani said in his low, monotone voice.

The priest understood him, but he also knew that Hiram and Clarissa had rarely slept together—they were both Catholic and twenty-four years of marriage had produced nary an offspring, nary even a possibility—though he kept silent and let his friend vent his hostility.

"I going kill him . . . one day," Kalani said.

The priest tried to calm his friend, telling him that there were other ways through which he could deal with the problem.

"No way. Ching took my mother from me. Even my own mother, she no like even look at me. Talk to me. My own mother. And every time I see her, I can feel dis—dis—dis deep kine hurt inside. I tell you, David, I wen carry dis hurt around fo' so long already. Too long. Since da day I found out, when I found out all about dis. And I not going carry 'em til I dead. I going get even. I going get even wit' dat fucking pākē scumbag."

When the signs first started surfacing on the theater's wall, Father Fonseca immediately called the prison to find out if Kalani had escaped. The prison official assured him that Kalani Humphrey was still in prison. But that was not satisfactory for the priest, for he knew that Kalani was always full of surprises. It was not beyond Kalani, he thought, to hire a hit man or some desperate street person to do his dirty work. But there was no way the priest could tell anyone about Kalani's murderous tendency, for he had taken vows that forbade his breaking the covenant of confidentiality between priest and confessor.

"Eh! You coming o' what?" grumbled George Hayashida from the outside front steps of his house. "We going be late. Hurry up."

"Oh, shut up, you old futhead," Joyce muttered to herself in the bathroom, where she was putting on the finishing touches of her eye makeup.

"Eh! You heard me?!" George shouted.

"Yeah! I heard you!" Joyce shouted back. Then, to herself, "Damn futhead."

Fifteen minutes later, Joyce came out of the house. She

got into the car that George had started and killed and started and . . . for a least five times.

"Who you think you are, Miss Universe?" George said.

Joyce was going to counter by comparing his face with a bulldog's but decided that it wasn't worth the effort.

Five minutes later, on their way to the party at the Kahalewais, George asked Joyce if she had remembered to bring the invitation. "No," she said softly, as if in a shadow, and thought how unnecessary it was to bring an invitation to a baby lūʻau but also knowing George's anxiety that made him think he needed to have the invitation on him just in case someone was to ask if he was invited.

George slapped the steering wheel with his heavy palms and heaved a burdening "sonavabitch." He pulled over to the shoulder of the road and made a U-turn, fueling the car's acceleration with his imprecations. After he had driven for about a hundred feet, Joyce said, feigning an expression of surprise, "Oh . . . I just remember I got the invitation in my purse." She was thereupon assaulted with another "sonavabitch."

The invitation was to the one-year birthday party of Sunshine Rodriguez, the daughter of Val and Laverne Rodriguez. There was really no need for an invitation, for everyone in Kānewai had been invited to the celebration by word of mouth, or in the case of the Hayashidas, by the written word since it was hard to get hold of them even for a short chat, as they both worked the split shift at the pineapple can plant in downtown Honolulu. The party was at Sunshine's grandparents' home, which was up an unimproved road that ran up a low hill just outside of Kānewai town in the direction of Waiola Valley.

Halfway up the potholed road to the residence of Mildred and Henderson Kahalewai, George noticed the long line of cars already parked along the side. "You see," he grumbled at his wife, "we so late. Now we gotta park all the way down here. Long walk." He parked behind a bright yellow Isuzu pickup, the precious property of Matilda Nunes's son, then turned off the engine with a sour twist on his face. "And what if rain?" he added sharply, looking straight ahead at Jason Nunes's truck.

Joyce sighed heavily, as if she were releasing a burden. "Then we get wet," she said. She gathered her handbag in her lap, waiting for George to make the first move out of the car. "What you waiting for," she finally said, looking out the steaming windows, "for the rain?"

George muttered one of his more profound and more ambiguous variations of "sonavabitch," then got out of the car. Joyce followed suit. Without a word, they walked up to the house that was the sure source of the wonderfully delicious aroma of kalua pig.

The Kahalewai house was a typical redwood tract home that originally had a living room, two bedrooms, a bath, and a kitchen. Another two bedrooms, another bathroom, and a large open-air patio were later added on to the house. Over a part of the spacious backyard, Henderson and his son-in-law and some of his son-in-law's friends had pitched a large tent, a remnant from the Korean War, which was borrowed from Henry Kila who in turn had borrowed it (for at least seven years) from his uncle, Gabriel Ho'okano. Long rows of folding tables rented from Kānewai Rent-All lined the area under the tent. The tables were covered with virgin newsprint and decorated in the center with wild ginger and ti leaves, vanda and wild orchids, and red hibiscus. Spaced periodically between five or six settings were generous handfuls of 'alaea, raw sliced Maui onions, and cut sprigs of green onions, set on large ti leaves. A paper bowl of poi and paper trays of lomi salmon, squid lū'au, chicken long rice, raw 'opihi, and raw crab were at each setting. Children were running everywhere, playing tag or hide 'n seek or whatever, and some of the older folk were sitting at the tables, though most of the menfolk were gathered in small groups outside of the tent, drinking their beer and making small talk. Some of the womenfolk were helping out in the confusion of the kitchen and at the same time were having a good time talking story.

Val Rodriguez was on the patio, dressed in a bright orange aloha shirt and white pants, and holding his daughter in one of his gigantic arms. Sunshine had an impressive, sparkling smile, winning hands down over her father's, though Val's smile at the time was somewhat tainted by the tardiness of the musicians.

His cousins from the other side of the island had promised to play their version of Hawaiian reggae—Jawaiian, as it was called—but had yet to show up for this manuahi gig. Val had called his auntie's house the night before for a confirmation, but the boys had taken off to the beach early that morning and had not come back. "No worry," Val's auntie had reassured, "they going show up. And so how's your little darling keiki?" But now that it was an hour past the designated starting time of the party, the possibility that the show would not go on as scheduled was definitely troubling Val's mind. He labored through the small-talk with the guests, his mind disturbed by the possibility of his cousins' no-show, but at exactly one hour and seventeen minutes past the projected starting time his cousin Everett entered the patio area, hauling a large amplifier and a bass guitar.

"About time, eh, cuz?" greeted Val with an enormous smile on his face.

"Eh, you know us," Everett said. "When we say something, we going do 'em. Our word is golden."

They shook hands.

"So where the rest of the band?" Val asked.

"Parking da van. So where da outlet?"

Val directed Everett to the area where the band could set up.

Then cousin Emerson and a musician friend, introduced to Val as Joe-Sloe, came into the tented area where they set up the mikes and amps and PA system. Val left them for a while, returned, and deposited into Emerson's palm three thinly rolled joints, Kānewai-grown Kona gold. "And this, fo' juice da chords," Val added, drawing a pint of Southern Comfort out of his back pants pocket.

When the band was warming up with their first song, an instrumental, Mildred complained in the kitchen to daughter Laverne about the music being too loud.

"But Mama, da music is freeing da spirit."

"What spirit?" Mildred returned.

Meanwhile, Joyce had settled herself at the farthest table from the music, next to Georgette Edwards and Mary Wahineokaimalino, though being the farthest away from the amplified guitars didn't help to lessen the volume. George had remained in the garage with Henry Kila, Quintin Lee, Tiny Vierra, and several others of the bowling gang. They talked about Paul Navarro's jackpot-winning score of 720 pins the past Thursday night, and as Paul wasn't present in the garage, talk drifted to his secret liaison with the town's librarian and spinster, Cassie Chun, though the "secret" was well-known among the menfolk of the bowling team since they were all part of the cover-up.

"But everybody know about them now," Henry Kila said, referring to a recent exposé on the theater's wall.

"Yeah, but not everybody believe in the wall," Dennis Umeda said. "And anyway, Paul's wife, she rather him go and get it on with her, anyway."

"How you know?" Henry asked.

"'Cause my—my ex-wife told me."

"But you know dat wall is something else," Quintin Lee said. "I feel like going down dere right now and tearing da frickin' thing down."

"I no shit you," Dennis said.

Claudio Yoon nodded his head. It was seldom that Claudio ever expressed his opinion, though it was a well-known fact that if you give him some talking room he was a very opinionated person. Ask him about fishing and no one could shut him up.

"Den *you* go down dere and break da fuckin', friggin' wall down," Henry Kila said.

"I tell you, that wall give me the shivers every time I go pass 'em," Dennis said. "J'like da stuff stay breathing on you."

"Maybe we should make one nada watch," Henry said.

"For what?" Quintin protested. "Never had one sign up for long time already."

"But that's why so scary," said Dennis. "You dunno when the next one going come up. You dunno . . ."

Each of them finished Dennis's last sentence in his mind. There was a momentary silence. A couple of the men sipped their beers.

Finally, George sighed. "Me, I still think da Humphrey boy making all dis trouble. And I tell you why I think so."

Four

"BUT HE GET one point," Henry Kila added, referring to George Hayashida, who had just left their circle for home after being nagged for several minutes by his wife Joyce. "After all, only the Humphrey boy know what's going on around here. Something about him. I noticed about him since he was one small kid. He get da kine extrasensory perception. ESP."

"Crazy, yeah, dat kid?" Watson said. "Heard he was one real bright kid, too. Cannot help but be smart when yo' parents schoolteachers."

"Yeah, I remember him as one real good kid. He always used to call me 'Mr. Kila.' I remember him like that. But all of a sudden he wen turn sour."

"I wonder what happened," Quintin said.

"Nobody going know, eh? The parents wen died couple years after he wen drop out of school," Dennis said. "Funny, yeah, they both dying the same time."

Henry Kila nodded his head. "I remember that. Was strange, the way they wen die. They wen ma-ke in their house. I think Harry Hoʻokano wen find them watching the teevee and both of them was dead. Harry tol' me that in all his years as one cop he never seen one spookier thing than what he saw at the Humphrey house. He said both of them was sitting in their chairs like nothing wen happened, their eyes still open to the TV."

The group was quiet.

Henry went on: "But the medical coroner report said they both wen die of natural causes. So there was no foul play involved. That's what they said. Odd, yeah, they both die natural causes at the same time."

"I wonder what really wen happen," Quintin said.

"What you mean?" Henry asked.

"I mean what *really* happen."

"Kalani Humphrey wen killed his parents," Claudio said.

"But how?" Henry asked. "The medical coroner report said they wen die of natural causes."

"I mean, maybe he wen scare them to death," Claudio said. "Or something like that."

"What dat mean, 'die of natural causes'?" Tiny asked.

"Dat means they wen ma-ke of *natural causes!*" Henry suggested.

"Heard, too," Watson said, "that in their will, the Humphreys never left even one single cent to Kalani. Not one cent. Their own son. Their own flesh and blood."

"You think Kalani was their real son?" Dennis said. "I heard the story he was adopted."

"He no look like them," Tiny suggested. "You no think he too dark fo' one haole?"

"So what you think 'bout what George wen say?" Quintin asked. "I dunno about George. He little bit getting senile or something."

"He get one point, but," Dennis said. "After all, I heard the story that Kalani get one twin bruddah somewhere."

"Das crazy," Henry said. "You mean after all these years one twin bruddah going all of a sudden pop out from nowhere and start painting up all dose frickin' signs? No ways, José. You gotta be outta yo' mind, talking dis kine nonsense. Making up story." He slurped up the remainder from his can of beer.

"Then you can come up with one solid reason why all dese signs going up on da wall," Dennis demanded. "I cannot figure it out, unless you believe in da ghost story going 'round."

"But there is one ghost in the theater," Tiny said. "My

sister saw 'em one night when she and her friend wen use the bathroom. Honest kind."

"Das full of shit," Dennis said.

"I dunno about that," Quintin said.

"I believe in ghost," Claudio said.

"I no care if you believe in ghost or what," Dennis said, looking at Claudio, then at the others. "The ghost not going harm you. It's da kine real kine people, flesh and blood, das da ones going hurt you. One ghost only made up gas and air. How going hurt nobody?"

"Then you go down the Hawaiian graveyard right now and tell me you no believe in da spirits," Henry said, folding his arms across his wide chest.

"I nevah say I no believe in ghost," Dennis rebutted. "But how da hell one ghost going grab one paintbrush and paint one sign? You tell me that. Only people can do that."

"Eh, I no like talk about dis already," Henry said.

"No, le's talk about it," Tiny said. "I tired hearing all dis same kine stories over and over again. I like get down to what is really happening."

"Well, we not going find out what's really happening if we jus' sit around here and talk about it," Dennis said.

"What you mean?" Quintin said.

"I mean all dis is hot air."

"I thought you said the ghost was all hot air?" Tiny said. He laughed at his own joke. No one else laughed.

"I mean le's do something about it," Dennis said.

"Like what?" Henry asked.

"Like we go down to the moviehouse and we go inside and see if there really is one ghost. Le's go take some raw pork and find out if really get one ghost."

"No fut around," Henry said, opening a cold can of beer. "I staying put right here and sucking dis can I holding right in my hand and I ain't going nowhere. You can go, fo' what I care. But me, I not moving from my seat. I feeding my face." And he quaffed the entire contents of the can in one swig. Then he belched wetly.

"Me, too," Claudio said.

"Then you guys chicken," Dennis said.

"I would go," Quintin said.

"And you, Watson, what you going do?" Dennis asked.

Watson Kamei had been silent for most of the night, slowly drinking the beers and eating the pupus. He shrugged his shoulders, scratched his balding head, then said, "If I was you guys, I leave all dis business alone. I was there on the watch wit' you guys down at the theater, but I think all dis business is worth the shit we talking about right now."

"I agree," Henry said resolutely, snapping open another can of beer, this time taking a shallow sip.

"I tell you what," Dennis said, interrupting his sentence with a final sip of his can. He crushed the can in one hand, then tossed it into a trash bag of empties. He wiped his mouth with the back of his hand, then grabbed Henry's beer out of his hand. "I going get up right now and drive down to that frickin' theater and I going catch me that ghost or no ghost. I going leave all you friggin' cowards all back here, drinking yo' goddamn beers like one bunch of māhūs. And I going catch me that ghost and I going bring 'em back here and shove 'im in yo' faggot faces."

"Eh, Dennis, no get too rowdy," Tiny chided. "Dis one baby lūʻau. Cool head, brah. Calm down. Sit down . . . sit down."

"No. I not going sit down. I no like sit down wit' you bunch of hypocrites, you old ladies. All you folks only like do is talk story like one bunch of old maids. Me, I like do something about it."

"As if we never try do something abou—" Henry belched. "What you think about all that time we spent doing that watch down there? That was all good fo' nothing?"

"Yeah," he said, then guzzled his beer.

Henry frowned, waving him away. "You full of shit," he said.

"*I'm* full of shit? Fuck you! Fuck you!"

"Eh, Dennis, keep it down!" Quintin said. "Dis is one

baby party. Get plenty people can hear. Dis is one baby lūʻau."

"I think Dennis, he drank too much," Claudio suggested.

"I tell you what I going do. Right this second I going leave you fuckers. I not going sit around here and talk to you fucken māhūs. Fuck you. I going straight to the theater and I going catch dat fucking ghost."

"No be so crazy," Quintin warned, watching Dennis stalk off into the darkness. "Come back here. You cannot drive in yo' condition."

"Let him go, dat sonavabitch," Henry said. "I nevah could understand him when he get drunk. Da sucken guy, he change when he get drunk. Me, I get mellow. But him . . . jus' look at him. He get da opposite direction. Da fire come outta him. Look at him, dat crazy sonavabitch."

Staggering into his four-wheel drive, Dennis sped off toward the town, but the car was sluggish down the road, as if something was holding it back. Was it . . . some kind of . . . spirit? Cold sweat broke out over him. Then he remembered what his grandmother had told him, as a seven-year-old, if ever he encountered a ghost: "No be scared, boy. Mo' bettah be hūhū! If you show the ghost that you're not scared, the ghost will not bother you," she had told him. Boldly he yelled, "Fuck you, ghost! No curse my car!" Moments later, about the halfway mark to the theater, he noticed the acrid smell of burning metal and realized that he had forgotten to release the parking brake.

Five

PERHAPS IT WAS instinct that guided a drunk, insensate Dennis Umeda down Kānewai's dark streets. And lucky that he had any kind of instinct, as his thoughts were not on driving but on the moviehouse itself and all the fun times he had as a kid growing up in Kānewai, watching low-budget Japanese science fiction movies with his friends. As he hugged the wheel around a turn, he chuckled, amused that he had once found entertainment in those Godzilla and Mothra movies. Of course, he and his friends knew that the monsters were fake, rubber costumes with men inside. But maybe that's why they had enjoyed those movies so much, because they had used their imaginations to make those monsters real. They had laughed at the silliness of the costumes, but they were still afraid of the eyes and the teeth.

And Dennis remembered he and his friends walking the mile or two or three to Kānewai Theater, and how they'd wait impatiently for the lights to dim in that corrugated iron-roofed moviehouse, and when it did get dark the screen would start flashing, and there'd be a roar of cheers and whistles from the young audience; the cartoons would roll; and then the monster double-bill would begin, the latest movies of latex monsters and aliens.

He parked next to the wall of the theater and left the engine running and the headlights on. The wall had recently been whitewashed, but whoever did the last cover-up had used cheap paint, for the underpainting had surfaced back to prominence, as if the lettering were messages from another world.

He got out of the car and approached the wall, his shadow cast disproportionately large on the wall, then diminishing to a pear's shape as he got close. He touched the wall. A jolt of electricity zapped his finger, propelling him back and bouncing him off the grill of his truck. He fell to the ground. Dazed, he struggled up. A chill entered his feet, spreading up his legs. He retreated to the cab of his truck and locked the door.

For a long, long while he sat, rubbing his legs, doubting his fortitude and commitment to his word. Was just my imagination, he pleaded drunkenly to his consciousness. Just my imagination . . . just like that song. He breathed in, then out, another in and out, then unlocked the door and stepped out.

———————

THE PROBLEM WAS getting into the boarded-up theater. But that was solved as he remembered how, as kids, he and Jimmy Hirota and his other friends used to get into the theater when they were short of money, which was the usual case: climbing in through the girls' bathroom window. And if the window was locked, all it took was a few firm raps on the lock to loosen the bolt on the inside.

But he stopped himself. Once in, then what? He told the gang at the baby lūʻau that he was going to get the ghost . . . but how? And what if there isn't any ghost? And . . . what if . . . there is a ghost?

Maybe he should have kept his big fat mouth shut. It wasn't the first time he had mouthed off something that he'd wish later he hadn't. That always happened when he drank too much. When would he learn his lesson? Maybe he should quit drinking.

All right, what's done is done, he told himself. He had to stick to his word. So now he had to have proof that he actually did get into the theater. *At least that going shut their fricking mouths.* No problem. Get inside and take something that anyone could identify as being from the theater. Like one of the seats. Or a lamp from the lobby. Better yet, he'd break into the old man's office and take one of his fat, smelly cigars, that nauseous trademark of Ching. If there were any in his office. Dennis knew that Clarissa Ching never allowed Hiram to smoke them in their house—wasn't she a bitch—so it was only at the theater that Ching would smoke. Every moviegoer knew that damn cigar smell that permeated the theater and exuded the strongest from the front seats.

Dennis went to the back of the theater and with a closed fist struck the lower edge of the women's restroom window a few times, but the latch wouldn't come undone. So Ching had fixed the lock. Dennis swore, then pounded harder and harder, and finally ended up cracking the wired glass. He swore again and glanced around to see if anyone had seen him or had heard the noise, a feeling of guilt coming over him. But then he remembered that the theater was doomed anyway for demolition, so why worry about old glass? He picked up a two-by-four that was on the ground and broke out a wide enough hole so that he could slip in his arm. He unlocked the window. Prying it open, he cleared the bits of broken glass off the inside sill and used a wooden crate that was conveniently placed right below the window to step up to the opening. He snuggled his body in, grunting and emitting a blast of gas when the hard edge of the window jamb pressed too hard into his soft belly. But alas! How the years had gone by. There was a time when Dennis and his friends could slip through the window like the wind and be in the front row, joining in with the yelling and whistling while the first cartoon flashed on the screen. From breaking and entering to sitting, it would take them no more than forty-seven seconds; they timed themselves once, using Charley Nakashima's brand-new Timex, a gift on his tenth birthday. But no more.

Dennis was stuck, right below his piko. He was caught in a wretched limbo, half in and half out, his feet dangling inches above the crate, his hands on the ledge propping the inside half of his body and easing the however increasing bite of the metal jamb on his tummy. He grabbed the edge of the ledge to pull himself in, but that didn't help at all. His well-padded abdomen was no help in buffering the bite of the jamb.

But then the air of the restroom stirred and quickly intensified, as if a mini tornado were passing through; moments later Dennis was sucked from the window and jettisoned across the restroom, crashing into the door of a toilet stall, his head striking the lip of the commode. He blacked out instantly. And it was there, approximately three and a half minutes later, that Clarissa Ching found him, crumpled like a marionette with its strings cut, one hand dangling in the ironized water of the bowl.

―――――――

CLARISSA WAS GETTING pretty disgusted, discovering crate after crate of pornographic magazines and books that her late husband had stored in the large closet of his office. And he never even locked the door! It was, nonetheless, a collection extraordinaire, of nearly every nudie magazine that had been in his reach. There seemed to be complete collections of such skin classics as *RamMan, Naughty Girls, Hump-ty Dumpty, High School Teasers,* and *Swinging Vixens,* each issue carefully protected from the elements by its own zip-lock plastic bag. Hiram Ching had sorted his magazines by date and issue number, and Clarissa even found a loose-leaf binder containing a typewritten inventory of his library. She also found, in a rack behind the dozen or so crates, thirty to forty cans of feature-length, triple-X film. Not knowing at first what the films were about as the cans had no labels, Clarissa unraveled one reel and found it to be the most disgusting twenty-five or so feet of 16 mm celluloid she had ever viewed. Sickened by its explicitly perverted nature as well as shocked and embarrassed by the discovery of this other side of her husband's character, she returned the reel to its canister and hurled it across the room; upon impact on the concrete floor, the can split open, and the reel was sent spinning, leaving a trailer of film on the floor until crashing into a wall above which an oil portrait of Hiram, which she had never seen before, was hung. He was grinning down at her, in a kind of dignified way, holding a pipe in one hand, while the other rested on the arm of a dark blue Duvouchy chair. He was wearing a velvet fuchsia bathrobe with a pink ascot tucked in white satin pajamas, apparel that Clarissa, again, had never seen before. She picked up the reel and heaved a perfect strike at the painting (which had been done by a well-known, impoverished, and alcoholic artist who lived in the bars on Hotel Street in downtown Honolulu), but it did nothing but tilt the portrait to one side. Then she rolled the cart of films out of the closet and, with three attempts and one final shove, successfully tipped over the cart, the cans of film clanging into a messy pile in the middle of the room.

Tormented, she sat on her husband's chair and cried a good cry, which cleansed her mind somewhat of all the filth that she had just been exposed to. She felt the sudden necessity to take a bath, to rid her skin of a layer of imaginary dirt that had come from the smutty, vinegar-scented films that were now putrifying Hiram's office, far beyond the pollution from his cigars. Staring at the wall next to Hiram's desk, where there was a calendar, compliments of Freddie Tanaka's Service, of a bikini-clad haole girl lying on her side and stroking a Siamese cat; a framed business license; and a hodge-podge of scotch-taped discolored notes and business cards, she could not help but imagine—with utter disgust— her husband viewing the pornography in the privacy of this very theater. He probably even ate popcorn while watching them *fornicate!*

The idea came to her that perhaps he wasn't alone while viewing the smut, that perhaps someone else might have been with him. But she tossed out the possibility of his unfaithfulness: He was never able to get it up for her for over a decade, so how could he have gotten it up for anyone else?

After a minute or two of feeling sorry for herself, she decided that the best thing to do with all the smut was to get rid of it all in any way possible so that others would never find it. It was not a matter of protecting Hiram's reputation—

Clarissa had no intention of protecting anything of his at this point—but, as the wife of a respected member of the community, it was a matter of protecting *her* dignity, *her* integrity, *her* reputation.

She quickly began stuffing the magazines back into the crates. Dumping out a cardboard box half-filled with dirty rags that she found in the closet, she started filling the box with the unwound reels and the other film canisters, then realized the magnitude of the work of moving such an enormous load. She thought about whom she could trust to help her with the task and she could think of no one. What could she do? If she sealed the boxes, would she be able to hire someone to cart them out? But what if that someone peeled off the tape and peeked inside? And what if that someone went back to where he had been hired to dump the boxes and salvaged them?

She decided that she'd have to do it by herself, no matter how long the job would take. She'd have to come back at night, parking her car in the side alley and loading as much as she could at a time, then dumping the boxes where no one could find them, perhaps in the ocean.

And so she started, filling a box and then pushing and pulling it over the worn carpet, down the long theater aisle. Finally reaching the side exit, she collapsed on the closest seat, perspiration streaming down her temples. It was the hardest work she had done in a long while, perhaps the hardest in her life. Her eyes rested on the dark crimson curtains that hung on one side of the screen, then followed the dark folds to the cobwebbed ceiling, then drifted down to the screen. And then, like a scene from an introspective French movie, a scenario came to her, of her late husband sitting in the theater all alone and watching his collection of pornography. And that vision shook her: She suddenly became very sad—truly sad. For her husband, though he was an incommunicable son-of-a-bitch, had worked hard to sustain his business (the theater and the various property holdings in Kānewai) and their more than comfortable standard of living, which had provided her with unshakable financial security throughout their married life . . . though he had not given her the one thing she perhaps needed the most, something that was denied her since the aftermath of her high-school pregnancy, that wondrous skin-crawling feeling called L O V E. (The experience of being shaken to orgasm was also denied by an incapable Hiram, but that's another story.) But—and a big *but*, for sure—he was very good to her, in this pecuniary way. He had given her a beautiful big house, a generous allowance, a late model Mercedes with all the extras thrown in. If "husband" meant "good provider," then Hiram Ching was the definitive example.

Clarissa could not hold back the tears that came from that soft part of herself deep down inside. She thought more of Hiram—of his strengths—and was impressed by that image of him as an efficient, business-savvy, hard-working, lonely—though perverted—old man. She envisioned him sitting by himself and enjoying perhaps one of the few pleasures he had in life: watching other people make love. (She was, however, only half-correct when she made her final assessment on Hiram's sexual incapability; although he could not get it hard for Clarissa or anyone else, he definitely was able to get a rise from the screen. The screen empowered him to an enormous potency.)

So she sat there and cried, trying as hard as she could to draw a picture in her mind of Hiram as a kind, honest, hard-working man. She closed her eyes to further her imagining, but when the only image of Hiram that came to her was his smiling oil portrait—a bit inconsistent with what she was trying to do—she opened her eyes quickly and continued her cry. And when her tears dried, her fond memories of Hiram as well evaporating but slowly, Clarissa got up, dusted off the back of her knit slacks, and gave the large room a lookover. Pretending that Hiram was watching from above somewhere, she said, "Hiram, you were a good man." A capricious thought came to her: As a last measure of appreciation for a man who had provided her financial comfort for all those years she would, instead of merely discarding the smut at the local dump, burn the entire lot so that the essence of those films and magazines would go to wherever Hiram was and give him some kind of pleasure in an everlasting kind of way. She devised a plan to take the collection home, bit by bit, and when she had collected it all, she would burn it up all in the backyard one night.

As she pushed the box out the exit doors toward the car, the sound of breaking glass came from a distant corner inside the theater. *What was that? A robber breaking into the theater? The ghost of the women's restroom? The theater's roof collapsing?* She jumped to the driver's door for a quick getaway, then realized that her handbag—and car keys—were in Hiram's office.

Reentering the auditorium, her ears pricked, she inched her way to the office and found her Vuitton handbag leaning against the box of *Saintly and Sexy*. There was a crash. Holding the bag as if it were a shield, she scurried back to the exit.

A loud, dry moaning slipped out through the last three inches of the closing side door. She slammed the door shut, leaning against it with all of her trembling weight.

———————

CLARISSA DROVE TO the other side of the theater and parked about twenty feet away from the truck, the headlamps from her car lighting up both vehicle and wall. A few cars passed by on the main road. *Whose truck is this?* Cautiously she slipped out of her Mercedes and approached the truck. No one was inside the vehicle. She returned to her car, took out a flashlight from the glove compartment, and went to the open window of the women's restroom. Shattered glass was everywhere on the ground. The flashlight beam shaking uncontrollably, she scanned the interior, then found two feet sticking out from under the door of a stall. *Who is that?*

"Who are you?!" she yelled. "Who are you?!"

There was no answer, but she could discern a soft, low moan.

"Whoever you are, I'm calling the cops!"

Again, no answer.

She hurried back to the car and got in, her heart pounding wildly, pondering her next move. She thought of calling the police, she did say she was, but quickly disregarded the idea, as doing so would probably bring more nīele people into the know of her husband's secret business. Perhaps Father Fonseca? No. There was no one to turn to. The only option she had was to confront the intruder herself.

BACK IN HER husband's office, she found a Louisville slugger in the closet and, taking in a few deep breaths, made her way to the bathroom, the bat raised above her head. A rat scurried across the lobby. She gasped, then bit her lower lip to silence herself. She went on, in the darkness, toward the entrance of the restroom, the door on the ground, having fallen from its hinges. The room was illuminated by her car's headlights, and Clarissa stretched inside and groped for the light switch but could not find it. (It was located outside in the hallway, inches from her other hand.) Hesitating, she entered the restroom, then realized that all along she was carrying the flashlight, which she now switched on, directing the light toward the intruder. Pushing back the door of the stall, she recognized him immediately. *Dennis? Dennis Umeda? What?!*

Clarissa prodded Dennis with the bat and jumped back when he stirred. A groan came from him. She prodded him again. This time he opened his eyes, blinded by the light. She noticed the drops of blood on the floor next to him. *Is he hurt?*

Dennis rolled to his side and rubbed the side of his head with the hand wet with the toilet bowl water. He sat up and looked into the beam of the flashlight. "Whas dis about?"

There was no answer from Clarissa. She was sweating as if in a terrible heat, her hand barely able to hold the flashlight, not to mention the Louisville Slugger wavering above her head.

"Where am I?" Dennis asked.

Again no answer.

"Whas dis about? Where am I? Who . . . you?"

With one elbow on the rim of the toilet bowl, Dennis began to prop himself up.

"Don't move!! Get back down—or I'll call the police!! I have a gun—pointed—at *you!!*"

"Who . . . you? Okay. Okay. Don't shoot. Where am I? What you want? Who . . . you?"

"Don't move! I have a gun pointed at you!"

"Yeah-yeah. I heard you. You see me moving?"

"What are you doing here?"

"Wha—? Whas dis all about? Where am I?"

"You tell me! What are you doing snooping around in my husband's theater?"

Clarissa Ching?

It took exactly seven seconds for Dennis to recollect his last conscious act, that of suddenly being undone from the window. He touched the tender spot on his head, looking soberly into the beam of the flashlight. "You were the one kicked me into the window?"

"What?"

"Never mind."

"You still didn't answer my question. What are you doing here?"

"Is a long story. I can . . . sit up?"

"All right. Go ahead. But tell me, what are you doing here?"

"I told you. It's a long story."

"I don't have time for a long story."

Dennis proceeded to tell his long story.

"So you see," he concluded, "we—I—was just doing this only fo' one joke. Fo' da boys back at da party."

"Some joke," Clarissa said. "You scared the daylights out of me."

Dennis thought her last comment was funny, but he

stopped from telling her that or laughing. He grinned, rubbing his head where it hurt the most.

"Are you . . . all right?" Clarissa noticed a trickle of blood on his cheek.

"Yeah. Jus' one bump on the head."

"Here," she said, plucking paper towels from a dispenser and offering them to him. "You got a bad cut on your head."

Dennis pressed the wad of towels to his head. "I sorry I made you all scared and everything."

Clarissa stopped herself from saying that it was okay, since it was not okay. Then Dennis asked her the expected question: "Don't mind me if I ask you, but . . . what are you doing over here at this time of the night?"

As calmly as she could, she explained that she was sorting out her husband's papers.

"Oh. So, uh, you need some help?" He stretched up slowly. Dizziness. He leaned against the wall of the stall.

"No . . . I don't need any help. Just . . . I want you to leave."

"All right. I will. Hey . . . can we turn on the lights?"

"I don't know where the switch is."

"It's outside. In the hall. I'll get it."

He went into the hall and switched on the lights.

———

THE FIRST THING that Clarissa noticed was the message written on the mirror in red paint. The paint was running down to the washbasin.

"Did you do that?" she asked.

"Did what?"

She pointed to the mirror. Dennis regarded the letter "U" and the number "2," which were separated by a comma and ended with a question mark. He shook his head.

"I didn't do that. I swear to God."

Clarissa traced a trail of red paint from the mirror, over the washbasin, and along the floor to the spot where Dennis was standing. She looked at the sign again, silently reading it over again, then reading it aloud.

With the understanding came a shriek, then the flashlight falling and bouncing on the ground.

Dennis caught Clarissa's head before it struck the floor. He lay her down. As he bent over her and tried to figure out what to do, a cold, tingling sensation crawled up his back. He spun around and saw a thin blue mist vanishing out into the dark hall.

Six

HIRAM OBSERVED THE painting of the sign in the women's restroom, and though he wanted to warn Clarissa about it, he couldn't since he was dead: He had yet to learn a method of communication with the material world. It troubled him that he was not able to warn her of his unearthly feelings, for earlier, as a ghost floating beneath the dry dusty rafters of the theater, he watched his wife crying, which touched him very much. He truly had not known how much Clarissa had loved him. It was an agony for him to remain silent, floating this way and that, not knowing which way he'd drift to since he also had not mastered the art of directional phantasmal levitation. If he could have cried he would have, for now he was deeply saddened and frustrated, having left Clarissa all alone to manage his difficult financial affairs. He knew it would be mind-boggling for Clarissa to sort out his business papers since he had kept every receipt, a record of every business transactions, in two large file cabinets, one marked "Old Business" and the other "New Business," though he had never really differentiated the two.

Right then and there, overcome by emotion evoked by Clarissa's expression of love, he pledged to her, to himself, that he'd protect her from any harm whatsoever whenever she was in the theater. He especially thought about that mischievous and noisy obake in the women's room. When as a ghost he first became aware of its presence, the noises—which sounded like the high whinings of bamboo shanks rubbing against each other in a forest—scared him. Though he soon got used to the sound, it still bothered him that he had no idea what the apparition looked like.

At the time when Clarissa was cleaning up his office, Hiram sensed an intruder. He wasn't able to move to the site of the break-in but was aware of its location, a phantasmic instinct picked up since death. He thought initially that the naughty apparition was up to one of its pranks again, but an infinitesimal fraction of a second later intuition told him that something else was in the works. He tried desperately to warn Clarissa of the danger—flailing his arms to stir the air (unsuccessful); making grotesque faces (don't ask him how he did it, but his lower jaw did stretch to the floor of the theater); moaning wildly (which gave him an earache)—all of which failed to attract even a mote of fear or uncertainty in Clarissa, who at the time was nervously wrapping and sealing in a cardboard box part of the evidence of her spouse's unhappy sex life.

But Hiram the ghost learned something useful from his failure at eliciting premonition. While imitating the mournful sounds of the restroom ghost, he accidentally took in a deeper breath than usual (ghosts don't need to breathe, but they're still able to perform the function) and found himself zipping across the ceiling to the other side of the theater. Startled, then arrested with elation at the discovery, Hiram faced the opposite side of the room, repeated the procedure, and found himself sailing across the room again. Applying this new-found technique, Hiram got himself by trial-and-error to the restroom, where he witnessed the intruder squirming through the gap in the window.

He recognized the intruder as Dennis Umeda, then wondered if it was he who had painted those nasty signs inside and outside the theater. It was hard for Hiram to conceive of Dennis doing all that since the Dennis he knew was a law-abiding, intelligent citizen. But . . . why is he now sneaking into the women's restroom anyway?

Hiram heard grunting and swearing. Dennis was stuck in the window. Good for him. But after watching a while, Hiram began debating whether to help him. He decided to help, though he wasn't able to physically push or pull him. Out of frustration, he took a small breath in, but it was a large enough breath to create a mini-storm in the restroom. He smiled to himself. Why not? Why not scare him out of the window? So Hiram steadied himself and drew in air slowly, then out, coming closer to Dennis, and then back out, then another in and out, fast and faster, and deep and deeper, until he felt he was about to burst. Then something unexpected happened. Instead of being drawn to Dennis, he drew Dennis in, for suddenly Dennis was a projectile impaling Hiram's vaporous presence, like a gravid jetliner flying right through a cloud. Dennis ended this very brief jaunt by smacking his head unconsciously against the toilet bowl.

Hiram was in shock. He was seized with guilt since his plan had hurt Dennis more than a simple scare. He begged an unconscious Dennis for forgiveness. But Hiram was not aware that his lament in English was being translated—or rather, transmutated—into the only sounds that were audible to human ears: moans and groans. And it was these sounds, following Dennis's crash, that reverberated throughout the still theater and brought terror to Clarissa.

———

WHAT IS THAT? At one moment Clarissa was pushing with all her weight against the exit door and the next moment she was in her car, searching for the car keys in her handbag, then fumbling and dropping them to the floor. She picked them up and then jammed the key upside down into the ignition slot.

———

HIRAM BECAME AWARE of his favorite black-handle paintbrush bobbing across the restroom to the mirror where a letter "U" was painted in drippy red, followed by a comma, a "2," and finally a question mark.

"Eh!" Hiram exclaimed. "Whachu doing using my paintbrush? And you destroying my property!"

With that outburst, the brush dropped to the floor.

A beam of light burned through Hiram. Screeching out of the restroom, he hovered below the ceiling of the auditorium, nursing his terrorized heart. And while calming his rampaging spirit, he came to a conclusion that it was not Dennis who was the sign-painter but the ghost of the women's restroom.

Drawing in a breath, Hiram took it upon himself to rectify the problem by expurgating the apparition from the theater by any means possible. Perhaps if he told Clarissa of the problem, she'd expedite the demolition of the theater. But he shuddered at the thought that the destruction of the theater might also mean his own.

He was confused. But at least now he was sure of who —or what—was responsible for putting up those damaging signs all over the theater.

Or so he thought.

Seven

G ABRIEL HO'OKANO SAT on his veranda the morning after a heavy rain, rocking his chair while gazing at the buffalo grass and the old abandoned Mustang. He was thinking about the last time he had seen his older brother, Jacob Ho'okano, the late kahuna of Waiola Valley. Gabriel had climbed the long overgrown trail that wound up to Jacob's place far back in the valley. At the end of the trail, on top of a sharp incline, which was impossible to climb if the trail was wet with rain, was a large kukui tree, which was also the tree from which hung Jacob's compact boxhouse. After about ten minutes of catching his breath, Gabriel had called out to his brother. He knew it would take a minute or so for Jacob to hear him—the sound of his voice would first reverberate all around the bush and trees and finally find its way into the tiny entrance of Jacob's house—and it would take a bit more time for Jacob's failing ears to hear it. After the fourth or fifth call, Jacob poked his head out, focused his eyes on an impatient and irritated Gabriel, then silently shooed his brother away with a wave of his hand.

The brothers had not talked for years, since the time of the ominous coincidence of a small earthquake and a great flood that had wiped out most of the taro patches in the valley, a disaster that seemed to be the portent of taro's demise in Waiola, with outsiders buying up most of the land in the years following or claiming ownership of property through shady but legitimate deals with the government, later leasing the land to sweet potato farmers. Jacob and Gabriel were two of many who could trace their ancestry to the original workers of the land. Jacob was also one of a few who had resisted the unscrupulous efforts of the outsiders in their attempt to take over the entire valley. Later, however, he succumbed to the political hegemony of the legal word, which he did not understand at all, or rather, ignored: Though articulate in English, he refused to speak or read in any language except for Hawaiian. He blamed his kid brother Gabriel for not helping with the family cause, an accusation that angered and haunted Gabriel painfully. Whenever he thought about the incident, especially those times of refracted reflection on the veranda, the frequency of which was seldom, he'd throw his hands up in the air and exclaim sourly to his girlfriend, Mary Wahineokaimalino: "Dat brother of mine! He always blaming me fo' the family's loss. But how I could help? Cannot fight da gov'ment. Shee—and plus they wen draft me go fight in da Pacific!"

That last time Gabriel had gone to his brother's was to inform him of their grandniece's wedding. Though he knew that Jacob didn't care a hoot and would completely ignore him, Gabriel thought it was his obligation to go to Jacob and give him the news whenever there was anything happening in the family. So when obstinate Jacob ducked back into his wooden shell, Gabriel cupped his mouth and began rattling off the specific points of interest, as he always did—in this case the particulars concerning Davilyn's wedding and reception. Finishing his announcement, he cursed his brother silently for making deaf ear and wasting his wordy efforts, and pretended to be sour and irritated at Jacob's inhospitality. Then he went down the trail, carefully stepping over surfaced roots and loose stones while feeling a small sense of duty accomplished. He also relished the possibility that perhaps his old, reticent, hardheaded brother might have the heart to attend Davilyn's party at their niece's home, which would bring smiles and touches of good feeling to the hearts of the family members. Of course, old Jacob didn't break with his silence and seclusion. And he died a few weeks after Gabriel's visit.

Mary called him from the kitchen, but Gabriel didn't answer. He wiped away the tears from his eyes and cheeks. After a few minutes, Mary, bundled in Jacob's old army jacket, joined him outside, sitting herself on the wicker couch.

"What you was asking me?" she asked Gabriel.

Gabriel slowly turned to her, then shrugged his shoulders. "I never said nothing to you."

"No . . . last night. You was telling me something."

Gabriel tried to remember what he had said. "Oh . . . last night," he said, though still searching through the misty arches of last night's already distant architecture for something to grasp. "Last night," he muttered with an affected sense of affirmation. "But last night was last night. Today's one new day."

Mary forced a cough. She folded her arms and looked out into the front yard. She seemed homey and content in the old army jacket and worn house slippers. Though her hair was whitening fast and her once smooth and unblemished face was now a victim of the slow but sure movement of time, there still was a serene, mature warmth and beauty about her, some essence that frequently was capable of infecting Gabriel with the amorous condition of chickenskin. "Up to you," she said placidly.

"What you mean, 'Up to me'?"

"Up to you. You tol' me you was going try make it better. But if you no like make it better, then is up to you."

Gabriel was puzzled. He wanted to know more about what he had told Mary. He tried to figure out a way to get clues about what he had said without letting Mary realize that he had forgotten. Though they had been together for decades, Gabriel still found his failing memory embarrassing. He, Gabriel Ho'okano, always had to be on top of things, or at least make it seem like he was.

Mary knew Gabriel very well, better than Gabriel would

ever know Gabriel. She knew that Gabriel's memory was failing, and she regarded this as something that could not be helped. "C'est la vie," she would say to herself, that phrase Gabriel had taught her years ago, a saying that he had picked up while fraternizing with an Australian soldier in the Pacific front. The slow deterioration of Gabriel's memory was not important. Well, not that not important. For Mary had *made up* the vague remark that he was supposed to have said the night before. She knew exactly what would go on in Gabriel's mind if he was told such a story. For the record, Gabriel had not said anything of much interest the night before. Her false statement was not really a lie or a form of entrapment: It was just Mary's way of making Gabriel respond positively to her next question.

"Honey," she said, "you want to drive me to the market?"

Gabriel mumbled something about having a lot to do around the house, but finally, seeing this as an opportunity to divert Mary's attention from his condition, consented to her inquiry. "When you like go?"

"In little while. About half hour from now."

"Gotta pick up Georgette?"

"Yeah, I asked her if she like go market with me and she said okay."

"Okay." Gabriel pretended to concentrate on something across the road. Then, grinning, he said, "But you thought I was going do it, then, eh?"

Mary wasn't sure how to answer him.

"Then I tell you what," Gabriel finally said. "I making my mind up right here and now that I going do it, once and for all."

Mary was going to ask him, "*What* you going do?" but she caught herself.

"Le's go then. You ready go or what?" He stood up, stiff but erect in spirit, ready to take on whatever it was that he was going to do.

Mary's eyes widened. The sight of Gabriel standing so strongly and purposefully was very becoming. She smiled.

"Well, we going or what?" Gabriel said impatiently. "I get lot of things fo' do. Take you and Georgette to the market. And I gotta do what I gotta do."

She answered him with a smile and a nod of her head, and went in and got herself ready. Gabriel went in, too, to get his jacket, wallet, and car keys. Then he went out back to the garage, an ancient, termite-ridden one-car structure set apart from the house. From the back of the garage he took a two-inch wide brush and the half-emptied can of paint, which Mary had bought him days before, and he placed them all in the trunk of his '58 Chevy Impala. He started up the car, got out, and waited for Mary.

Gabriel looked over the wire fence across his cousin's pasture, and once again he began thinking about his late brother. "Dat sonavabitch brother of mine," he said sourly, "I dunno why he nevah come Davilyn's wedding."

————

WHENEVER GEORGETTE EDWARDS and Mary got together... watch out. Words were exchanged with a flurry, like an orgy of hungry mynah birds flying undecidedly between two fruit-laden litchi trees. Gabriel never learned to like listening to them. Over the years, he had devised a method of shutting them off completely from his hearing mind. It was an effective method and it was fool-proof, 99 percent of the time. That morning—while Gabriel was driving Mary and Georgette to the market—was one of those times when that one percent ruled.

Of course, Gabriel, as he would have adamantly insisted, *chose* to listen to their talk. Three words of Georgette's gossip were immediately grabbed by his ears: "painting" and "paint thing." He pretended that he wasn't listening: Occasionally he'd make believe that something passing—a tree, another car, a freshly painted fire hydrant—was catching his attention, or he'd whistle along a couple of bars with the tune on the radio.

The women didn't mind or care that old Gabriel was listening, and they went on and on, talking about how the painting on the wall was desecrating the town and how one day the young Father David had gone down to the theater and had blessed the site, but how that seemed to have failed, too, since something seemed to have possessed the Father, stunning him and making him stiff and speechless for a long while until Cynthia Cordeiro finally had the sense to shake him up good. Then he had fallen backward but got up quickly and staggered away, mumbling something about "blood" or "Holy blood" and some other such ramblings in a language that Sandy Kim suggested as being Latin.

"So what happened after that?" Mary asked, who was sitting in the front seat next to Gabriel.

"I dunno," said Georgette, who was sitting right behind Gabriel. "But later on, they wen go to the church and they nevah could find Father David."

"Really? They no could find the Father? Where he went?"

"I dunno. But somebody told them later on he went downtown fo' talk to the Bishop."

"About what?"

"About maybe how the theater really stay haunted, about how maybe one evil spirit possessing the theater. Maybe they gotta go find one priest, like you know the one in the movie, *The Exorcist*. You know, maybe something like him."

"Oh, my Virgin Mother Mary."

"I tell you, Mary, all this business is not so funny like how it all started out first. Something real bad is in this town. I no joke. Something real bad. I dunno what it is, but it's bad. Evil. Kinda spooky."

Mary turned to her boyfriend. "Gabe, what you think about all this?" Mary had to repeat the question twice, as Gabriel had to snap out of his pretended trance, which Mary knew about all along anyway.

"Wha-what? Whachu talking about?" Gabriel asked.

"All this business."

"All this business 'bout what?"

Mary sighed. He was taking this pretension a bit too far. "You know what I mean. About the theater."

"Oh . . . 'bout the ghost? The evil spirit?" Gabriel paused, taking in a breath as if to energize his thoughts. "What I think about all of this? Well, I think all this is nonsense. You know how I feel. Somebody pulling the rug from under everybody else. You know what I mean? Is like everybody talking about the cat with the mouse but never had the cheese before to attract the mouse in the first place. You know what I mean?

"But this thing about Father David, well, I tell you this. You know when he was one young kid around here, das was the time of the damn hippie days. You remember those hippie days, eh? Well, you know that Father David used to be David Fonseca before. You know, Harold and Dorothy Fonseca's kid. Eh, that kid, believe it or not, used to smoke da kine *pakalolo*. You nevah know that? I think the drug effect wen all come back to him. What I mean, the pakalolo influence still in his mind, and it wen come back and make him hallucinate. See things. Das what I think. The Father, even though he one priest, he still cannot run away from his past, befo' him one badboy. You unnerstand? Even God not that merciful. The Father was seeing things. The Father was *hallucinating*.

"Das what I think wen happen to him at the wall by the theater. He got one big flashback. Das what dey call one dah kine . . . dah kine . . . wachu ma callit? Dah kine psai-key . . . psai-key . . ."

"Psychedelic?" Georgette offered.

"Yeah—yeah—psychedelic trip. He was so much in shock. Das what happened to him, if you asking me."

"But Cynthia Cordeiro and Sandy Kim said they wen feel something strange coming from the wall," Georgette interjected. "Jus' like had one presence over there. Spooky kine."

Mary nodded her head in agreement.

"But you know what I really think," Gabriel said, as if he had not heard Georgette, "what I really think is that—"

"Gabe? Where you going?" Mary said. "You wen pass dah market."

Gabriel looked into the rearview mirror and saw the sign for Leong's Market about half a block behind them. He pulled to the side of the road, then made an illegal U-turn.

"Gabriel, what you was going say?"

Gabriel had forgotten what he was going to say. He searched in his mind for the frayed end of that thought, but he couldn't find it. Just as he was running out of time to make up an excuse for his absentmindedness, an excuse was delivered to him—you could say—by God Himself. On a bus.

Having just gotten off the bus from Honolulu, Father David Fonseca was waiting to cross the street at the intersection when the blue '58 Chevy Impala came cruising by. He saw Gabriel pointing at him.

"There him—there the Father!" Gabriel said. "Why you no go ask him all about it!"

The womenfolk would have asked, "About what, Gabriel?" But they were embarrassed by Gabriel's pointing, and to cover their embarrassment they waved at the Father, and the Father waved back.

When they had gone a safe distance past the priest, Mary turned to Gabriel and chided him. "You shouldn't do dat kine stuff, not at the Father."

"Do what kine?" Gabriel returned.

"You know . . . point finger at him. He going think we was talking about him."

"But we was," Georgette said matter-of-factly.

"But we wasn't. I mean, not like that."

"Yeah, we was talking 'bout him," Gabriel minutely remembered. "And what you mean, 'not like that'?"

"You know what I mean," Mary said.

"No. I dunno what you mean."

"Oh, Gabriel, I no like fight with you. But you know what I mean."

"No. I dunno what you mean."

Georgette cleared her throat. "E kala mai, Mary. E kala mai, Gabriel," she said. "But Gabriel, you wen pass the market again."

Georgette began to laugh, and the laughter spread to Mary, then to Gabriel. And by the time Gabriel parked his car in the stall two places away from the front entrance—his usual parking place—tears were flowing from everyone's eyes.

Eight

ATHER FONSECA WAS the only passenger on a bus headed to downtown Honolulu. The bus was about halfway up the climb to the first of two tunnels that connected Kānewai with the city, and Father Fonseca, with one hand holding onto the handlebar in front of him, the fingers of the other hand anxiously rubbing a fold on the side of his black pants, had his head turned to the quickly passing trees and wild grass, though his eyes were focused on his semi-transparent, shadowy image reflecting inwardly off the window.

He had had a sleepless night, that vision of coagulated blood bubbling from the theater's wall haunting him until morning's first light, the sun giving him but small courage though enough to challenge the nightmare and chase it from his immediate consciousness. In the stale, solitary air of the early evening chapel, he had prayed; and again in the early morning hours when he realized that sleep was impossible; and again after the break of dawn. He had decided to go to town later that morning and confer with Monsignor Bickens about what course of action he should—needed to—take. Perhaps they really had to look into the possibility of getting an exorcist.

As he looked out the wide, water-stained window of the bus, his eyes now directed to the dense foliage that was flying past, he wondered why this evil happening was occurring so suddenly, so forcefully, in Kānewai. Was this a message from the Lord? Was He trying to punish certain unrepentant individuals? But why was the entire community being chastised? He turned from the window and was startled by the sight of a disheveled old Portuguese woman seated across the aisle from him. He had not noticed her before; in fact, he did not remember her boarding the bus. She was holding an unlit cigarette and watching him with a smile that squinted her eyes and brought deep wrinkles around them. Her mouth opened, as if searching for necessary words to say, exposing a mouthful of bad teeth. She swallowed dryly, her eyes calmly swaying to the side then back. Then, smiling, her gravelly voice dusted with anxiety, she said, "Father, you have one light, please?"

Father Fonseca was struck by the red sparkle in each of her eyes. "No . . . I don't smoke. I'm sorry."

The old woman nodded, as if she had expected the answer. She looked forward, masticated dryly, then rose from her seat and tottered up to the front, struggling against the swaying inertia of the moving bus. She settled in a seat behind the driver.

Father Fonseca looked out the window, the old woman's eyes disturbing him. He was afraid to look at her again, afraid to see her eyes looking back at him, eyes that had, in a matter of seconds, seen deep inside of him. But he pulled himself from the window and forced his eyes to the front. The woman was not there. He had a sudden, bottomless feeling. He could not feel his feet, his legs were but paralyzed stalks of vegetable matter connected to the floor. He gripped the handlebar hard with two hands and yanked at his legs to be free. Like trying to wake himself from a bad dream, he struggled to stand, to walk away from this hold of miasma that he was sinking in. Finally he burst up, body quivering, a sudden light-headedness overwhelming him. Trembling, he sat back down and touched his crucifix, crossed himself, and took a deep breath to steady the shake in his body. He got up again and dragged himself to the front of the bus but stopped halfway. He sat.

There must be some explanation for this. He kissed his crucifix, crossed himself again, closed his eyes, and prayed. When he finished, the bus was entering the darkness of the first, shorter tunnel. The interior lights flickered on. There was a gap between the tunnels and a flash of daylight lit the bus; then it was the longer, darker tunnel. A chill entered his body through the small of his back, spreading quickly and numbing his senses. He was losing consciousness, but he didn't fight it. Bright sunlight bursting through the front windshield purged his mind of darkness. As he slouched in exhaustion, gently nourished by the warm light, a thought came to him about where he might find the answer to his hesitations.

At the very next stop, he got off, walked across the highway, and waited at the closest stop for the next bus back to Kānewai. He waited for half an hour before the bus came by. Climbing on board, he dropped a quarter in the coin box and seated himself halfway toward the back. As the bus again climbed the Pali, now going in the opposite direction, he began to reevaluate his faithful position about Kalani, his good friend since elementary school, as not having any connection to the evil. If there was an embodiment of the devil in Kānewai, it had to be Kalani Humphrey. But the Father knew that he'd have to go back to the theater and find out for sure. It was necessary to clear up this mystery once and for all, for the sake of the community. And for the sake of his own faith.

He got off in the middle of Kānewai town and while waiting for the traffic light to change saw Gabriel Ho'okano's old Chevy lumbering down the main street. Gabriel had a packed house in his car. The Father knew that in the car besides Gabriel (or, as the Father would say, Uncle Gabe) were Mary Wahineokaimalino and Auntie Mary's friend and second cousin, Georgette Edwards, and that they were probably going to the market. Or perhaps the two women had persuaded Gabriel to take them for a pleasant morning drive somewhere.

Waving hello at the car, the Father tried to remember the last time he had heard any of their confessions. He could not remember. Though the church still played a large role in the community—the steady increase in enrollment at St. Mark's School attesting to this fact—still he had noticed a visible drop in attendance at Mass, and in the number and frequency of confessions. Perhaps the dark events in Kānewai were really an expression of God's wrath, His anger at the people for their hypocrisy and sins. People illegitimately sleeping with one another. People cheating one another. People lying. People stealing. Perhaps the blood that he witnessed at the wall was the blood of Christ, warning them that the town of Kānewai was soon to come under Judgment. Perhaps the malefic manifestations at the theater were the work of the Devil who had realized, with the steady demise of faith in the Lord, his growing power and influence over the inhabitants of the town.

The thought shook him. It so petrified him that his arm remained raised in recognition of Gabriel's Chevy Impala even though the car had passed him at least fifteen seconds before. He lowered his arm and crossed the street, the internalization of that horror blinding him from a car that came to a screeching stop eight and a half feet away from running him over. Unshaken by the near accident and waving a "Sorry" to the driver, he ambled toward the theater, greeting people along the way with unconscious hellos and smiles, finally standing across the street from the wall.

His eyes widened with the immediacy of a new vision. New blood was on the wall: bright, red blood. Never mind that it was a new sign painted with red paint (done by Dennis Umeda at Clarissa Ching's direction; "No Trespassing," it said). For Father David Fonseca, the paint was blood.

Father David meditated on the vision for a long while, concluding that his fears were real. And it wasn't until little Tammy Nakashima, a third grader at St. Mark's School, came pedaling her bicycle next to him did he snap out of his stonelike trance. Tammy greeted the Father, and when she found him unresponsive, she impatiently grabbed him by the pants and gave a solid yank. Father Fonseca looked at the girl, his eyes searching for some clue to the familiarity of her face. He said hello, and then she bicycled away. Only when she was too far for calling did he remember her name.

But he came to a resolution.

Shading the crucifix from the sun that was an hour from setting behind the theater, the Father prayed silently, whispered three Hail Marys, then trudged away, laboriously carrying the weight of his confession to the nearest bus stop, where he awaited the next ride to the city.

Nine

AT THREE MINUTES to eleven, a warm and windless night, Quintin Lee's phone rang. Quintin leaped across the living room, where he was watching a video, with the volume turned down very low, and grabbed the receiver in the middle of the first ring, making sure his wife would not be stirred out of her sleep.

"Quintin, is me. Henry Kila."

Quintin looked nervously at the television screen. "Hold on," he whispered, panting. "Wait."

"What you doing?"

"Nothing," Quintin answered, then, using the remote control, stopped the VCR, which was playing *The Sizzlin' Sexties,* one of several videotapes he had borrowed from Dennis Umeda. "Yeah, what you like?" he said, barely audible to even himself. "What you calling me at dis fuckin' hour fo'?"

"Gotta talk to you."

"About what?"

Quintin heard Henry sigh.

"Da signs going back up again," Henry said.

Quintin scratched his head. He asked Henry what was so new about that.

"What's so new about this is," Henry said, "the signs talking about us."

"And who *us?*" Quintin remembered the message about Paul Navarro, but that had seemed to be an exception. "About who the signs talking about?"

"Everybody. Dennis, Paul, even Claudio." He paused for a blink. "And you."

A chill entered Quintin. "Me? So . . . whas the sign saying about me?"

"The sign saying you fucking your hand every night after your wife go sleep."

There was a telling pause on Quintin's side of the line. "What—and—so—what dah signs stay—ah—saying—"

"You know what dah signs stay saying about Claudio?"

"What?"

Despite clearing his throat of the impediments of guilt (if there was one thing that Henry never liked to do, that was being the source of gossip), he gagged on the last word of his next sentence: "The thing is saying that Claudio is one . . . fag."

"Claudio . . . one *fag?* Eh, is dis fo' real kine?"

"You asking me? He was yo' buddy in high school, not mines."

"Eh—you calling me one fag?"

"I not calling you nothing. I jus' calling you up telling you dah facts. Dah frickin' wall stay acting up again."

Quintin cast a leery eye at the VCR, then at the television: *And he-r-r-r-re's Johnny!* "So . . . what you going do?" Quintin asked.

Quintin could hear Henry breathing. "What *you* should do? Yo' name is up there, not mines."

The idea of his solo nocturnal submission going public angered Quintin and, of course, embarrassed him. "Damn! Whoever is that frickin' buggah putting up those signs is one fucking liar!"

"Tell me about it."

"I thought you said everybody's name is up there? How come yours not?"

Henry shrugged his shoulders, which Quintin, obviously, could not see. "Dah fucker who doing all dis is not after me, directly, but is me that is getting attack too, through association with the names on the wall."

"What you mean? What I did? I never do nothing."

"You wen fuck Clarissa Ching. Maybe it's the old man's ghost haunting you now, trying get back at you." Henry laughed.

A thin rascal grin came to Quintin's face. "Eh—what you mean?"

"Brah, everybody knows about that night wit' you and Clarissa. Except that old pākē. But maybe now he knows. Maybe now he knows because he in that spiritual world where you can know about everything. Maybe he haunting you."

"I never sleep with Clarissa Ching," Quintin said in a decibel just above a whisper. He checked across the living room toward the hallway to make sure his wife wasn't listening in.

"No fut around, Quintin. Everybody, maybe with the exception of your wife, knows about that. Maybe even she knows. And why you whispering like dat fo' anyways?"

"So what you proposing to do?" he said.

"We go down there and whitewash the frickin' wall. Again. And if we have to, again and again. Until da buggah doing all dis geevs up. I meet you down there. Right now. Bring some white paint." Henry hung up.

Quintin imagined the snickering laughter of the people after reading about his nightly doings. He swore. He regarded the VCR for a while, wondering what he should do, then deciding—first things first—to return immediately all the pornographic videotapes to Dennis. Borrowing all of those tapes had put a curse on him. And how the hell did Dennis get so many tapes all at once? Where the hell did he get them in the first place? And who was that frickin' sonavabitch sign-maker?

While he ejected the videotape, he felt heavy breathing on the back of his neck. He spun around. There was no one. The curtains covering the far window shivered, then stopped. Shaken, he pulled out the videotape, dropped it, picked it up, and slipped it into the case, then stashed it with the others in the Pan Am bag, which he stored in a secret spot in the garage. But there were eyes on him. There was someone watching him. He jumped to the front door and opened it, switching on the floodlight. There was no one outside. He settled back in, dumping himself on the couch. Perhaps who-ever-it-is was able to listen in to his thoughts. Perhaps who-ever-it-is knew about the lie he had spread anonymously about Clarissa Ching being so promiscuous that she had even paid Kalani Humphrey to do it to her, and also about the lie (which he also had spread anonymously, via innuendo) about him and Clarissa doing it in the Chings' garage in the back-seat of her brand-new Mercedes. Whoever-it-is also probably knew that it was he, Quintin, who ratted on Paul Navarro (he had called Pat Navarro on the telephone and told her in a voice muffled with Kleenex that Paul was having an affair with the librarian Cassie Chun) a day after Paul had made him look really small in front of the boys at the lounge, Paul bragging about how much more money he was making than Quintin even with Quintin working more years; but that was only, as the saying goes, the tip of the iceberg, since Paul Navarro and Quintin Lee always had a minor feud going on, ever since that intrasquad football scrimmage when he hit Quintin on the blind side (for no good reason, Quintin con-cluded, but to show how tough he was in front of the onlook-ing practicing cheerleaders), giving Quintin a concussion that cost him the season; to more recently when Quintin had positively seen his wife and Paul Navarro make eyes at one another at Val Rodriguez's baby lūʻau. And whoever-it-is also probably noted, of course, the tapes he had been borrowing from Dennis, those naughty tapes of men and women doing it to each other—whoever-it-is must have watched him watch those tapes all this time, and now the entire community would know about it! The shame! The embarrassment! Quin-tin Lee masturbating in his living room when he was sup-posed to be sleeping with his wife!

He rushed to the windows, hoping to catch the spy. And again, there was no one.

Damn asshole, probably left already, I'll get him.

He sat on the couch, not knowing what to do. First things first, he told himself, the sign gotta come down.

His eyes drifted to a crucifix that was mounted over the kitchen doorway. For seven long seconds his eyes beheld it, first with mild indifference, then in desperate appeal.

He took the crucifix off the wall and pressed it hard to his chest. He squeezed his eyes closed, praying for forgiveness.

IN THE BEDROOM, his wife mumbled something unintelligible to him, and Quintin told her that he needed to go out for an errand. She rolled to her side and went back to sleep.

Quintin dressed, then left the house.

In the bed of his Toyota pickup, he placed a half-used can of white enamel paint, rollers and pans, then drove to the theater.

WHEN QUINTIN ARRIVED, Henry Kila was already painting the wall in hasty, sloppy strokes. More paint was on the sidewalk than on the wall, and paint was dripping down from his elbows. Quintin was about to laugh, Henry usually being such a meticulously neat person when it came to work habits, until he saw the sign that, in his mind, made him look worse than a cuckold. Quickly he opened his can of paint and began plastering over the sign with a haste and waste that was noticeably inferior to Henry's effort. Swearing, grunting, and whining, Quintin covered the sign with two coats of his cheap paint. He stepped back, making sure that he had covered every stem and curve of the letters (especially those of his name), then swore at the thinness of the paint and went over the sign another two times. He noticed Henry giving him a stink eye.

"What the fuck you spending so much time on that puny

sign?" Henry growled. "Com'n and cover the rest of the signs."

Quintin gave his sign another working over, then began painting over the others. The two men worked silently for about half an hour.

"Who you think doing this?" Quintin asked the fire-fighter.

"I dunno. But whoever the punk is, if I find out who it is, I going give the punk one dirty lickin'." Henry stopped, stepped back and studied the wall. He shook his head. "I dunno . . . I dunno why I doing all this. I like geev up already. Maybe I shouldn't."

"Shouldn't what?"

"Shouldn't do all this, covering every damn word, every damn time dis thing happens. It not talking about me. Maybe . . . maybe I should just let 'em all go. Maybe everything should just hang out, let everything go the way it has to go. I sick and tired of covering up the truth."

———

IT TOOK THEM another half hour to finish the wall. Dennis Umeda and Watson Kamei had come down to help. Paul Navarro had refused to get out of bed, and Henry had decided not to call Claudio Yoon, even though it wasn't for certain that Claudio had the kind of orientation that the wall had suggested he had. But Henry wasn't taking any chances. And after they got through, the boys decided to get some coffee at Breezy's Drive-in and talk about what they should do to confront the problem. Two coffees later, they decided that they would send a scout out every morning at 5:00, armed with a bucket of paint and a roller, just in case new lampoons were plastered on the wall, for they came to the conclusion that the signs were done only under the cover of darkness. They each took responsibility for the next few mornings, then volunteered Richard Pimente, Tiny Vierra, and Paul Navarro for the mornings following, with Claudio Yoon as the single—and only—alternate. Then they left for home.

Henry Kila was the first to monitor the wall at 5:00 the next morning, and he found, over the fresh paint, the exact signs that had been covered up approximately twenty-seven hours before. It was as if the signs had been resurrected, bursting through the whitewash to live again.

Ten

THEY WERE ALL talking about the Bowling Brigade checking the wall every morning, and the general consensus
among most of the residents was that the brigade's efforts
were fruitless. Gabriel Hoʻokano thought them a bunch of
fools. Flora Goto didn't see the logic in their going there and
trying to find the sign-maker; she remarked to her husband,
who wasn't listening to her but watching a favorite TV game
show, that whoever was making all of those signs was
"smarter than all of those jackasses combined." Earlier that
same day, Freddie Tanaka of Tanaka's Union Service said to
Matt Goto as they sat on the back seat of the '69 Dodge Dart
that he thought the bowlers were crazy, but that sometimes
craziness had to be paired with what was right, that sometimes craziness was just the same as being right.

"But if you ask me," Freddie added, shaking his head,
"they should jus' bus' down the wall, the theater, and forget
all about it."

Matt reflected for a moment on a sign hanging sideways
by one nail on one of the posts that held up the roof over the
gas pumps. The sign read, "TURN ENGINE OFF."

"But, you know," Matt said, "get the ghost."

"You mean, you think the ghost going haunt somebody?
It wen take his revenge already. Hiram Ching ma-ke. And das
dat. So all dis other things is crazy. Fo' da birds. As long as I
not involve."

Matt crossed his arms over his chest, fingers anxiously
tapping the elbows. "But you involve."

"What you mean?"

"The whole community involve in this . . . in this lōlō thing."

Freddie waved a fly from his face. "I nevah do no harm to nobody. So why should I worry about that?"

"You get one point. I hope you right."

Simultaneously both sets of eyes wandered up the quarter block of street to the theater, to a full viewing of the wall with all of its layers and layers of signs and whitewashing attempts. But what had caught their attention was Harriet O'Casey, whose old bent body was unmistakably recognizable from any distance. She was pointing at something at the very top of the wall for a long time.

"What she doing?" Freddie asked.

Matt shrugged his shoulders. "Beats me."

Harriet lowered her pointing finger as if counting rungs of a ladder. She stopped her countdown, her finger stuck on a spot for long while about three feet from the bottom of the wall.

"What the hell she doing now, dat crazy wahine?" Freddie said.

Again Matt shrugged his shoulders, adding an inarticulate mumble that sounded like a "beats me."

"What you said?" Freddie asked.

"Nothing."

"I think she counting how many feet down to the bottom of the wall," Freddie offered, "but what fo', I have no idea."

"I think she cursing the place," Matt said matter-of-factly. "She making all that motions like she cursing the place."

Freddie coughed. "Maybe she blessing the place."

"Could be. I dunno."

Harriet broke away from the wall and began hobbling down the street, away from the men. But before disappearing around the next corner, she stopped, turned her head a quarter of a turn, and laughed, as if laughing at the men. Then she continued on.

"I dunno whassamattah wit' her," Matt said weakly. "I dunno."

FATHER FONSECA WOULD have interpreted, correctly, what Harriet O'Casey was doing. Or rather, he would have known what someone like her, whom he had always considered a "good person," would have done in the face of the Devil. The Father would have explained that Harriet was laughing in Satan's face.

Eleven

IN THE SOLITUDE of his small room, Father Fonseca strummed his guitar with no song in mind. He had just come back from the state prison, from visiting Kalani Humphrey, his old high school friend, and was bothered by what had gone on there. Talk between them went well, right up to the second to the last thing that Kalani said. That penultimate sentence went something like this: "So, you see, David, jus' like how I wen tell you befo' da second half, I ain't in the game because of the game, but then like I said before they wen arrest me, the time I saw you at the church, all this is one big game and the point is how to make it seem like it isn't a game."

Father Fonseca was about to ask for a translation of what seemed to him a riddle when Kalani stood, extended his hand for a shake, and said, "Thanks for coming, David, but I gotta go." They shook hands, and the Father watched the guard escort him through the barred door.

When he got back to the parish, the Father went into the chapel to pray. Then he lumbered up the steps to his second-floor room and sat on a chair next to the window that opened to Father Rosehill's vegetable garden below. Watching Father Rosehill prepare the soil for another roll of string beans or tomatoes, Father Fonseca pondered the significance of what his old friend had said, thinking perhaps Kalani had unintentionally given him a clue to why things were happening the way they were in the community.

He chided himself. He turned from the window and

raised his eyes to the crucifix above the threshold of the doorway. Had he not already found the meaning of life through the salvation of Jesus Christ, the Son of God? And instead of receiving a message, wasn't he supposed to be delivering the word of God to Kalani? His thoughts rambled on in length, spiked by the troubling events of the community. He looked out again over Father Rosehill's garden, where the older priest was turning over the dark moist soil in one corner. At first sight, no one would have guessed Father Rosehill was a servant of God. He was wearing a faded tank top, tattered Bermuda shorts, and a beat-up pair of tennis shoes with no socks. A wide-rimmed coconut hat shaded his face. Father Rosehill tried almost any type of vegetable under the Hawaiian sun with near perfect success. The transplanted Iowan for more than thirty-odd years had come from a longtime farming family, and even in his sermons he used words figuratively, drawing from his pastoral background: the repeating, the harvesting, the nurturing, the watering, the planting, the ripening of God's Glory in Heaven and on Earth.

As Father Fonseca studied the elder Father's simple laboring—his simple hoeing of a singular short furrow in which seeds would be dropped and with the blessing of the Lord through His winds and sun and water, and, with the nutrients of the soil, life would be raised—he came, again, to a ravenous admiration of Father Rosehill's stoic expression of belief in the life and work of God and His Son Jesus Christ.

Father Fonseca leaped to the window, fearful that the profound feeling would escape, and burst forth: "Thank you! Father!"

Shaken for a moment at Father Fonseca's bombastic blessing, Father Rosehill stopped his work and shaded his eyes with the cup of his hand, looking in the direction of Father Fonseca's window. Then, smiling with recognition, he waved a greeting and shouted, "Oh, I'm all right! The sun is good today! And how are you today, Father?"

A MINUTE AFTER Father Rosehill returned to his gardening, Father Fonseca sat down again with his guitar and began to play a favorite song that had been popular during the time he first decided to become a seminarian; and it was probably that song on a couple of occasions that had served as a euphonious compass directing him across the chaotic river of Sin to the beatific shore of Sacrifice and the Lord. The guitar was out of tune, the honey-colored soundbox having stood in the direct wrath of the afternoon sun for several days now. He carefully tuned it, feeling the warmth of the wood, then picked the first chord of a song that he knew oh so well. He closed his eyes and turned inward to the time when he was attending a seminary located just outside a small farming town in California, to those antiwar days when he was a follower and later organizer of the Concerned Catholics Against the War. Effortlessly, as if time was not an eraser of memory, the words of the stanza flowed out, then the chorus:

> *The answer my friend is blowing in the wind*
> *The answer is blowing in the wind.*

———

AT APPROXIMATELY FIFTEEN minutes to eight that evening, Father Fonseca received a surprising telephone call. It was from Clarissa Ching; it was the first time Clarissa had ever spoken to him since his return to Kānewai in the late seventies.

"Father, I want you to come to the theater right now, please, if you can."

"How can I help you? What seems to be the problem, Mrs. Ching?"

"There's no problem. I mean, there is a problem."

Thinking that she wanted to give a confession, he suggested that she come to the church.

"No. You must come to the theater. Right now."

"All right." The Father checked his watch. "I'll see if I can use the seminary's car. I'll be there in ten minutes."

The car was not available; Brother Epiphanio had gone to town for a meeting of the Catholic Schools Council. So he walked, taking double the time that he had predicted. When he got to the theater, he found a worried Clarissa Ching waiting outside the front entrance.

"What is it that is troubling you, Mrs. Ching?" he inquired.

"You and Kalani were best friends, right?" she asked calmly.

The Father nodded his head. "We still are."

"Do you know that Kalani Humphrey is really my son?"

The Father studied her face, anticipating a confession. "Yes."

"Come with me," she said, and she led him into the theater. They entered the main auditorium, and halfway down one aisle she stopped, turned to the Father and said, "Well? What do you think?"

The Father hadn't observed anything out of the ordinary, other than the sharp, wet odor of mold, so he asked what it was that she was referring to.

"There . . . up there." And she pointed to the arches above the curtains. "Do you see it now?"

Large white letters had been painted on the façade above the screen. It read, "The Father of Kalani Humphrey is responsible for his parents' murders."

"Do you know what that means?" Clarissa Ching asked with a tremor in her voice.

The Father read the sign a couple of times to himself. "Kalani's . . . father is to—"

"You don't know what it means?" It was a statement rather than a question.

"I think it's saying that Kalani's father is—"

"Don't you know what it means?"

He saw the fear in Clarissa's eyes, heard the urgency in

her voice. Perspiration formed visibly on his forehead. "No, I . . . I don't know exactly what it means. If I am to understand it for what it's saying, it's saying that Kalani's father is responsible for the deaths of Mr. and Mrs. Humphrey, which, legally could mean Mr. Humphrey, or it could mean . . . " For a moment, the Father remembered the mysterious way the couple had been found dead in their living room.

"No! No! No!"

"I'm sorry, but I don't understand. Can you tell me what it means, then?"

"It means you're going to kill me!"

Father David looked gravely at a horrified Clarissa Ching. He felt his heart pounding, harder and faster, like it did a few nights back, at a little past 3:00 in the morning, when he had wakened out of that terrifying dream of washing his hands of blood that would not wash off.

———————

THE ONLY THING he could ask was if she wanted him to bless the place. She didn't answer, her face bleached of emotion, almost ghostlike in the dim lighting of the theater. It was the first time that he had seen her face close up, and though the light was weak, he saw the deep wrinkles that she had tried unsuccessfully to make over. And he could also see the white roots of her black hair. She looked so miserably old and vulnerable in his eyes. It was not compassion that he felt for her; it was pity. It was a pity of the kind that he had hoped to have purged himself of during seminary.

Priests are not supposed to pity people, but to understand them, to feel compassion for them, as Jesus Christ and all the Saints through history have felt.

The thought had haunted him through his student years, though with his entry into the priesthood he had disavowed any claim, purposely or otherwise, of it. But now he felt a wave of pity gripping his internal cloak and tearing it from his soul, exposing his inner self to himself again, that internalized conflict that he had forgotten or ignored for such a long time.

It was immediately troubling; it pained him; and yet, he could not help but feel the intensity of that pity growing and growing as his eyes scrutinized Clarissa's face more and more. Her eyes were now huge and glossy and fearing, and he felt a huge urge to grab her, to wrap her in his arms of a beast and crush her while sinking his teeth into her neck.

He gasped, his body lurching forward then back, the rocking between the heels and toes of his feet lengthening, though imperceptible to Clarissa. But he caught himself, stopped his rocking, shook off the trance, then turned to the front of the stage, crossed his heart, and offered a silent prayer to the Lord for the theater and for Clarissa, but, more so, for himself. Then, with a nod of his head as a goodbye, he quietly left the auditorium.

He took the long walk back to the seminary, a route that passed Gabriel Hoʻokano's house and the old Hawaiian grave-yard. He took this route purposefully, for about halfway home on the shorter way, with his mind clouded with ambivalence, he turned his thoughts to his great-grandmother who had died seven years back at the age of ninety-eight and was buried in the old cemetery, alongside her husband of sixty-seven years, eighty-two years if eternity was included. Father Fonseca had been very close to his tūtū; it was her advice that prompted him to enter the priesthood. He remembered well, that time.

"Tūtū," he had said, his eyes reddened from tears, "I did something wrong. Real bad."

"ʻAe," she had agreed, smiling with understanding.

"I don't know what to do."

"You not thinking wit' you naʻau."

"I don't know how fo' do that."

"Manaʻo kou puʻuwai. Lohe kou naʻau. No think wit' you mind, keiki-boy."

"But if I don't think with my mind, I don't know what to do."

"Heh-heh-heh! Keiki-boy! The stream run dry and you think no mo' water again."

"But you don't know what I did. I tell you."

"'A'ole. Akua knows and das nuff. If you lohe Him, He tell you what fo' do."

———

HE WALKED UP the dark dirt road to the wooden gate of the cemetery where, pausing for a moment, he breathed in the stillness and dampness. He heard the collective mourning of Harriet O'Casey's cows. Scanning the sky, the stars and clouds and the moon in its last quarter, he pushed through the gate and entered. Though the cemetery was overgrown with grass, Father Fonseca knew the pathways well, where the grave-markers were, where the interred ground was sunken, for he visited his great-grandparents at least once a week. His family plot was near the back of the cemetery, close to the fence of the pasture. He came to his great-grandparents' gravestones, brushed them off, and kissed each, then settled cross-legged on the small clearing he had made during the last time he had visited, which was yesterday. Then, facing his tūtū's stone, he said, with head bowed, with fingers folded together, "I never told you before, Tūtū, but this time I have to tell you what really happened."

Twelve

JUST AS MATT Goto inserted his videocassette of the 1981 Super Bowl (the Oakland Raiders versus the Philadelphia Eagles—the Raiders won with the aging Jim Plunkett; Matt always glorified the fact that Plunkett had come back as a has-been and became the hero of the game), the electricity went out. Cursing in the darkness, he groped for the eject button, pressed it, then remembered that the outage also affected that feature. He managed to find his way to the kitchen to a drawer of odds and ends. He found a candle stump and lit it.

Meanwhile, Flora had come out of the shower. The water was all right, but it was funny to shower in the darkness; she felt—and this could have been her own words—naked in there, as if someone was watching her. She dried herself quickly, wrapped her wet hair in a towel, and came out of the steaming bathroom in a faded old mu'umu'u, her skin moistened from the steam. "What happened?" she asked Matt in the candle-lit living room.

"The lights went out. Here." He offered her the candle.

"We get nuff candles?"

Without a word, he went back to the kitchen to search the drawers again. "Yeah," he said from the kitchen. "Get couple mo'." He lit another one and came back into the living room and picked up the phone. "At least the phone still work," he grumbled, then began dialing.

"Who you calling?"

"Dennis. Dennis Umeda. He work fo' da electric company, right? Maybe he know what da hell is happening— Dennis? Eh, this Matt . . . Yeah, yeah. You, too? . . . So what?

You think going last long or what? . . . Da electricity. Da electricity went out . . . Yeah-yeah-yeah . . ."

Flora went into the bedroom and sat on the edge of the bed to dry her hair. She couldn't dry her hair with the blower now, and the TV and VCR were out. What could they do tonight? She unwrapped her shoulder-length hair and began drying it by taking locks in the fold of another dry towel and rubbing out the moisture. That was the old way she used to dry her hair, before all those new electric appliances came into existence. That was the way she and her three sisters did it back in the old plantation days. On Saturday mornings, they'd all wash their hair and sit in the bright sun, rubbing their hair with towels and combing them out, helping each other. She was young and firm then, and her hair was black and thick and shiny, and her face was brown from working alongside her mother and father and her two older brothers and her two older sisters in the pineapple fields. They lived in the plantation camp, and before setting off to work, the girls would bundle their hair tightly in scarves, using wide-brim straw hats to hold the bundles in place. But the red dirt would still permeate the coverings, and there were times when after a long day they'd come home early enough to wash their hair, but there were times too when it was too late to wash their hair, their mother forbidding them to sleep with wet hair in the cold night, and for Flora those nights trying to fall asleep was a discomfort, and as a way to make herself sleep she'd think of Saturday mornings combing out wet, clean hair.

It was very long then, those days when one way femininity was measured was by the length of a woman's hair, and after she and her sisters washed their hair (twice with Ivory soap), they'd rinse with the nectar of unopened bulbs of ginger that grew wild on the slopes behind the camp. The ginger had a fragrance that was unmatched by any of those new shampoos or rinses; even those so-called herbal treatments smelled too medicinal. And now, as she rubbed-dry her hair, which was curled by chemicals and rollers and heat and cut to a "manageable" length, she wished for one of those bulbs of ginger in her hand, what they used to call "shampoo ginger"; if she had one right now, she'd squeeze it over her head and let the juice run down, then she'd rub it gently into her scalp.

And she remembered the letter that Matt had written to her from the European front, and that was the only time—ever—that he had written, or said, for that matter, something romantic. "I miss the ginger in your hair," he had written. (He had jotted down that memory during a brief lull of gunfire before his unit was to take an Italian hill. He had addressed and sealed the letter, then gave it to his commanding officer. Several of his buddies had been either killed or wounded that day, and Matt thought that this approach was going to be the last for him. Being romantic before dying had given him a strange but honorable sense of fulfillment.) As she eased into this soft, expansive mood, she began to feel young. She became aware of the peripheries of her body: fingers wet from the hair; feet on the worn carpet, toes digging into the stitching; moist skin tingling warmly under the muʻumuʻu.

She remembered that one late morning sitting with her second oldest brother on the front porch of their plantation workers' home when Matt came by to talk story with Akira, a couple of years before the war; there was something different about the way he behaved that time as compared to previous occasions. Before she had been Akira's younger sister, but now Matt seemed more aware of her and yet avoided looking at her; despite that his eyes were directed at Akira, she felt a strange, embarrassing sensation that he was studying her. Finally there was an exchange of animated words between Matt and her brother, with Akira bursting with laugher. Matt was obviously bothered by this and left without a word. But that early evening when Akira had gone to work, Matt came back, and she wondered why, and he politely greeted her father and mother, and they were all in smiles. And then Matt began talking to her, his eyes never meeting hers, even after asking her out for a date to see a movie. And when she said yes, that it would be all right for the next evening, if it was all right with her parents, Matt's face softened, he smiled though still not looking at her. He thanked her parents. Then, without another word, he left, walking into the darkness toward his home. But she was thrilled, thrilled that someone had been considering her for a mate, for marriage . . . that's what he wants, no?

Matt was watching her by the doorway.

"Whas the matter?" he asked. "How come you smilin' like dat?"

She swallowed the smile and turned her face away from the candlelight. "Nothing. Was jus' thinking."

"Thinkin' 'bout what?"

"I dunno. Jus' thinkin'. How long dis electric outage going last? What Dennis said?"

Matt shrugged a shoulder. A roll of hot candle wax dripped on his hand. He switched the candle to the other hand, rubbing off the wet wax on his pants. "He dunno what happened. No storm, nothing to make da outage." Looking toward the ceiling. "Nowdays, cannot tell what going happened next. Things jus' happening by themselves."

"What you mean?"

He rolled his shoulders and leaned against the doorway. "Things jus' happening by themselves." He stared at the candle's flame. "Like down by the theater. They jus' happening. What can you do about it? Can't do nothing. Dis world turning upside down, inside out. What can you do about it?"

Flora saw clearly the old lines on Matt's face, the candlelight deepening his wrinkles. But she refused to see an old man. She closed her eyes and searched for a picture of a youthful Matt: thick black hair; short wiry arms; thin but muscular build; a dark, clear complexion. The Matt of yesteryears. But she couldn't find that picture. She opened her eyes. "Matt, you remember that letter you sent me when you was in Europe?"

"What letter?"

"The letter you told me you wrote in the army before you guys was going take over one bridge?"

"One bridge? You mean one hill." Pause. "No. I no remember writing you one letter."

Flora felt old all of a sudden; Matt had forgotten the letter. She went back to drying her hair. "So how long this going last . . . the power outage?"

"I dunno. Dennis said he not sure what wen happen. Mechanical failure, maybe. Cannot watch teevee."

But there was something ambivalent in the way Matt had said the last sentence. Flora watched Matt watching the candle and saw a familiar glow his eyes. Her skin began to tingle again.

She got on her side of the bed, setting the candle on the nightstand. "Let's go sleep early tonight," she said. "No mo' teevee to watch."

Matt nodded his head, then went to the bathroom to brush his teeth. When he came back, the room was strangely bright, as if the luminescence from his candle had doubled. He blew the candle out and with his hands found his side of the bed. And he asked her what kind of shampoo she was using, that the stuff was nice smelling like the stuff she used to use a long time ago. Flora smiled. It was dark, and Matt couldn't see her smile, but she began to giggle, and Matt could hear that, and Flora had the comforting belief that Matt hadn't forgotten the letter after all, that he was just being Matt thinking how embarrassing it was to write a letter like that and more embarrassing if he was to admit that he still remembered it.

So Flora lay on her back patiently, motionlessly, listening and feeling every stir of her husband, and finally, after a long deliberation, he began to touch her, something he hadn't done for at least the past two years.

———

IT WAS EARLY the following morning, a workday, when the electric company finally was able to restore power. The linesmen had to wait until the firemen could separate the late model blue Datsun pickup that was wrapped around the stump of a shattered utility pole; the top of the termite-ridden pole had fallen on the cab of the truck, crushing it. The accident had occurred around 8:30 in the evening, and the lone occupant of the pickup, who had been drinking heavily, was killed instantly, or at least he was dead by the time the ambulance arrived at the scene. The city morgue report cited that the possible cause of the accident was a combination of drunk driving and speeding. But every one of Claudio Yoon's friends knew that Claudio never drank more than two beers at a sitting. Claudio, they all contended, never got drunk.

Thirteen

Father Fonseca gave the eulogy at Claudio Yoon's funeral. Claudio was described as being quiet and kind, and having much love for his family and friends. After the service, while in the gathering room lunching on a plate of sushi, fried sesame chicken wings, and house noodles (slivers of char siu pork, roast duck, chicken, egg, and an assortment of vegetables on cake noodles, all smothered with a special Cantonese sauce that included oyster sauce, mashed black beans, Chinese Five Spice, corn starch, and water, among other things) catered from Fung Lung Chop Suey House, Quintin Lee made a remark to Henry Kila about what kind of loving Claudio was probably into.

"You think is true or what?" Quintin mumbled through a mouthful of food.

"Huh?"

"I mean," swallowing, "you know . . . what the sign said. That he one, you know, one da kine . . . acey-deucey."

"You mean one fag?"

"Eh! No talk so loud."

Henry sighed. "Why you talking like dis fo' at the man's own funeral? I would shut my face if I was you."

Quintin accepted the suggestion. But that didn't stop him and the other bowling members at the funeral—even Henry himself—from considering the facts about Claudio, something that nobody had ever done before since Claudio was a low-key kind of guy, never in the spotlight. For example, it was now deemed odd that Claudio had always been a bachelor; no one recalled ever seeing him with a woman.

Also, it was now decidedly strange that he enjoyed being "one of the guys" on any of the men's athletic teams (e.g., the bowling and slow-pitch softball teams) since, by common consensus among the players, Claudio could play for shit. Someone with a bit of background in drugstore Freudian psychology asserted that the cause of Claudio's "deviance" was probably because of his shaky childhood and that he never had any strong male models. He never knew his Korean father, though he took the man's surname, and his Filipino mother died when he was eleven, leaving him an orphan of the state up to a little past his sixteenth birthday, when somehow he finagled his way into the armed services. He was stationed at an air force base in France (post–Korean War), was honorably discharged, and got a job as a merchant marine on ships crossing the Pacific, finally leaving that job to be a repairman for Richard Pimente's home appliance sales and service shop.

"You know dose guys," commented Henry, in reference to Claudio's tenure at sea, to Quintin and Richard Pimente at a nearby Korean bar after the funeral, "sometimes they can get funny kine, all by themselves on the high seas wit' no women around."

"I wonder what he used to plug it in—ha ha ha!" laughed Quintin.

Henry gave him a sour look, then wolfed down the half-glass of beer and suds.

Richard made a disgusted face at Quintin's occupationally incorrect comment about his former friend and employee. "What the fuck you talking like dat fo'? Da guy dies and all of a sudden all of his so-called 'close' friends start talking stink 'bout him."

"I wasn't no close friend of his," Quintin affirmed.

"But you was in da same teams wit' him. You wen bowl wit' him. You play softball wit' him. Dat don't mean nothing to you? Fo' Chrissakes!"

Henry sipped his beer, remaining silent. Richard had a point.

"Christ, when I die," Richard fired, "you guys going talk stink 'bout me?"

"Eh, partner, cool it," Henry said. "You know as well as me what the rumors are dat going around 'bout Claudio, dat he one māhū."

"Māhū or not, da buggah was my friend. One good friend. He was one good worker. Never complain. Das a lot more than what I can say 'bout some people I know."

"Like who?" Quintin retorted.

Richard grinned, then sipped his beer. "Like who the one when make one pass at one fag down Hotel Street?"

Quintin rose from his seat. "You fuckah! You going bring dat up—hah?"

Richard glared back with challenge at Quintin. "Bring what up? Everybody know 'bout that. And look at you, dah very one who bring up dis business anyway!"

"Eh, sit down," Henry ordered. "No make one scene."

"You fuckah! No fuck wit' me!" Quintin sat down, but not before pointing a threatening finger at Richard.

"I jus' speaking da facts. Das all."

"I was drunk that night, all right? You know that. Henry was there, too. Right, eh, Henry? I was drunk, right?"

Grinning, Henry shrugged his shoulders and took a chug of his beer.

"Henry, no act. I was drunk. And da fuck!—she wen look like one she. If wasn't me, would be somebody else get fooled."

Henry belched oppressively, then smiled. "To each his own," he said.

"Eh, fuck you, too."

"But I could tell 'she' had one big prick under that skirt," Richard said soberly. "Not my fault you so goddamn igno-rant."

"Shit. Remind me no ask you come wit' us when we go out again."

"Eh, enough said already," Henry said. "Both of you

wrong. You shouldn't make fun of Claudio. He was my friend, too. And you shouldn't bring up the Hotel Street thing. One honest mistake."

"Yeah. Was one honest mistake."

"Henry, tell me something. If we went down Hotel Street again and you got stinkin' drunk, tell me if you could tell if da wahine was one man or not."

Henry raised his eyebrows. "Yeah. I could. I wasn't born yesterday."

"See!" Richard gave a hard look to Quintin, then laughed.

"Eh, shut up already," Henry said. "Da fuck, I nevah come here fo' get into one argument. I came here to relax, pay my respects to Claudio, *our* friend. Peace, brah, peace. Shake hands."

Reluctantly, Quintin and Richard shook hands.

"Okay," Henry said with satisfaction, lifting his glass. "Now le's drink one toast. Here's to our friend, Claudio Yoon. May he rest in peace."

The men toasted and guzzled their beers. They were silent for a while, listening to the music playing on the bar's radio, Owana Salazar's rendition of "Sweet Memories."

Quintin, his eyes moistening, said, "Here's one nada toast to Claudio. And this toast is with my apologies."

The two joined in. And they toasted more, drinking several more rounds, each toast dedicated to someone whom they all had known but was now deceased.

Fourteen

I T WAS THEIR fifth meeting at the Falls. Clarissa was counting. Almost every minute. It was wonderful.

Never had she felt this way since the time before graduation when, as the head cheerleader of Wilson High's pep squad, she was asked out by practically everyone on the football team, even though everyone knew that she was going steady with the halfback, Carson Sumida, who later in life went into the construction business on a neighbor island; and, of course, while going with Carson, she had succumbed to the dashing romanticism of Richard Pimente. She adored the curls of his hair; she thought he looked like Caesar Romero.

Then it was those long years of sacrifice with Hiram, which nonetheless benefited her immensely by helping her to salvage her pride and reputation as well as by providing her with unwavering financial security. Her liaison with Hiram was surely the best economic move of her life. But it had become evident—and this had become more apparent to her in the last few years before Hiram's death—that her acclaimed beauty of the past was quickly being lost. Now no heads would turn when she entered the drugstore or market. Now no conversations would stop as she passed pockets of men at the shopping mall. Now no prank calls came to the house (before, Hiram often changed the unlisted number—in one year he did so four times). She dreaded the coming of the years now more so than at any other time. Each time she'd meticulously examine herself in the full-length mirror in her dressing room, she'd become more and more concerned about the irreversible loss of her youth and natural beauty. Even with her stable situation in life, she began to question whether it was all worth it and for what purpose did it serve.

All of that had changed. Fate had paid her well for those years of frustration, celibacy, sacrifice, and more. She would always remember that particular night when good fortune dropped itself on her front steps. Or rather, the night Dennis Umeda fell into the women's restroom.

They were parked alongside the road that led to the entrance of Wailana Falls. The view of the Falls was best here, better than the designated scenic spot. But the view was the last thing on their minds. Besides, with the quarter moon hidden behind a cluster of lazy clouds for most of the evening, they couldn't see much of the Falls, though they could definitely hear it—if they were outside Dennis's four-wheeler. Instead, their legs and arms were entwined in the air-conditioned ambiance of Dennis's car, since buzzing outside of the car were swarms of mosquitoes, each dying to get in and dine on two warm bodies. One satisfied mosquito, however, did find its way in, or perhaps had already been the guest resident of the car. But that didn't bother the middle-aged practitioners of unending passion. Clarissa didn't care if she got a bite somewhere she wasn't supposed to. The point was that she was having the best fun in her entire life, and getting bitten where she wasn't supposed to was really a small trade-off for the pleasure of the moment.

They did it in so many wonderful positions that Clarissa had never thought possible or never could have conceived of. In past excursions they did it in the driver's seat (though that got too noisy with the horn), in the passenger's seat, in the backseat, on the back floor, upside down, sideways, crossways. Of course, most of the time it was uncomfortable for Clarissa, but that was the second or third or last thing on her mind; the first thing, of course, was that she was doing the thing.

Though the first three meetings she hadn't reached orgasm, Dennis did something different the next time that helped her attain that ethereal state of exhausting pleasure for the first time in her life: He had gone down on her. At first, she was frightened, disturbed, even repulsed, thinking that what he was doing was an absolute taboo. But with the noise of the Falls in the distance and even the buzzing of mosquitoes all sounding bizarrely romantic (they were on a blanket on the warm hood of his car), she found a tiny spot between her thighs expanding and swelling to the center of a sensuous universe. She grabbed Dennis by the back of his head and pushed his nose and tongue in deeper. Her head began to spin and fly away, and a warmth grew from the outside and spread inside to that center, until finally the stars around her exploded, basting her with tingling silvery dust. Oh, this Dennis must have had a lot of girlfriends, she jealously thought while absorbed in the diminishing warmth of dripping pudendum pleasure. But, she concluded, whatever scope of experience that Dennis had was really best for her.

What Dennis would never tell her was that all of his "experiences" were actually learned from textbooks. Or rather, from slick sex magazines. And triple-X-rated movies—some of which he had viewed recently and were none other than pre-owned by Clarissa's late husband.

He really had no fucking finesse. He was married once (no children) for three years, and the only position he used was the old missionary. If judged by the standards of a twenty-level video game, he would have gone no farther than the third level: His approach was awkward and rough, and his maneuvering was clumsy; in short, his lovemaking was repulsive. But fate—that good old word—had also fallen into his lap—perhaps more accurately, on his head. For both Clarissa and Dennis fell into each other's presence at just the right time, place, and circumstance.

They finished their lovemaking and were warm all over, laying in an exhausted state on the front seat and catching their breaths. Clarissa was smiling languidly, making spiraling circles with her finger from Dennis's piko to his nipples.

Then she sat up, looked out the window, and declared that a walk outside would be nice.

"I feel comfortable here," Dennis murmured.

"Oh, com'on. It's real nice out."

"With the mosquitoes?"

"Don't be a party pooper."

"But we have to put on our clothes."

"No, we don't. Let's run around naked. Com'on, Dennis."

"Where we going go?"

"Let's go look at the moon."

"We can see it from here."

"Com'on." She used her sweetest, sexiest voice, her fingers crawling on his stomach.

"Okay. Okay." He started to put on his underwear.

"What you doing?"

"Putting on my clothes."

"No. Why do we need clothes?"

"Hah?"

"Let's go out like this."

"Naked?"

"Yes. *Naked.*"

"Why?"

"I don't know. It'll feel good. I never did that before."

"But the mosquitoes."

"I don't care."

There was a definite change in Clarissa, and it was shocking Dennis. Though there had been a steady change of her personality since the first evening, the one tonight was most dramatic. This was definitely not the Clarissa he knew, that prudish wife of Hiram Ching, the richest and proudest and most powerful man in all of Kānewai. Even in the darkness, Dennis saw a Clarissa that was not Clarissa. Her eyes glittered, and she seemed so comfortable with her clothes sloughed off. Not like the first couple of times being self-conscious about her body, covering it completely after they had made love. She reminded him of one of those characters in the video he had recently viewed—what was the name of the movie, *Naughty High School Girls?* He was frightened for a moment: This woman whom he never thought he had a social chance with, whatsoever, was now begging him every day to take his pants off for the use of his thing. He felt uncomfortable, perhaps used. But wasn't he also having the most fun of his life?

"But what if somebody sees us?" he asked weakly.

"Silly. There's nobody out here but us." She kissed him.

"All right. But I gotta wear my slippers."

She leaned over and hugged him. They went outside. Dennis felt utterly ridiculous and self-conscious. He had never done anything like this before. For him, this dark, desolate road was lined with hundreds of hidden eyes, this road that absolutely nobody came on at night because of a local superstition.

According to legend, an unfaithful woman was murdered by her husband at the Falls. Her vengeful spirit now roams the area at night, looking for unsuspecting lovers, and if she finds a couple, she kills the female by entering her body. The male lover never knows what has happened and continues on with his business until the woman reaches orgasm, whereupon the spirit leaves the body, leaving the body lifeless. The male is not unaffected by this phantasmagoric liaison: His phallus becomes lifeless for the rest of his life. All of this, of course, was a lot of bullshit to Dennis Umeda, as he emphatically remarked to Quintin and Henry after Henry had told the story at Myra's Lounge, though now holding hands with Clarissa as they walked along the dark road, his other hand was cupping his genitals; he was hoping that Clarissa could not see what he was doing.

———

NOBODY—ESPECIALLY DENNIS or Clarissa—would have guessed that of all the possibilities the one ghost haunting the area would be Claudio Yoon's. And indeed, Claudio's spirit was roaming the bush at the Falls right at that time.

The last remembrance Claudio the ghost had was that of drinking downtown at a nameless Korean bar; it was the first one he found along a strip of lounges. That afternoon, at exactly 3:37 P.M., he entered the premise, his face long and nearly touching the floor, and without a word walked past an eager, welcoming, and rather touchy hostess and set himself at the bar, drinking heavily up to around 8:00 P.M. He couldn't remember how many beers he had drunk, but the smiling, wide-cheeked, clean-shaven Korean bartender served him as many as he wanted. The next thing he knew he was in the middle of nowhere, or rather, in the midst of bushes and trees. How he got there he had no idea.

He heard the mad buzzing of mosquitoes and murmurs coming from all around him. It frightened him. He thought he was in a bad dream and pinched himself to get out of it but felt nothing. The feeling was worse than a terrible dream, a nightmare, the worst that he had ever had. But he began to doubt that he was in a dream when he took a deep breath and found himself floating inches above the moon's wavy reflection at the pool on the top of the Falls; touching it, a coolness spread throughout his being. Something was terribly wrong. What happened? Was he . . . dead? He took another deep breath and found himself suspended above his wrecked blue Datsun pickup. The last glimpse of life as a living person—the truck's steering wheel turning into the utility pole—flashed in front of him.

Why did he do it? Why did he turn his wheel into the utility pole when in actuality he always harbored a great fear of dying?

It was a saddening realization for Claudio that perhaps he might be eternally trapped in this anchorless, dream-like existence—this state of being, or nonbeing?—that was wedged between the real world and the other world, which he really didn't know anything about other than having the idea that there might exist an "other" world. He dreaded the possibility that this predicament was a form of punishment, implemented by whom he did not know. Perhaps there was really a God, and it was God punishing him for taking his own life. But he regarded himself as leading a good, clean life, free of sins (well, except for those few times he had paid for carnal satisfaction down on Hotel Street); and besides, wasn't God supposed to be merciful?

But no, things never work the way they say they're supposed to. And wasn't he always the gullible victim? Someone always conning and deceiving him, lying to him. That was the way of his life. But would the church lie to its congregation about the afterlife? He didn't think so. If a person led an honest life, wouldn't he be rewarded at death with a ticket to Heaven? If God was merciful, then why was he in this depressing limbo? He sighed grievously, and his moans were so loud and hollow that they scared him. But he quickly got used to his new sounds, finding them pleasant and useful for draining himself of anxiety from this involuntary exile in a nightmarish world.

———————

"WHAT WAS THAT?" Dennis was motionless, listening to the bush.

"I didn't hear anything," Clarissa said. "But I can hear your heart beating."

"There—that noise! Listen."

Clarissa strained her ears. "I don't hear any—"

"There! Didn't you hear that?"

"Oh, that's probably a mongoose. Dennis, are you afraid of a mongoose?"

"Let's go back to the car."

"But I want to go down to the pool and take a swim."

"Swim? The water is too cold."

"How do you know?"

"It's too cold. And the mosquitoes not botherin' you?"

"No. Oh, all right. Let's go back." She hugged him, then giggled and tried to goose him. "Why are you holding those . . . things?"

"The cold. It's cold. Let's go back."

A mist-like figure crossed their path, stopping. A horrid moan came from it. Clarissa grabbed Dennis, and he grabbed her, and for that brief two or three seconds, the cold darkness of night entered their hearts. Then: "AARGHHH!!"

The next thing Dennis knew was his hightailing it back to the monster black four-wheeler with Clarissa trailing behind pleading with him to wait up. Dennis, running as hard as he could while clutching his genitals, could not hear her, for all that mattered to him was that he get into his car and get the hell out of there. He didn't want any retribution-seeking wahine ghost cutting off his 'olos. That was the last thing he could afford to lose.

He jumped into his car and started it. Then he wrestled on his underwear. Clarissa jumped in and covered herself with her clothes. Jamming his foot on the accelerator, Dennis raced the truck down the dirt road in reverse, then straight-ened out and sped to the St. Matthew's school parking lot (where the police never checked on their routine patrols). Dennis cut the engine and the lights, and coasted to a stop next to Clarissa's Mercedes. They sat silently, until Clarissa began dressing herself.

"We've got to stop seeing each other," she said. "That was Hiram's ghost we saw. And I think he wants to kill me."

Fifteen

FLOATING AMONG THE dusty old rafters of the theater for an eternity was no idea of fun for Hiram, especially when sunny days made the ceiling unbearably hot. He could not *feel* the heat, but knowing how hot the ceiling should be *made* him hot. He had quickly gotten bored with this "life" (if the word could be used liberally). How would anyone like to be restricted to one location for the rest of one's . . . ? Nary a soul would. Find one, and Hiram would unequivocally declare war on that individual; he'd take whatever means possible to haunt that poor embodiment of thought and feeling to death so that he or she could join Hiram in this existence and experience firsthand one of the most uncomfortable eternities ever between worlds. Hiram never knew the existence of the "other" world that Claudio, innately, was aware of. He never had a clue that there was more to an afterlife than what was contained within four coral-brick walls, a corrugated iron-sheeting roof, and a cracked concrete foundation. He had given himself into an eternity trapped in an impervious perimeter of timelessness. It didn't help that he was the kind of guy that just accepted things as they came, whether it be a sexless marriage with the once most beautiful girl in town or the startling fact that—yes, how strange that a thoroughly human adage can be proved truthful even in the afterlife—it was impossible for him to take all of his hard-earned money with him.

Even in the existence after death, one's personality never changes. There is no real need to change one's temperament since there is no one to change it for. And, besides, by this stage of the game, one should be satisfied with one's self—or rather, essence. But sometimes as he drifted from one side of the immense ceiling to the other, or to one of the restrooms, or to the hot dusty attic, Hiram went against that grain, wishing that it would be possible to escape the confines of the theater. He had tried to leave several times, but each time the attempt was aborted since he simply just didn't know how to get out; there was some kind of invisible force that kept him there. Sadly, he began accepting the fact that he was to go nowhere but would forever haunt the theater.

Sixteen

T HE BUS RIDE was too long and cramped for Father Fonseca, for he was in the asphyxiating confines of anxiety, both fretful and optimistic about the possibilities that might arise at the end of his present journey. And when he finally got to his destination, the state prison, his talk with Kalani Humphrey was just too short; even though he was a man of the cloth, the guards didn't give him enough time to deliberate on his friend's verbal riddling. As he rode the bus back to the Kānewai, he found himself even more confused about the matter of who—rather, what—was responsible for the lampoons. Back at the parish, after leaving the chapel following a session of heavy praying, as he walked down the cool main hall of the dormitory, he had a sudden insight into the riddle that was plaguing him for nearly fourteen years, since the halftime of that game in which Kalani Humphrey, after rushing for nearly a hundred yards and scoring two touchdowns, had suddenly unsnapped his helmet, threw it on the sidelines, and stomped off the field without saying a word to anyone. After the game, David Fonseca, the quarterback of the team, found a note written on a paper hand towel on the bottom of his locker. It said, "David—No believe in the Ghost."

He stopped in the middle of the hallway and touched his crucifix, his fingertips trembling.

———

HE MOVED HIS desk chair to the window overlooking the garden and sat down, watching Father Rosehill methodically hoe in the mid-afternoon sun. But a minute later, his lips parted. A revelation—or perhaps better, a resolution—came to him about why the pestilence was cursing the community. He shot up from his seat, the blood of ages rushing from his head and temporarily darkening his mind. He felt like shouting, but all he had could mutter was a cry muffled deep in his stomach. Gripping the window sill, his nails digging into the wooden jamb, he spat out something too soft for Father Rosehill to hear: "The Holy Ghost."

———

FOUR HOURS AFTER finishing his last confession (Matilda Nunes had admitted to stealing three loaves of bread two days ago from the bakery), Father Fonseca went to the common room and telephoned Clarissa Ching.

"Hello, David. Oh, I'm so glad you called. There's something I've been wanting to ask you. But first, how can I help you?"

"I'd like to ask you some questions about the theater."

"Yes . . . what do you need to know?" she said uneasily.

"Is the developer still interested in the property?"

"Right now they've put the deal on hold. Why are you asking?"

"They're still interested in the theater?"

"I suppose so. They haven't talked to me lately, but they're always in touch with my late husband's attorney. Why are you asking me this?"

"And what is the name of the corporation again? It's from Nevada, isn't that so?"

"Yes, it is. The name of the company is . . . is . . . it's on the tip of my tongue . . . uh . . . oh . . . Trinity. Trinity Corporation."

A silence on the Father's end.

"David? Are you still there?"

"Yes. Yes, I'm still here."

"David . . . Father Fonseca, can I ask you why you're asking me this?"

"Well, uh, I'm just curious. It seems that the entire community is concerned about what's happening at the theater. You know, the wall with all that graffiti."

"Yes. But why are you asking me all these questions?"

"I think I have an understanding of what all this is about."

Clarissa was silent.

"Mrs. Ching, are you still there?"

"Yes. I am. What do you mean about 'all of this'?"

The Father fixed his eyes on the crucifix nailed above the entrance of the common room. His eyes drifted to the Coke machine next to the entrance. One of the buttons was lit: "SORRY PLEASE MAKE ANOTHER SELECTION."

"What I mean," Father Fonseca said, "is that all of this that is happening to the community is really everyone's own doing."

"What do you mean by that?"

"What I am trying to say is that the theater is the embodiment of evil in the community, and we must do something about it."

"Like what?"

"I really don't know. But something."

"Look, Father. It's late and I'm a bit tired. Can we talk about this later, tomorrow?"

"Oh, I'm sorry. Yes, it's a bit late. I'm sorry."

"Goodbye, Father."

"Yes, good—"

After the click on the other end, the Father listened to the silence for nearly a minute, then hung up. He sat for a few more minutes in the ill-lit room, then sprang up and searched through his pocket for four-bits and bought himself a can of orange Diamond Head soda. He stopped briefly for a chat with Father Geoffrey and Brothers Vincent and Leopold in the library, then went up to his room. Picking up his guitar and opening the window to the night, he began strumming and humming a sixties peace song that he did not know the words to though the tune evoked a nostalgic memory. He remembered the girl—Caddie Hager, from Akron, Ohio—whom he had met at a Berkeley demonstration, and he remembered well the pleasant webs she had spun around him. They hadn't slept together, but it was the first time he had ever thought strongly about withdrawing his vow of celibacy and perhaps getting married. And now he wondered what it would've been like if he had left the seminary and became a layperson: Would he have children now? Would he still be happily married? Where would he be living?

The present moment was the first time in a long time, since that time with Caddie Hager, that he considered leaving the priesthood. What was making him think this way? There was definitely something in the community that wasn't healthy, that was making people think and act badly. Was he getting affected, too? Yes, he thought, it's affecting me, too. But wasn't he happy here at St. Matthew's? The seminary was good to him, and, if he could be a bit self-appreciating, he was good to the seminary. And the seminary was good for the community, for it provided the spiritual guidance that influenced a large, significant part of the population. Yes, he felt good being part of the seminary; of a church that was parent to St. Mark's School, which gave a quality Catholic education to many children in Kānewai; of an organization that was the rock-solid, moral foundation of the community.

But there was that something bothering him. Was it really . . . ? He was confused. He stopped playing the guitar—he wasn't sure how long he had stopped strumming—but when he glanced at his watch it was already 11:30. The night had gone by fast. He needed to talk to someone. Maybe Father Rosehill was up. No. The Father was already sleeping; he was always in bed at 8:00. Promptly. Maybe Father Geoffrey or one of the Brothers. No. It was just too late. But he needed to do something, he needed to go somewhere to air out his thoughts, to breathe the clean, cool air so as to aerate his mind. He needed to go for a walk.

————————

A WANING MOON gave him ample light to walk the empty main street of the town. Few cars passed. A couple of cars slowed down, recognizing the Father and tossing out surprised greetings. He passed the old theater and inspected the wall for any new messages. Yes, now he understood the riddle of it all. But how could he deliver this understanding to the community when they were all, for practical purposes, a part of the problem? They all had lost faith in the Holy Ghost and were now reverting to a type of pagan worship: Each was creating their own kind of "Holy Ghost." That was the crux of the problem. That was his profound understanding.

As he turned from the wall, a hand touched his shoulder. He jumped away, nearly crashing into the wall. It was Harriet O'Casey.

"David Fonseca!" said Harriet, rather gleefully. "What brings you here? Welcome!"

Welcome? "Auntie Harriet? My . . . you gave me a startle right now. What are you doing out here so late?"

"Just doing my everyday business."

Father Fonseca nodded his head. He knew of her eccentricities, especially that of keeping company with her cows. But at this late hour?

"But you, David, what you doing out here so late? What problems? What kind pilikia you get?"

The Father's eyes widened uneasily.

"Somebody dying? Who dying now?"

The Father relaxed. He smiled. "No. No problems. I just wanted to get some fresh air."

"Ohhh . . . so you *get* problems."

"I just needed to get out of my stuffy room."

"Everybody get problems, you know. I know you for how

long, David. You can't hide anything from me. I know your family for how long now. Your great-grandmother used to babysit me. Das how long. Where you walking to? I walk with you. Come on. We can talk story. I don't have to be anywhere at anytime for anybody." He told her that he thought of walking the length of the town and back. "Good enough with me," she said. "I need more exercise."

So they began walking.

"Auntie Harriet, how come I'm not seeing you at church at all?"

"Oh, I don't wanna hang around those . . . hypocrites. Sorry to say this, David, but you got one hell of a congregation full of hypocrites. And anyway, I always pray to God every day. Twice, in fact. After I get up in the morning and before I go moe."

"But it's important that you come to church."

"Don't tell me what's important, David. People in this town think I'm crazy, that my mind just snapped. I'll tell you something. My mind is sharper than most of the people living in Kānewai. That's one fact. In fact, God Himself knows this. That's why He made me privy to the secret. He knows I'm straightforward. He knows I don't lie and sin and do whatevers, like the others in the town. And they do it in the name of Our Father!"

"What secret are you talking about?"

A smile came to Harriet's face. Her face began to glow almost preternaturally. Father Fonseca had to blink a few times before realizing that her rosy glow was from the neon sign of a closed drive-in across the street. She laughed. Father Fonseca did so too, but reservedly.

What kind of secret is she going to tell me?

"As if you didn't know?" Harriet said, followed by a "Whoop!" "My, Father, they really taught you good manners, eh, in seminary!"

"I really don't know what you mean. I mean, about the secret."

Softly Harriet began singing a song about guys and dolls, something the Father guessed to be from the big band era. Or something like that. Harriet became so involved in the song that she began dancing and acting out lines from the movie that the song was from while leading a silent and perplexed Father Fonseca to the road that led past Gabriel Hoʻokano's home and the old graveyard, and then to her own pasture. Then she stopped, a bright smile coming to her face, brighter than the illumination of the moon.

"Father David, I had a good time with you tonight. But before I leave you for you to do your business, tell me this. I've always wanted to ask you this. Why did you leave Gloria Pasho? You know, I always thought you two would be a very nice couple. Weren't you two going get married after graduation? Tell me, David, why you leave her?"

He didn't know how to answer the question. The question was usually never asked, the answer being so self-evident. And if he ever was asked it, his answer was the obvious, that he had responded to a calling from the Lord. But the way Harriet asked the question was vastly different than the other few times he had been queried. He had the feeling that she knew what the answer was already. But what could he say? The real truth, for the record?

"I went into the priesthood," he mumbled.

At first Harriet regarded him quizzically, as if trying to figure out his words, then a look of betrayal flooded her face. But a moment later she smiled, smoothing the front of her mud-splattered jacket. "Oh you, David! Always trying play games with me again!"

Father Fonseca tried to remember when he had ever played "games" with her. He could not recall ever doing so.

"I know what you're thinking about," Harriet said. "After all these years, you still wishing you were Gloria's husband. Right? But you know—and I know you know—people can change. Especially Gloria. I know you were a little bit offended when she got pregnant by your best friend."

The Father's face darkened. What did she say?

"But you know how to forgive, don't you, David? That's what they teach you in seminary, right?"

The Father nodded his head. *What is she talking about? My best friend? What best friend? Gloria pregnant?*

"Oh, David, even for a man of God, you still get planny lot more learning about life."

But enough is enough, even for a priest. Especially for a priest with unsettled thoughts.

"Auntie Harriet, tell me about this 'secret' you mentioned a little while back."

"Oh, David, always changing the subject."

Who's this person whom she's always referring to? Games? Best friend? Gloria pregnant? Changing the subject?

"All right, if you really want to know," she said. She unzipped her jacket and fanned herself with the flaps. "Hot tonight, eh?"

The Father hadn't noticed. But he now realized that he was perspiring profusely.

"You want to know who is doing all this muckraking in town? I'll tell you. Everybody." Then Harriet turned her back to him and began walking in the direction they had come from. "I'm going home," she said. "I'm tired. Go ahead, David, go visit your tūtū. Go and do what you have to do. Go and do what you were going to do."

Father Fonseca was speechless, wanting to say something to her but not knowing what, as he watched Harriet's bent figure plod on back down the road until she merged with the darkness of night. Then he thought of a question he wished he had asked her: *Who's this "everybody" and how are they doing it?* But it was too late. Even if he ran and caught up with her, the timeliness of asking the question had passed. *It wasn't worth trying to salvage what was already lost to time, right?*

He decided to take Harriet's advice and visit his great-grandmother's grave. Though he had come out of this meeting with her confused, he was kind of glad that he had talked with Harriet.

He spent an hour talking with his great-grandmother about his predicament and the situation in the community, and when she became a bit sleepy since warm nights always made her sluggish, he kissed her and left the gravesite.

Before reaching the corner where he and Harriet had parted, he saw an apparition turn up the road, holding what looked like a severed head by its long hair.

Seventeen

WHAT IN HELL is Gabe Hoʻokano doing here so late in the night? wondered Hiram Ching. *And what is he doing with that bucket of paint? And why is he trying to break into my theater?*

Hiram heard Gabriel tap on the window of the women's restroom. It sounded like some kind of code.

He's trying to get in touch with that ghost.

Hiram hovered inside the open window, hoping to see the spirit of the restroom that he had heard so much about but had never seen.

But what's he doing with that bucket of paint? Damn Hawaiian . . . I bet he's going to paint a sign on the wall.

Watching and listening for Gabriel's next move.

But all Gabriel did was continue tapping a rhythmic pattern on the window. After a few minutes, he proceeded farther down the wall. *(Damn, now I can't see him make his sign.)* A minute later, Gabriel reappeared at the window, tapped on it again, then left. Gabriel saw a cloud-like sheen in the window, which he dismissed as a reflection of the quarter moon.

There . . . that rotten buggah. He's the maker of the signs.

He was caught red-handed. But how could Hiram tell anyone of his discovery when as a ghost he had absolutely no channels of communication to anyone? *I gotta tell Clarissa,* Hiram declared to himself. He knew she was returning since the stuff she had packed in cardboard boxes was still in his office.

Damn Gabriel. I wonder what he wrote on the wall this time. So he's the one doing all of this. I should have guessed all along. *Only he would do this. And all this time I was blaming Kalani Humphrey. Couldn't figure out how the punk could get out of prison, make his trouble, then go back in. No make sense, eh? All this time I blaming the Humphrey kid. And all this time it was—is—actually Gabriel Ho'okano. That damn, no-good old fox.*

ALL GABRIEL DID was to leave the small pail that was three-quarters filled with white paint at the back corner of the building and take the other bucket, now empty but once (three days before) three-quarters filled with the same kind of white paint. He never lifted a paintbrush to the blasted theater wall. Whoever was the creator of the signs was unknown to Gabriel. All he was doing, the only function he had in all of this, was to supply the paint that would mysteriously find its way up on the wall in the form of large letters, as the latest lampoon focused on someone special in the community. As long as he did his part of the bargain, Gabriel thought, his name, or his girlfriend's name, would never grace the old brick wall. It was a bargain he kept faithfully. Every three days he brought another fresh bucket of paint (twice he purchased a gallon from Thrifty Hardware, but most of the time he bought from various stores in town, away from the eyes and gossip of Kānewai), taking back the empty pail for refilling.

Who was actually putting up the signs was anybody's guess. Gabriel didn't know who or what it was that was doing all of this mischief. But one thing was certain to the old man, and that was that if he stopped bringing the paint, all hell would break loose in Kānewai. That was how he interpreted the recurring dream he had been having months before the first sign was discovered on the theater's wall. The dream went like this:

Gabriel has just dropped off Mary and Georgette outside the market when suddenly he is inside, in one of the aisles, pushing a cart behind the two women. In the cart is an assortment of red fish: kumu, āholehole, aweoʻweo, opakapaka. One of the fish, a sizable kumu with clear eyes, begins to open and close its mouth as if to speak. Gabriel can't hear or understand the squeaking of the fish. Cautiously, he reaches down to touch the fish but, before touching it, finds himself in the living room of an old friend, the late Harold ("Hana Hou") Jennings. Hazy white light streams through a large window that is rather four smaller, square windows. No one is home. He leaves the house through the front door and steps into the nave of St. Mark's Church. Columns of newspapers are uniformly spaced apart on every pew. In the front, dressed in a black robe, is a tall, bearded priest whom Gabriel cannot identify. The priest calls in a sonorous, accented voice for Gabriel to come forward. Gabriel totters to the front, a hand trailing on the ends of the pews. He stops next to the front pew, close enough to see the deep pores of the priest's face. The priest is an old haole, and Gabriel sees something familiar about him. (Actually, it is Harriet O'Casey's deceased husband, whom Gabriel had met just prior to Jimmy being shipped off on the ill-fated battleship that was sunk by Japanese torpedoes in the Pacific. Why Gabriel can't immediately recognize Jimmy O'Casey is simply because the O'Casey in Gabriel's dream is not the twenty-three-year-old man-boy Gabriel met in 1943; the man in Gabriel's dream is pushing seventy, and the European accent is definitely not his.)

"Whas—whas dis all about, Father?" Gabriel asks.

The Father looks over the pews of newspapers and says, "Dees es your life, Gabriel. Here es de collection of ev'ry day of your life since de day you vere born."

There are lots of newspapers. But Gabriel notices that the first two rows are empty.

The priest notes Gabriel's disturbing observation of the penultimate and ultimate rows of his life. He smiles and nods his head. "You've had a good life, Gabriel, on dees world," the priest says. "But you have two more rows to go. So make de best of dem."

Though Gabriel has been pretty much content with the

way his life has gone, he is a bit disturbed about the emptiness of the two rows. It would be nice if all the rows are filled.
Or completed. "How," Gabriel begins, his voice trembling,
"can I finish my life in one good way, Father?"

The priest turns to the long crucifix hanging on the
wall behind the chancel and crosses himself. Murmuring, he
turns to Gabriel. The priest has changed into a young man. A
stunned Gabriel recognizes him vaguely, though still not able
to place the face with a name. (The young man is Kalani
Humphrey, whom Gabriel had spied upon when he was ditch-
ing that stripped Ford Mustang one night in the empty lot
across his house.)

"Go home," says the young priest, "and finish up what is
unfinished."

———————

When Father Fonseca bumped into Gabriel Hoʻokano at
the bottom of the street, Gabriel, who was returning from his
self-appointed work with destiny, was humming a tune he
had just made up, hoping that later, with the right words,
he'd teach Mary to sing this song at his funeral. The Father
stopped, an immediate apprehension stiffening his body and
aborting the thought in his mind. But he soon recognized the
slumbering gait of one of Kānewai's oldest and almost uni-
versally respected citizens. He relaxed and, with a cleansing
breath, blew out the chill that had tightened his heart.

"Uncle Gabe?"

Gabriel froze, then ditched the empty paint can into a
bush next to the sidewalk before whoever it was could see it.
To the Father, Gabriel's silhouette was like a stone statue.

"Who you?" Gabriel demanded.

"Me. David Fonseca."

"Da priest?"

"Yes—yes, Uncle Gabe."

"What you want?"

"Nothing. What are you doing up so late?"

"Doing my monkey business. But what you doing here? I thought you priests supposed to be sleeping already?"

"I was just at . . . the cemetery."

"Doing what?"

"I was visiting my great-grandmother's grave."

"At dis hour? You gotta be pupule."

Father Fonseca wanted to laugh to ease the tension, but at the last moment, he didn't think Gabriel would have been humored by it. "I just had to do my business."

"What kine business, meditating about the Father and Son?"

Of course, he knew Gabriel meant it to mean God and His Son, the spoken-for, Heaven-appointed Savior. But a bluish mood clouded his mind, and Father Fonseca interpreted Gabriel Ho'okano's utterance to mean something else. He could not rid his mind of the name of *his* son, who would be twenty years old in December.

"Yes, you could say so," the Father said, his eyes lowering. To change the subject, he lifted his eyes and said, "But tell me, Uncle Gabe. How come I haven't seen you at church for a long time?"

"Eh, you know me. I not da kine religious type."

"But you were before."

"Before is before. After is after. Actually I still religious. But in one nada way. But now"—taking in a deep breath—"I content wit' what life tells me to do. Not to take anything away from you—no, I no want to do that—but I no have to go someplace and have somebody tell me something I already know. You know what I mean?"

"Oh."

"But you . . . something must be troubling you, eh? Funny fo' one priest walking around like this in the dead of the night."

The Dead of the Night. The Dead of the Night. The Resurrection of the Dead. Jesus Christ rising from the Dead. In the Dead of the Night. In the Night there is Light and the Light is

Our Father in Heaven who knows of no Name for Himself.
YHWH.

"So how's Glor—Auntie Mary doing?" A bead of sweat running down his cheek.

Gabriel Ho'okano studied the turmoil in David Fonseca's face. He read isolation and uneasiness in his eyes. He laughed to himself. "So you still thinking about her?"

"Of course. Auntie Mary is always in my heart. She comes to the church every Sunday for Mass. I always tell her to bring you along."

"No. You still thinking of *her*, eh?"

"You mean Auntie Georgette?"

"No—no—no! Her! Ah! Forget about it!" Gabriel laughed. "You see, even you, David, trying make one fool out of me. But no can. You like make one fool outta me, you dah fool! You gotta talk sense, David. Talk what in yo' heart. Not what in yo' mind." Gabriel hobbled passed the priest. "Good night."

Father Fonseca watched Gabriel Ho'okano's figure join the night. Then he ran after him, calling his name.

"What now?" Gabriel said irritably. "You going try preach me again? I tol' you I no need dis kine stuff." He retraced his steps and recovered the empty can of paint from the bush.

"No," the Father said, panting. "What were you saying? What do you mean by that?"

"Mean about what?"

"That."

"That? Oh . . . that. Well, David, if you don't know by now, I feel sorry for you. You one priest and all that. Here you talking about the Father and the Son, somebody else's Father and Son, when you one father already. To me, no make sense. If you like talk 'bout dah Father and Son, you yo'self gotta act like one father and son." And then he continued on to his house.

Father Fonseca watched him until he disappeared into

the darkness of the road, then he turned and walked slowly away. But he stopped and turned to hear a declaration shouted by Gabriel Hoʻokano at the top of the road: "And if you like know, I took one bucket white paint to the movie-house! And now I bringing back one empty bucket! And I going fill 'em up wit' mo' white paint and take 'em back down there again! Tomorrow! My bucket runneth ovah!"

Eighteen

T HOUGH THEY SEEMED to be in the same room, the ghosts
of Claudio Yoon and Hiram Ching could not see each
other since, conditioned by differences in date, time, and circumstances of their deaths, they could never exist in the same
dimension. Yet despite these metaphysical-temporal-spatial
considerations, it was still possible for them to sense each
other's diaphanous presence.

A simple explanation for all of this: When Hiram Ching
saw the physical act of writing on the mirror in the women's
restroom, that night when Clarissa discovered an unconscious Dennis Umeda next to the restroom commode, what
he was perceiving was the physical manifestation of another
spirit's metaphysical action, an activity that Hiram was incapable of doing (as yet). The episode in the women's restroom
as experienced by Hiram Ching was the work of the legendary
ghost that haunted the women's restroom of Kānewai's one
and only moviehouse.

Exactly twenty-two years, five months, and twenty-one
days before, a woman by the name of Vera Kobashigawa died
in her sleep, alone in her spartan, dustless studio three blocks
down from the theater. It was funny that moments before she
succumbed to her final sleep, as a result of her ingesting a
handful of tranquilizers, her mind had taken her to the chalk-
smelling restroom of Hiram Ching's theater. Perhaps the reason for this was a particular sudden remembrance of being
outrageously sick there, after having vomited all over Hiram
while performing fellatio. It was a time when her insides had
come undone, floating between the states of mud and light-

headedness, a similar nauseous reaction she would later experience with her stomach full of killer pills (though this time she rebelled against her stomach to heave out those half-digested pills and to deliver her from a flat-line existence). The spillage on Hiram was in the projection room, during a private showing of one of the first XXX films that ever graced any screen in the highly Catholized town of Kānewai. Hiram thought it was his ultimate duty to educate the unenlightened masses of the town—well, a selected few of the masses—in the art of sexual intercourse. Vera had come for her—God knows the number—lesson, and though she knew about the news for weeks, having tested positive not once but twice (just to be sure), she figured the best time to tell Hiram about an incipient Hiram (or the probable close look-alike) was after he came to a threshold of some satisfaction, at which time—she sincerely hoped—he'd be welcome to new ideas, in particular, the circumstantial outcome of his purposeful teachings. At that spot of time when Hiram was experiencing a cosmic blast of stardust, Vera's biological clock was malfunctioning, and she became suddenly engrossed with an overflowing feeling of distaste: Morning sickness struck her at a little past 9:15 in the evening. Using her clothes to wipe her mess on the then-erupting and erupted-upon Hiram, she apologized tearfully to a twisted-face Hiram, then hurried nakedly to the women's restroom while holding back the progressing peristaltic motions until, hanging over a wash basin, she burst forth explosively multiple times.

Eventually, a week later, she told Hiram about his destiny, this time before another educational session, and Hiram coolly refused to believe that his destiny was in the dark folds of a woman two years his senior whose only dowry was whatever came with a counter job at the local bakery. He persuaded her that it was in the best interest of their special, fate-created relationship that she rid herself of that inside interest so that she could be better responsive to the future they were both making (whatever that meant, Vera couldn't figure out, but it sounded hopeful to her). He then promised her a brand-new car that she had been dreaming about for at least five years. Vera asked him, "What kind of interest are you talking about?" Hiram quickly responded that he had a good friend, a very-very-very good friend, in downtown who knew exactly what he was doing, a very intelligent friend who had, in fact, gone to a very-very-very good school in the Midwest ("Where that? California?" Vera asked). So reluctantly, oh so reluctantly (she had a vision of herself in a light blue '55 Chevy Bel Aire convertible, with the top down, driving along some sunny, cactus-dotted stretch of highway), she accompanied Hiram one early Sunday evening to downtown Honolulu, and there through a back entrance they went into a tall dark building, catching the elevator from the basement level to the floor of the office of a well-known M.D. (Vera didn't know about that fact, and she never even saw his face since it was always hidden behind a white gauze mask, although she could see that he was Oriental), entering quietly the M.D.'s office, and it was here that Hiram Ching's threatened destiny was saved.

Vera did get her car, though it wasn't that brand-new '55 that she was promised. And she was also dumped unceremoniously by Hiram Ching one week after his future was secured. Vera went back to school and became a licensed practical nurse, and every so often she'd be called on to be a midwife. One rather warm September evening, in a strange turn of events, you could say, she guided Kalani Humphrey down that long wet, slippery channel of life. Months later, days after Hiram's marriage to Clarissa and a week before her death, while still vengeful after all of those years at the loss of her own half-life and at the treatment she had received from that asshole Hiram, she warned Mr. Experienced Educator on the phone about something that would directly influence his destiny. Hiram didn't say a word and hung up gently. His mind went blank for a minute. Then he picked up the phone and called Clarissa's parents, who had moved from Kānewai to another part of the island, asking them how everything was and thanking them a second time for their generous wedding gift. After the brief, forced conversation, he picked the phone up again and, after two minutes of deliberately dialing and canceling and redialing the number, called another friend in downtown to finish off the unfinished business.

JUST BEFORE HE died, there was only one major uncertainty in Claudio Yoon's life: He didn't know who had written that slanderous sign on the wall that was to become his unofficial epithet for his entire good life. He wasn't a homosexual, or at least didn't think he was. But to be called a faggot, even if it was not true, was a serious offense in Kānewai, a total damaging of one's character. He never dated anyone, he was too shy with women, though he did occasionally slip out of his cautious mannerism and play a bit of macho man every other month or so down on Hotel Street (yes, he had his regular girl, and her name was Trés Bleu). During the middle of his last drink on the night he crashed into the utility pole, Claudio pinpointed who it was—the only person in his life—who had called him a māhū: Hiram Ching.

Claudio remembered well that night when he had run into Hiram—of all people—in a stale-smelling bar on Hotel Street. Hiram had at first turned his back to Claudio, trying to hide from him. But Claudio, being a good-natured, nice guy and ignorant of the social fineries of the hai-mucka-mucks, went up to old Hiram and said hello in a tentative voice that was overwhelmed by the loud jukebox music. Hiram pretended that he hadn't heard Claudio, but when he looked into the mirror behind the bar counter and saw Claudio's smiling face looking straight back at him, he turned and put on an ostentatious greeting that intimidated Claudio. They began to talk. Claudio was puzzled how amicable Hiram could get all of a sudden. Perhaps it was the alcohol that was loosening old Hiram up, he thought. Their instant camaraderie led to an invitation to Claudio for a special, private screening of

Hiram's Selected Works of Skin on Skin. At first, Claudio didn't quite understand what Hiram was saying, and Hiram had to reinforce his explanation of "fuck films" with a rudimentary demonstration: He made a circle with the index and thumb of his left hand while inserting his right index finger in and out. Then he adorned this primal sign-making with a wink and a smile. By then Claudio understood exactly what Ching was alluding to, though it came as a shock and an enigma to him why Hiram Ching, one of most prominent citizens of Kānewai, husband of the sophisticated, aristocratic, hai-mucka-muck Clarissa Ching, was acting this low. Claudio, of course, politely refused. Hiram took this as an insult, for who was Claudio to refuse him? The theater owner regarded a smiling Claudio coolly, took his eyes off of him for a moment, took a glance at a transvestite coming into the bar with her/his sailor boyfriend, then blurted out, "What you, Claudio? One faggot?" He turned away from a voiceless Claudio, who was not sure whether to take the comment as a joke or an insult.

He decided that Hiram was serious about the accusation. He became so disturbed about it that he left the Street without seeing Trés Bleu. And the thought of the incident drained him of all attentiveness in other things, including work, for an entire week, until a temporary turn came when Trés Bleu gave him a service call, sweetly persuading him to get himself down to the Street for a taste of her homemade cooking, so to speak.

Yes, that last sip had loosened the painful memory, making it float to the surface of his cortex, where it now played havoc by jeopardizing his other thoughts. But how could he determine if it really was Hiram who had written that message on the wall? Besides, he was dead. But was it, perhaps, his ghost that wrote it? Or did Hiram make public that comment before his death?

Claudio insisted to himself that he was not a faggot: *I'm not a faggot, I'm not a faggot, I'm not a faggot, I'm not a faggot,*

I'm not a faggot, I'm not a . . . Yet in his drunken stupor, it was a hard thing to convince even himself, even though objectively he really wasn't a homosexual. Public opinion—especially in the hands of one Hiram Ching, the Father of Cinema and Multimedia in Kānewai—was too strong to fight against.

Claudio took out his thick wallet, fingered through the twenties, fifties, and hundreds—part of his life's savings that he had withdrawn fully three days earlier—and left enough under his empty glass to pay his tab in addition to a hundred dollar tip, then gave Chester the bartender an envelope addressed to Trés Bleu with a generous monetary gift and a short note of thanks. Then he left the bar, drove off in his truck, and shortly thereafter forced his way to an early retirement from this world.

Now in this bizarre afterlife—or rather, the way toward one—Claudio found it necessary to find Hiram and to expurgate from him the reason(s) why he had put that slanderous sign on the wall. It wasn't revenge that Claudio was looking for; it was freedom. He entered this limbo with an a priori understanding that if he proved his point well—that of his involuntary complicity with his own death—his spirit would be released to the next desynthesizing stage of existence, or rather nonexistence.

It was hell to be confined on earth and not be able to grasp it sensuously. A sojourn in a three-dimensional world in Claudio's (or Hiram's) state was torturous. It was like—and this was Claudio's own analogous explanation—an all-out local boy being forced into a tuxedo to deliver an acceptance speech at the Oscar awards. Or going to a French restaurant and wishing for a Spam musubi. He desperately needed to confront Hiram and get the truth out of him. It didn't matter now that Hiram had been in a higher social class than him. The painfully important fact was that both he and Hiram were dead, and having lots of money couldn't make Hiram more alive than him. And Claudio Yoon knew that.

ALL THIS ATTEMPT to communicate was, however, useless since it was a near impossibility for Claudio to deal directly with Hiram. But he accidentally came upon one method that enabled him to talk to Hiram—well, sort of—and that was through Hiram's wife of his previous life, Clarissa Ching. Unlike Hiram, who was confined to the theater, Claudio was able to roam on other turf, though it was chance and not choice that determined the location. He tried to approach Clarissa shortly after his death, but—manners still a strong part of him—stopped himself when he witnessed his friend Dennis Umeda and her getting it on one night in the back seat of her Mercedes while parked in the isolated St. Mark's School parking lot. He decided to wait for another opportune time, some night perhaps when she'd be alone at home, but every chance encounter with Clarissa, which, inexplicably, was usually at night, was a night of pleasure in the company of Mr. Umeda.

So he waited and waited for that break, though it felt like "an everlasting impossibility," a phrase used sparingly and with caution by even the most inexperienced of ghosts. Then, one early evening, he found her leaving the house for the theater. Yes, that was a good place to approach her, he thought. And he followed her there, and inside the semi-dark auditorium he tried to materialize himself. But he couldn't. It was one of those things that he knew he could do, having done it at least twice, but one of those things that was governed again by chance and not will, at least at this point of his ghostly existence. For the most part, it was one of those secrets that he was still ignorant of. He tried to make a sound or topple something that would draw her attention. But he was unsuccessful on both counts. Frustrated, he rushed out of the theater, leaving behind a small, lusterless whirlwind, and roamed the streets and brooded disconsolately on his enervating condition.

THAT MILD CURRENT of air that Claudio left was felt by Clarissa. It gave her a shudder. She glanced around Hiram's dim office and noticed papers flapping and settling on his desk. Then she adjusted the sweater covering her shoulders and returned to her business of carefully packing her late husband's vintage collection of pornographic films into the sturdy cardboard boxes that Dennis Umeda had supplied her with.

Nineteen

THAT WAS THE last straw.

If George brings home another nudie video, thought Joyce as she gripped the handle of her coffee cup, *I'm going to kick him out of this house. Out of my life. Divorce him.*

It didn't matter what anybody thought anymore. It wasn't going to be "shame" anymore to be a divorcée. None of this anymore. And that was that. She was fed up with his eyes being glued to the television screen watching those disgusting movies of people doing it to one another. One night she went to the kitchen for a glass of water and George was watching one of those videos that he had borrowed from Dennis Umeda's store. *That Dennis, I knew it was him all along!* Dennis had quit his job as a mailman to open a business, the selling and renting of movie videos. With a generous cash gift from his sweetheart Clarissa, amounting to just a bit over ten grand, he was able to open a small store (constructed with the help of some members of his bowling gang) in the middle of Kānewai town and stock his shelves half-full of the latest releases and classic movie videos. What was hidden from the public eye was the other half of the store that was contained behind the back wall, a room and a small screening area that warehoused Dennis's collection of adult movie videos, all adapted from Hiram's 16 mm films to VHS format by Dennis himself. Using a state-of-the-art video camera that he recently purchased, he videotaped the actual screenings of the films. Of course, the resolution wasn't great, but then again, it gave the videos a kind of illicit, daring texture. *Damn that Dennis*

Umeda! There George was, eating corn chips and drinking a beer and looking with huge eyes of a crazy man at that shameless woman putting her face right into the man's you-know-what! *Oh!* That one glance at the screen almost gave her a seizure. Trembling all over from a combination of disgust and embarrassment, she hurried back to the bedroom, forgetting her thirst.

It made her miserable to think that something so evil, so disgusting, so *contaminating*, was being shown in her very own home. She was mildly relieved by the fact that her two children were not living at home now, the girl away at college and the boy in the U.S. army and stationed in Korea. She would die if any of them saw their father watching one of those naughty films.

She went to bed, but she couldn't sleep, her head throbbing and her skin covered with a sticky sweat. Oh! was she the maddest ever at George!

But today, this morning, she resolved to put her foot down. There would be absolutely no more viewing of girlie videos in this house. And if George refused, then that was it. She didn't need him. All this time before she was convinced that even if he was the worst man in the world, she needed him: How can a woman exist without a man in a man's world? There had been no alternative thought on the matter. But not anymore. *No, sir. George Hayashida, if you want to stay in this house, you can't watch those naughty movies! You hear?*

She resolutely drank the last sip of her cold coffee, then got up to put the empty cup in the kitchen sink. She looked out the window above the garage roof at the cloudy sky. George was in the garage, probably tinkering with his car. She could hear him rubbing, maybe sanding something. *When he comes in,* she thought, *I'm going to tell it to him, right to his face. And that's that.*

Flying in a curve across the sky, from right to left, was a flock of pigeons. They were flying their wide spirals over the neighborhood. They were Father Rosehill's, and the Father let them out every morning and early evening. Joyce watched them for a while, and her thoughts went to the church. Perhaps George was turning this way because they had not kept up with their faith; they hadn't gone to church for years. The younger priest, Father Fonseca, used to come over and persuade them to attend Mass, but it was at least a year ago when he last came. Their excuse had been the lack of time as a result of working the evening shift at the can plant. She and George also customarily worked the Saturday night shift, getting paid time and a half, and though they woke up in time for Mass, it was just too much for them to gather the energy to attend the morning service.

"But you can come to the late morning Mass," the Father had suggested.

"We'll try, Father," she had responded.

Perhaps if she started going back to church, she might persuade George to come, too, and maybe that would make him give up watching those disgusting movies. It would make him ashamed to be doing what he was doing. *Disgusting. Oh . . . so disgusting!*

Yes, maybe that's what I'll do. I'll make George go back to church.

But, what was also going wrong with the community? Before things were so nice and simple and clean. Now there were people like Dennis Umeda opening up a store that rented nothing but trash. Maybe she'd call some state agency today, or tomorrow, maybe the police, and tell them what Dennis was really selling at his store. *What is his store called? One-Stop?*

And all the things that nearly everyone—with the exception of her and her husband—were doing nowadays. How disgusting! Husbands and wives committing adultery. Married couples fooling around with other married couples. Homosexuality. Kids on drugs. Teenage pregnancies. Was she glad that her two children had been raised the right way. She had kept a tight lid on her house. Discipline was the rule. She never spared the rod when it came time to use it. Her father used to always beat her and her other brothers and sisters if they were bad, with the exception of her oldest brother, who always got away with everything; he always got praise and the biggest share of the meals and never the stick. Herbert was the naughtiest of all her siblings, and yet their parents always thought whatever he did was good. Always. That was really unfair. Her father always used to beat everyone else if they were naughty, especially Harry, her second brother. Oh, she used to feel so sorry for him. Even if it was Herbert's fault, Harry used to always get it. The oldest was never wrong.

And that wall. Who was responsible for all of that obscene graffiti on the wall?

A hesitant smile came to her face. She looked about the kitchen, then settled back into her thoughts, about that night after another routine work shift when, with George snoring in front of the TV after slurping up his large bowl of ramen, his usual fare after work, she sneaked out of the house with a can of house paint from the garage closet (George wouldn't notice it missing, *he's got so many of those other cans*) and painted on the wall the truth about Richard Pimente and Clarissa. And she didn't feel guilty at all, at the time and even now, about what she wrote since what she wrote—and she'd swear this on the Bible—was nothing but the plain, honest truth.

During high school when she used to walk home through the athletic field, she often would see Clarissa waiting for Richard under the bleachers or sometimes Richard would already be there and they'd be loving it up. They never saw her—she was just that bug-eyed Takamine girl, the pig farmer's chunky daughter; she was invisible to all the boys in school, as well as to most of the girls. Even George never noticed her. It wasn't until Mr. and Mrs. Hayashida, who were sweet potato farmers, and her parents had made an arrangement that George began paying any attention to her. And even then it was just an arrangement, not romance. If anything, their marriage could be described as being symbiotic: Joyce always wanted a family life and she got a son and a daughter from George; and George, drawn to that dogged tradition, wanted a son for a family namesake, though he never was aware of another need, something that he took for granted, perhaps the most important for him without him even knowing it, and that being the necessity to have someone available as a sounding board since nobody ever took his opinions on anything very seriously. And so, for over twenty-two years, the marriage was workable. Until this morning, when Joyce realized that she really didn't need to have George around.

Now that the children were out of the house, why did she have to cook breakfast and lunch and dinner and a late night snack for someone whom she really didn't love? Why did she have to wash his dirty underwear? Why did she have to listen to all of his complaints about life? Why did she have to bear with his slobbery in the kitchen and especially in the bathroom? Or have to deal with his incessant snoring and teeth-grinding? Or . . . or . . . or—and yes, this was the last straw: Why submit herself to the most basest of immoralities, the showing of sex films in the sanctity of her own home, in her own living room, with her husband watching this filth while sitting on her brand-new couch from the last summer's sale at Sears?

Enough is enough.

She was boiling over inside, steam venting out through her ears. She was so agitated that her entire body shook; her hands were shaking so badly that she dropped the empty coffee cup into the sudless dish water from the night before with a splash that reached her neck. Wiping herself, she searched the sky, now parting of clouds, for the spiraling pigeons, but they were gone, probably back to the cleanliness and security of Father Rosehill's holy coop. She would start attending Mass, she resolved, even if it meant knocking off a couple of hours of her beauty sleep on Sunday mornings, and she'd drag that hollow-headed husband of hers to the church, too, whether he liked it or not. Or maybe she'd kick him out of the house first. Then she wouldn't have to waste her time and energy persuading that lunkhead.

But one thing was certain, and that was that something

needed to be done about the disgusting, overall behavior of the community. Father Fonseca must be informed of what was happening, and in turn he must communicate this information to The Lord, The Father. Then, perhaps, God could correct all of the sinful doings in the town and make it a decent, peaceful place to live in again. Get rid of all the smut and sinners. Get rid of them all and bring a good, simple Christian life back. It had to be done. There was no other way of getting around it.

George was grumbling loudly about something in the garage, and she heard his angry footsteps climb the wooden stairs to the garbage can that was below the kitchen window. She hated that can being there; sometimes when George forgot to cover it, the rotting smells would get to her while she'd be washing dishes. She told him often about putting the lid back on, but he never paid any attention to her. She moved away from the window so that he wouldn't be able to see her and listened to him uncover the can, throw in something that struck the bottom with a heavy metallic sound, then slam the lid back on with a "Sonavabitch!" The lid fell to the side. He went back down the steps.

She peeped out to see if George was out of sight, then regarded the sky again, her attention caught by a lone pigeon that had somehow lost the trail of its brethren. It was flying in small, fast circles, as if fighting against a sucking vortex. Just when Joyce gave up hoping that it might win its resistance against the invisible force, the pigeon broke its circuitous pattern and flew away in the opposite direction of the seminary. *Maybe it isn't a pigeon of Father Rosehill*, Joyce thought. And all along she thought that it was. *That goes to show*, she noted to herself, *that what you see is not what you always get.*

As she turned from the window, a sudden, burning pain emanated in her chest. A numbing sensation spread throughout her body. She became faint, her arms becoming alienated from the rest of herself. She leaned over the sink, called for George or rather warbled for him. The world began to spin.

She collapsed, falling backward and striking her head on the edge of the kitchen table.

————

When George came in to get the keys for the storage room, swearing and grumbling as usual, hoping Joyce was nearby to hear him, he found her sprawled body on the floor, her eyes closed but her lips trembling, as if she were mumbling a Buddhist chant. He shook her, called her name with a voice crying from the bottom of a dark, deep well. Then he ran to the garage for his car keys but could not find them. Returning to the kitchen for the spare, he carried her to the garage and set her in the front seat of the car, changed his mind, and laid her in the back, then jumped into the driver's seat. Then, and only then, with his eyes bulbous and tearing and staring terrified through the sawdust-covered windshield, with his throat dry and knotted, did he have the sense enough to run back into the house and call for an ambulance.

Twenty

DURING THE NIGHT, someone had hauled away the '64 Ford Mustang that had sat for seven years in the abandoned lot across the road from Gabriel Ho'okano's. Gabriel had not noticed the missing car when he first came out to the porch to fetch the morning newspaper, but he had felt odd—an emptiness—as if something important had been purged from his life. He didn't know what it was that was making him feel this way. He went about with his daily routine, picking up the paper, tossing it on the old rattan chair for Mary's perusal (mainly for the sales), sitting himself down in his chair, rocking in it uncomfortably slowly, then starting his daily list of complaints to himself interspersed with his good observations of the weather, the air, the surroundings. ("The grass so green 'cause last night's rain.") He still could not understand why he had this empty feeling until he finished his fifth complaint, which was, "I wonder when dose buggahs going take away dat piece of ugly junk they wen dump here." It was then that he realized the why of his discomfort.

Gabriel perked up in his chair, his neck stretched out like that of a curious turtle, then returned to his deliberate, steady rocking, the chair and the termite-eaten floorboards creaking in a kind of discordant unity. For the next fifteen minutes or so, he stared straight ahead at that patch of sun-deficient, yellowed grass and dirt, wondering how the hell was he going to tell Mary about the vehicle being stolen.

Mary came out, having finished her morning chores in the kitchen, and sat on her chair with her usual pleasant air, giving her customary thanks to Gabriel for getting her the newspaper. She took the rubber band off, dropped it in the collection of other rubber bands in a mayonnaise jar at the side of her chair, then unfolded the newspaper and began reading. Gabriel studied her face for a hint of discomfort or anguish. He found none. Everything was the usual, it seemed, for Mary.

Gabriel's eyes returned to the bare spot. Clearing his throat, he said, "Dis weather no like change. Going be one nada hot day."

Behind the newspaper: "Wen rain last night. I heard. About three, four o'clock dis morning."

"Yeah, but . . . das last night. But speaking of heard, you know what I heard?"

A momentary silence. Then: "What?"

"I heard something strange last night. Like somebody dragging off something."

No answer. Mary lowered the newspaper. "You know what I heard? I heard Joyce Hayashida had one stroke. Georgette tol' me on the phone dis morning. And she so young."

"I not talking about that. I talking about somebody wen take off with da car last night."

Mary sat up, folding the newspaper into her lap. "Somebody wen steal yo' car?"

"No—no—no! Dat car." And he pointed across the street.

For about fifteen seconds, an unfazed Mary studied the spot of 'āina that was formerly held by the Mustang, then turned to Gabriel. "Oh, that. Well, at least you get something fo' be thankful fo'."

"What you mean?"

"Your wish is granted," she said. "They wen take away that junk, jus' how you was wishing fo' dah longest time."

Gabriel lowered his eyes, his face showing exhaustion, as if he were blowing up an enormous balloon and had run out of wind halfway there. He looked up, his eyes focusing somewhere above and beyond the fuzzy tips of the buffalo grass. "I was jus' getting used to that old junk," he said weakly.

After a minute of silence, Mary said, "She going be in the hospital for a while."

"What you talkin' about?"

"Joyce. Joyce Hayashida. She had one stroke. You listening to me?"

"I always listening to you, Ipo. So how long she going be in there?"

"For as long as it takes fo' fix her up."

"Auwē. Stroke. Das bad stuff." His eyes were fixed to the vacant spot.

"Now they get da kine modern medical tech-a-nique," she said. "They going fix her up no time."

"You think so?"

"I feel sorry for her husband."

"Who? George? Not me. Da buggah and his wife, they never get along too good. Dem guys always fighting, over every little bit of anything, like cats and dogs. I never see dem any one time smiling at each other. Not one time."

"They good for each other," Mary said, folding the newspaper.

"Hah? All they good fo' each other is fo' one guy irritate da ada guy like hell. And vice-versa."

Mary weighed Gabriel's comment, then asked, "I wonder what Richard going do with da car?"

"What you talking 'bout?"

"Richard. Richard Pimente. What he going do wit' da car?"

"Wit' what car? What you talking 'bout?"

"Da car. Da car across the street. Da junk."

"Was Richard Pimente?"

"I thought you said you heard him dragging da thing off?"

"Yeah-yeah," answered a deflating Gabriel. "I heard . . . but I never see."

"'Cause you was in bed all dat time. I thought you was sleeping. I heard you snoring. I wen get up in the night, drink some water, then I heard them moving the car."

"How you know was Richard?"

"'Cause I was looking out the kitchen window and I saw his face in the truck's headlight."

"So . . . was Richard . . . da one," murmured Gabriel. "Then he must've wen use Freddie Tanaka's tow truck."

"I no think so. Looked like he wen drive the car away himself."

"How can? The tires was all gone."

"He could've put air in the tires," Mary said, yawning. "Maybe I wrong. But it look like someone wen drop him off and he wen drive da car away."

———————

LATER THAT MORNING, Gabriel thought it necessary to confront his cousin, Harriet O'Casey, concerning her role in the confiscation of the abandoned vehicle. He waited on the porch all day, eating his lunch there and taking quick retreats to the bathroom when necessary. His eyes were constantly on the lookout for his famous, not-all-there-in-the-coconut cousin. Finally, at about half past four, he saw her shadowy figure ambling up the road.

He glanced at his watch. "She never on time when you want her be on time," he grumbled. Then he rose from the chair, stretched his limbs and courage, and decided to confront her before she passed the house.

Harriet noticed him coming, so she crossed to the other side of the road to avoid meeting him head-on. Much to her chagrin—and to Gabriel's old brittle legs—he followed her across. She stopped, and with eyes darting and narrowed, yelled as he was negotiating around a large clump of crabgrass, "And now what you like?! My blood, too?!"

Gabriel was undaunted by her sudden outburst, having actually expected something more violent all along. He continued at his steady, wobbling pace, stumbling on a small stone but keeping his focus on her face, which was turning from a rosy anger to a pinkish apprehension. She withdrew a few steps; and before she could act on a complete retreat, Gabriel burst into bombastic retort, perhaps as voluminous and brassy as the blast of the biblical character that he was the namesake of: "You mother-of-a-cousin of mine! You stop right there in yo' tracks and come and have one cup coffee wit' me! Befo' I turn yo' cows into hamburgah!"

Harriet's fading pink turned to a disdainful cherry. "You are not going to do anything of the sort!" she yelled. "And over my dead body you going take my pasture and turn it into one fast-chain hamburger joint!"

Gabriel stopped, tilted his head quizzically for a moment. "I said I going make yo' cows into hamburgah."

"I know what you mean. But I don't want to talk about anything with you. This is the limit of my talk with you."

"Wait a minute," Gabriel said with a nervous chuckle. "You get me all wrong—"

"You wrong? Hmph! Since when does my always smar-tass cousin admit he's wrong?!" She began to re-cross the road.

"Since . . ." He stopped himself. Why admit that he was wrong when he wasn't? But a split instant later, after recon-sidering the circumstance: "Since now! Yeah—now!"

Harriet stopped in the middle of the road and looked at him from a half-turned face. "Are you Gabriel Ho'okano?"

"You damn right das me!"

"And aren't you the one trying to get your greedy hands on my pasture and turn it into a fast-chain hamburger res-taurant?"

"There you go again." He tossed his upturned palms in the air. "I never said nothing like that."

"Yes, you did. I just heard you say that. But not only that, somebody told me of your plans. So don't lie to me, Mr. Ho'o-kano! I have ears everywhere!"

"Who that somebody?"

"Somebody," she said smoothly, with the ease of a cardplayer holding a trump card. "Somebody who you don't know but who knows you well."

"Cut wit' dah crazy talk."

"You calling me crazy?"

He silently chided himself for saying that. "No. You not crazy. We all crazy."

"Damn right, all of you are. Don't you remember you calling me 'four-eyes' all the time at Auntie Bessie's?"

Four eyes? No. Gabriel shook his head, then nodded. "I remember Auntie Bessie." With the swimming hole in back of her house behind the guava bushes. "You remember the swimming hole?"

Harriet sighed, but a fond image of the hole, with its frigid water and swinging vines over the deep section, flourished in her mind. The earth-taste of the mountain water came to her mouth. Then she felt Gabriel's prying eyes and immediately deleted the blossoming nostalgic smile on her face. "No. I don't remember," she said emphatically.

Gabriel smiled, his eyes glowing. He braved the few steps to her. "You remember, Harriet. I know you remember. Look the way you smiling. Ha—ha—ha!"

It was impossible to hide the feeling; thinking about that time did make her feel good. But of all people to show that feeling. She didn't want Gabriel, that selfish, arrogant cousin of hers, to get anything out of this moment. "I'm not smiling now. Look—I've had enough of you. Goodbye."

"Hey—wait one minute," Gabriel pleaded. He took her by the arm.

"Let me go!" she yelled, pulling away. "Don't you ever touch me again!"

"Look. I jus' like talk wit' you. Das all."

"I have nothing to say to you!"

"Com'on. Fo' old times sake."

"About *what* you like talk about?"

Gabriel couldn't hold back the darkness and hurt from his eyes. "About why you wen get Richard Pimente to move da car."

"What car? What car you talking about? You're crazy."

"Okay. I da one crazy. But why did you get Richard Pimente to move da car? Fo' bug me?"

"You're crazy. Let me go. I'm going home. You've already ruined my day. Thank you very much. Aloha!"

She strolled away in the opposite direction of the pasture, her strides taking her briskly to the bottom of the road. She was making the turn at the corner when Gabriel issued a call that resonated with bloody intent: "If you like find out how to stop yo' cows from becoming hamburgah, you better come drink coffee wit' me right now!"

———

MARY BREWED A fine pot of coffee, not too strong and not too weak. It was the best cup that Harriet had had for at least a decade, since the time she found, among personal items in a footlocker of her husband, a small tin of government-issued coffee. With trembling hands, she had opened that can right there and then, and after whiffing the contents several times, percolated herself a cup. After one sip, she swore to herself that the coffee was as fresh as the day after the beans were roasted. Every day for almost a month, she drank a cup of that coffee, using less and less per day to conserve the supply. And when she had just enough for one more cup, she saved it, promising herself (and writing this on a piece of paper in case someone would have to carry it out if she was incapacitated) that she would drink that last cup on her deathbed.

But this cup that Mary served her was so soothingly bitter and robust, what an exemplary cup of coffee should taste like. How Mary could brew such a fine-bodied cup of coffee from stock taken off the shelf of C. Chang's Supermarket, Ltd., was beyond her comprehension. She was tempted to concede that some kind of strange magic was embodied in the coffee, something that gave her an instant ease-of-mind. She sat on Mary's chair and gazed at the wild buffalo grass across the road, but now she didn't see food for her beloved cows but a vibrant green color. And life. And when Gabriel asked again uncharacteristically and patiently why did she hire Richard Pimente to take the car away, she lathered him with a soft smile and said, "I did it because I thought it was the best damn thing to do at the moment."

Blinking with confusion, Gabriel's eyes followed Harriet's to the buffalo grass, but he only saw the patch of pale grass that had grown bonsai-like beneath the belly of the Mustang. *Soon,* he thought, *dat grass going come back wit' color and going grow tall, and I not going have nothing to remind me of dat car dat used to be ovah deah.* He turned to his cousin, saying, "So you really did dat fo' piss me off?"

"I don't do anything to piss anybody off. What I do is to please people, whether they know it or not."

Mary brought out a chair and sat diplomatically between them, but just a bit askew off Gabriel's and Harriet's line of discussion.

"Then why you no clean yo' cows' mess?" asked a perturbed Gabriel. "When Kona wind come, I always getting one good sniff of yo' goddamn stink pasture."

There really must have been some magic in the coffee, for a second after getting terribly mad at her cousin's blunt comment, she smiled and laughed. "You're right, Gabe," she said. "You're right. Tomorrow I'll get Kalani Humphrey to clean up the pasture for me."

Gabriel gave Harriet a look of distrust but could not come out with his honest feelings. It was a dilemma he never liked: knowing he was being conned and yet having to bear with it. All he could say was, "I think das one damn good idea."

Harriet took her last sip and got up. "Very well, then," she said gaily. "I'm glad to be able to please you. You don't know how much I enjoyed drinking coffee with both of you, Gabe and Mary. It's been a long time. Mary, thank you so much for making me this superb cup of coffee."

"Oh, that's all right," Mary said, smiling sincerely. "Please come back again."

"Where you going?" Gabriel asked.

"I better go see my family," she said, looking toward the pasture. "Then I must get home and call Kalani Humphrey's house." She started down the porch steps.

"Hey—wait," Gabriel said, now with the thought that Harriet perhaps was really being honest. "You know about da pasture smell, well, actually I don't mind it at all. I was jus' making talk wit' you. You know me."

"I don't know you, Gabe. It's been many years. Seventeen? I forget. But many. But I really enjoyed visiting with you and your wife. Can I come back again? We can start off where we left off."

Gabriel couldn't figure out what had suddenly come over Harriet. Was she drunk? On coffee? On drugs? On sniffing too much cow manure? He was oblivious to both his nodding head and answer: "Yeah . . . sure . . . come back tomorrow . . . come back anytime . . ."

"Good! Then I'll come back tomorrow after I visit my nephew and niece, and then we can talk story."

"All right . . ."

"And thank you very much again, Mary." Another smile from Mary. "Mahalo nui loa me ke alo-o-o-ha." And then Harriet was off to visit the four-legged members of her family.

Mary's smile remained unshakable as she and Gabriel watched Harriet move slowly and ably down the porch steps and onto and up the dirt road, disappearing around the corner.

"You wen figure all dis out?" Gabriel blurted out, referring to Harriet's unexpected behavior. He sighed.

It took Mary a long, suspenseful twenty seconds to answer. But she did so with her smile intact and in a tone so simplistic and full of aloha, so Mary-like. "Of course," she said. "Always going get good in anybody who talk to animals."

Twenty-One

I T NOW WAS customary for Harriet O'Casey to stop at her cousin's house every day before visiting her children in the pasture. And Mary made sure that Gabriel and Harriet were supplied with a nice pot of freshly brewed coffee while they sat and reminisced about their childhood. But for that poor soul Father Fonseca, any dialogue he had was restricted to himself and God. It was a self-inflicted condition forced by his increasing mistrust of his fellow Kānewaians. Even Father Rosehill did not hold a mantel of trust, as he once did, ever since that time when Father Fonseca, his mind tucked into a nostalgia of the sixties, was singing songs of civil disobedience, and Father Rosehill, taking a mid-morning rest from hoeing in the garden, looked up smiling at the singing from the window and uttered a booming exaltation, *"Gloria in Excelsus Deo!"* Father Fonseca's face became ashen, and he quietly put away his guitar in its usual dustless corner; and as he walked from the room, down the cool somber corridor, he promised himself never to pick up a guitar again.

It was also about this time that Father Fonseca became familiar with the strange force that was emanating from the theater. He had thought Cynthia Cordeiro and Sandra Kim were perhaps exaggerating a bit when they had come to him with their claim that the theater was haunted. *That old story,* he thought while listening to the two. But now, since his accidental meeting with Harriet O'Casey, his recent scrutiny of the community, and his meditation at the wall, he came to the conclusion that something utterly evil had settled in the community, centering itself in the old abandoned theater, something so strong and malefic that any comparison with its power and evilness to that of the Catholic Church would be like comparing a starving tiger shark with a pregnant mosquito fish.

He harbored a terrified heart. He was encompassed by fear yet showed this to no one but God. In a number of self-confessions, he portrayed himself as a coward who would shamefully flee at the advance of Satan's surging waves that were being empowered by the birth of every sinful thought in the community. He was ashamed to admit to this weakness, but there was nothing else to do. For he also knew that fundamental to this weakness was the resurgence of his past: The temptations of mortal life, he found, had been only dormant, not thoroughly purged as he thought drinking the daily waters of the Holy Scriptures would help him to accomplish; and now they had regenerated into a monstrous, vigorous, and unrelenting state in him. At nights, it was now uncommon for him to fall into God's embrace; instead, he would toss and turn while haunted by the burdening thoughts of his displaced, neglected progeny. Sometimes sleep was impossible until later in the day, when he sometimes paid the price for its lack in his life with embarrassment. Such a time occurred while listening to a confession of a troubled adolescent girl: He had fallen asleep and was aroused by Sister Hyacinth who had been informed by the confessor that she had heard steady, heavy breathing behind the grille.

Satan was working his evil by infusing doubts and sinful thoughts in Father Fonseca. The Father finally reached his lowest point when one unusually chilly summer morning he woke up in a sweat after a dream of having sex with Clarissa Ching in the middle of the football field while Kalani Humphrey was watching from the announcer's booth. He was compelled to give a confession to Father Rosehill, his superior, but changed his mind, as he was too ashamed of exposing his fast eroding faith. Everything came to a head for Father Fonseca when Clarissa Ching mysteriously disappeared from town, leaving behind her household of valuables.

She had been efficient in settling most of her accounts, mailing remittances and letters of termination to the gas, electric, water, and telephone companies, while giving complete power to her lawyer to take care of necessary business during her absence. It was a remarkable achievement, accomplishing all of this within twelve hours. But yes, haste gives room for careless mistakes. Three days later, an uninformed Georgette came to the house to do her routine, a twice-a-week cleanup. As she was about to insert her key into the lock, she found the front door ajar. She entered the house, calling for the matron, waiting for a silent minute for Clarissa to show herself before deciding that she had probably gone out and forgotten to lock up. Georgette donned her cleaning apron and began dusting the living room. The fact that there was no house current to run the vacuum cleaner was not enough to give her suspicion of something wrong in the house. And she didn't think it strange when she found no water in the bathroom taps and no buzz on the phone and three bureau drawers open and half empty of clothes in the bedroom. But she was puzzled to find the stove top immaculately clean; and when she discovered the food souring in the refrigerator, a gap in Clarissa's favorite section of her wardrobe, and her bed undisturbed, Georgette grasped the idea that Clarissa might have been kidnapped. Trying to control her panic-stricken breathing, she finally broke away from the house and scurried down the quiet, isolated street, her heart rising and falling like a stormy beach break. She paused at the first intersection, undecided whether to use the phone at Harriet O'Casey's house or the one at the church. She chose to go to the church since it was closer, and there she found Father Fonseca praying in the chapel.

"Something wrong—wit' Mrs.—Ching!" The words erupted out of her mouth. Then she collapsed to her knees in front of the Father.

The Father helped Georgette to a pew. "Please calm yourself. What's wrong? What is it that you want to tell me?"

"The house—is empty—and—I dunno where—is Mrs. Ching!!"

"Is something wrong with Mrs. Ching?"

"She's gone."

"Where?"

Georgette fainted. Father Fonseca carried her to a side room where he lay her on a hard sofa. Then he got Sister Estelle to look after her. He borrowed the seminary car and drove to the Chings' house. Nothing seemed strange or suspicious to him. But he did find a sealed envelope affixed by magnets to the door of the refrigerator, addressed to "My Son." A pink Post-It was attached to it: "To whoever that may find this note: Please make sure that Kalani Humphrey gets this. CC."

———

THAT AFTERNOON FATHER Fonseca went to see his old friend but was informed that Kalani was hospitalized as a result of severe wounds from a knife fight and thus unable to see visitors. The warden assured Father Fonseca that the inmate was in stable condition, but that it would be at least two days before he would be allowed visitors. Something about the eyes of the warden stopped the Father from transferring the letter to his care; the Father left the facilities promptly. He called the next day and was informed that Kalani Humphrey had developed unspecified complications the day before and was now in critical condition. The Father pleaded for visitation rights and was flatly refused. Desperate to deliver the letter, the Father demanded to see the inmate so that he could provide him with spiritual strength but was again denied.

At approximately 8:00 the next evening, Father Fonseca received a call from Father Rosehill's desk requesting his services at the correctional facility, to perform the Last Rites for inmate Kalani W. Humphrey. He quickly dispatched to the prison, and at Kalani's bed performed the rites for his comatose friend. He then read him Clarissa's letter:

Dear Son,

I will never see you again and this is why I'm writing you this letter. You have never done anything wrong in your life and you alone have the power to change things for the better. You have been condemned to a life of discrimination and unfair treatment before you were born. It's so unfair what these people have done to you. And what they are doing to me. I must leave because I must. There is something bad going around in the town. And the people don't even know about it. They don't really care. They are so much a part of it that they are blind to it. But it's up to you to make it better. Only you can do it. Everybody thinks you are evil. But they don't know you like I know you. I have never hugged or kissed you. But I've done that so many many times in my thoughts and dreams. Believe me, my Son. You need to free yourself where you are, any-way you can, and get rid of this evil in Kānewai. Only you can do it. I know only you can. Then, when you defeat this evil, I will come back. I know you don't have any feelings for me because of how your life has turned out. But I am truly very very sad about all of this. I wish I could have done something. No, I wish I <u>did</u> some-thing. I know I could have. But my weakness stopped me. But you're not weak. I know that. You are strong. Very strong. I love you very, very much, son. Very much.

your Mom

Kalani's condition didn't change, but Father Fonseca's did. That night, after thinking and rethinking for hours in the darkness of his room, he flipped on the light and dragged his old trunk out of the closet, opened it, and took out his old foot-ball jersey (#12) and a pair of colorfully patched, faded blue jeans. Wrapping his head in a blue bandanna, he switched off the light and climbed out of the window.

He returned two hours later, his hands covered with red paint, cleaned himself and changed, then slept soundly for two-and-a-half hours before rising for his morning rituals. And he followed this pattern for the rest of the week while checking daily on Kalani Humphrey's condition, which remained unchanged.

Twenty-Two

IT WAS A hard decision, but a decision that had to be made. Quickly. For what could be lost in a blink of an eye was the opportunity of an eternity for Claudio Yoon the ghost. A full moon was coming, and with the planets and the stars and other heavenly bodies just in the right alignment with one another, Claudio Yoon was to be given this chance fleeting opportunity: a meeting with Hiram Ching. And this is how he found out about it.

The day before this transmutation was to occur, Claudio's spirit began slipping in and out of Hiram's dimension. He'd see Hiram's ghost floating in the theater and the next moment he wouldn't. But the frequency of this occurrence increased and intensified. He began to see Hiram for longer periods of time.

It wasn't the same, however, for Hiram. But Hiram's situation did change suddenly an hour before the perfect unity of stellar and planetary intercourse. Claudio began to note an apprehension in Hiram's eyes; Hiram was noticing more and more of Claudio's manifestation though he did not know exactly what he was looking at.

For Hiram, Claudio's image was at first two cloud-like moving veils, one behind the other. At first he didn't think it strange, for in this afterlife he had already—very quickly—gotten used to frequent phenomena like this; he would have described the experience as a misting of a camera's lens that eventually evaporates. So he regarded it with some curiosity, but nothing more.

Yet with the approaching synchronization of the galactic

intercourse, Hiram noticed the two cloudy veils coalesce and focus into a human-like figure. He wasn't sure who, or what, was being formed, but his curiosity was now piqued. But that wasn't all that he felt.

There was something else that he was sensing, some kind of change in the polarity of his—for lack of a more precise descriptor—being. He began to feel an ecstatic shift in mood, a transformation that he knew he was powerless to deter. And yet, it was a paradoxical switch, for though apprehensive of this new direction, intuition told him it was necessary to welcome the change. Hiram would have described it as "having butterflies in your feet." With this emotional swing came an inscrutable suggestion that he may be moving toward a kind of fulfillment.

When Hiram first entered the realm of the afterlife, he cherished the thought that somehow he had been elected to "live" again. But after a span of interminable moments existing in meaningless containment, continually floating from one area of the theater to another and back, he came to the instinctual sense that until his existence was completely selfless and unaffected by progressive time, his soul would never be free. In this present existence, Hiram was in a perpetual rot of irresolution; deep down in his vaporous heart was the understanding that there was needed a complete release of all human essences.

He also sensed that no one, or no thing, was able to forewarn when he would experience this liberation, this transcendence of the soul; this freedom from all material contradiction, he intuited, was necessarily independent of his own free will.

Now, as he studied that flourishing, lingering, then vanishing manifestation, he harbored a hope that perhaps *it* might give him a chance for absolute transmittance.

Twenty-Three

How did Harriet O'Casey know that the Father was responsible for those new signs on the side of the theater?

One night, she discovered him with a can of white paint and a brush, fitting his lampoons in one corner of the wall. She herself had brought a can of paint and a brush to the theater, and when, from across the street, she saw the Father dressed in battle fatigues, she thought at first that it was Kalani Humphrey. She was glad that it was Kalani, for she remembered promising her cousin he could clean up the cow dung from the pasture. (She had forgotten that Gabriel had later told her to disregard the suggestion.) So she deliberated for a minute, watching him paint while thinking how she might persuade Kalani to take the job. When she finally thought of a plan, she crossed the street and was about to call out to him when he fell to his knees and began to pray. She was startled. It was only then that Harriet realized that Kalani was Father Fonseca. Quietly and quickly she scurried back across the street and hid behind a newspaper stand. From this vantage point she watched, thoroughly astonished that she was witness to Father David Fonseca commit a crime that she thought only herself and Kalani were responsible for.

Crossing himself, Father Fonseca picked up the can of paint and brush, scanned the quiet streets for the prying eyes of any lonely person walking off insomnia, then scampered into the darkness behind the theater.

Harriet remained firm in her hiding place, her heart pounding so loudly that she had to scold it in a whisper to shut up. She finally fled when a newspaper delivery truck pulled up to the curb to fill the stand with the morning edition. The sleepy agent, craving for that wakeup cup of coffee at Breezy's that he'd get after his deliveries, and cursing his head for rebelling at him because of the excessive drinks he had taken with the boys after last night's bowling, did not see her blend into the dark telephone pole nearby (he should have noticed the pole's unusual bulge), and after he left for his next stop, Harriet hurried off to her cousin's house.

When she got to Gabriel's house, she sat patiently on the front porch, mumbling to herself, trying to make some sense of what she had just seen. The delivery boy passed by on his bicycle and tossed the morning paper on the steps. She waited until the boy reached the main road before standing, stretching and yawning, then retrieving the newspaper. She knocked on the front door until the kitchen light went on.

"Who's that?"

"It's me, Gabe. Harriet."

The door opened with Gabriel's sleepy and unbelieving eyes scrutinizing her uncomfortably. "Godfanit! What you doing here so early?" he demanded.

"I came here to deliver your newspaper," she said.

Gabriel looked at her with puzzlement. Then, yawning, in a sober tone, he asked her in.

———————

When Father Fonseca returned from his mission, he found a note taped to his door. It read: "David, Please see me immediately. Emmet." He cleaned himself and dressed in his robe, then went downstairs to Father Rosehill's office. The Father was reading behind his desk.

"Come in, David, and please sit down," Father Rosehill said without looking up from his book.

Father Fonseca complied. Father Rosehill slipped a bookmark in his book and closed it. He took off his reading glasses and folded them on his desk. Then he looked up and began, "Actually, David, I don't know how to start. You and I know that this seminary provides the community with the spiritual guidance that is necessary to make it . . . a well-meaning community."

"Yes."

"The Order has done this for over eighty-three years. We were the first church established on this side of the island. And the school, it has been in existence since 1941."

"Yes, Father."

Father Rosehill's eyes glanced uneasily over his desk, then rested on the book he was reading. "As you know, I don't like beating around the bush," he continued, looking up. "What I'm trying to get at is—and I'm sure you know what I'm trying to get at—is that this business you're doing at nights has got to stop. It is against the Holy Canon of the Catholic Church . . . what you have been doing."

"What do you mean, Father?"

"You know very well what I mean. It is something that we have talked about in the past. What have you to say about all of this?"

The young priest buried his gaze in the folds of his clasped hands that barely touched his lap. He felt the scrutiny of Father Rosehill's eyes upon him. Then, deliberately, he raised his eyes until they met Father Rosehill's. Both men's eyes locked into each other's in a kind of territorial struggle until Rosehill's conceded. He touched his book for no reason, then looked back at the younger priest and said, his voice having lost that edge of absolute authority, "You must understand the consequences of your actions."

"I'm sorry, Father," Father Fonseca said, his eyes still directed at Father Rosehill's now disquieted face.

"And I'm sorry, too, but it's imperative for the Order to take necessary measures in response to the actions that you have perpetrated. Quite frankly, your actions have brought some degree of embarrassment to the church. You do understand that?"

"Yes, Father. I understand."

"Very well." Father Rosehill rose from his chair. "As of

this moment, you are suspended of all pastoral duties to this seminary and parish, until further notice."

"Yes, Father."

"And you are forbidden to leave the premises of this seminary unless for reasons of official church business."

"Yes, Father."

"And while we're on the subject . . ."

"Yes, Father?"

———

"How come you carrying one can paint?" Gabriel asked, his eyes suspiciously watching for a reaction.

"Oh . . . this. I was going to paint my fence." Harriet nodded in the direction of the pasture.

"Funny time to paint, eh? And how come you painting da fence now? Never in my entire life I ever saw that fence painted. Not even once."

"Well, there's always time for change, right, cousin?"

Gabriel sipped the freshly brewed coffee. Mary was sitting at the kitchen table with them, reading the morning paper.

"Time fo' one change?" Gabriel's left eyebrow arched thoughtfully. "Well, I guess so. I kinda hope so. You sure you going paint yo' pasture fence?"

"Yes."

"Then le's go. I go help you paint."

"No, Gabriel." Harriet tittered. "That won't be necessary. I can do it myself. Besides, it's too early in the morning."

"No trouble at all." Gabriel was again suspicious.

"No. I insist that you don't help me. In fact, I think I'm going to change my mind about it. About painting my fence."

"Then what you going paint?" Gabriel gave her a hard look.

"Nothing," Harriet said resolutely.

Gabriel pressed on. "You sure you going paint *nothing?*"

"Yes. Nothing."

"Look at this, Gabriel," Mary said. "Get one sale on the

kine white paint you like use. Six dollar ninety-nine cents."
She opened the newspaper flat on the table so that Gabriel—
and Harriet—could see. But Gabriel was looking at everything but Harriet's eyes, and when he glanced at her face and
saw her eyes laughing at him knowingly, the corners of his
eyes creased with the hint of laughter. Then he did laugh. And
Harriet did, too. And soon, though she didn't know why at
first, Mary was laughing.

And before they knew it, the three had turned their
innocuous coffee-drinking mornings and afternoons into
guerrilla meetings to plot out the tactics for the night activities, which they didn't worry about others surveying. For with
the fall of Dennis Umeda's personality and business, along
with Clarissa Ching's mysterious disappearance, people in the
town began to forget—at least for the moment—about the
nature or message of any fresh paint slapped on the wall.
Besides, there came a long period where nothing new—or
rather, nothing interesting—was transmitted. The topics of
the signs were considered "old business," your everyday nonsense and common knowledge that everyone knew already,
such as "Clarissa Ching and Dennis Umeda get it on every
night" (outdated news), or "Kalani Humphrey's parents are
alive and well in Kānewai" (a fact everyone born pre-1950
knew) or "H. O. loves C.O." (H.O. had painted that one). None
of the messages talked about death or other similar topics,
and members of the community were, thus, becoming less
and less amused by the lampoons.

And it also became common knowledge that there was
no mysterious stranger or ghost who was creating the signs;
for each person involved in the sign-making knew that if he or
she was capable of generating havoc or formulating truths,
then everyone else in Kānewai could be responsible. But this
they acknowledged very discreetly among themselves.

Now that the venerable trio had sat around and confessed to each other's involvement in the crime of truth-mak-
ing, there came openly the reasons for their complicity. For
Gabriel, it was a matter of being conscientious: "I had to do

it," he confided, "to set this community straight. You see, if I neva do this, then somebody going think somebody from the outside doing this, or one ghost, or maybe even God. Then if this thing got big, eh, all hell would break loose. Everybody going start thinking that Kānewai town stay going down the tubes and everybody start getting all panicky. You know what I mean? So das why I da one was doing all the major graffiti on the wall. I take full responsibility."

But Harriet objected. "No, my silly cousin. You might have done some of that writing on the wall. But I must take responsibility for the most outrageous ones. And besides, Gabe, I saw, with my very own eyes, Father Fonseca, my cousin's grandson, my own flesh-and-blood, himself painting some of those signs on the wall."

"No forget, he my flesh-and-blood too," quipped Gabriel.

"Poor boy! I know exactly what he's going through. He has been a priest for such a long time already, but he still thinks about his Gloria and their son. My! The boy is so big now. I saw him and his mother one day when I got off the bus in downtown. That was three months ago, I think."

"What you saying?" Gabriel responded with disbelief.

"That's true," Mary added. "I know that, too."

"What you talking about?" Gabriel chided at Mary. "All you talking 'bout is nonsense. Nothing but nonsense. The Father is one priest. They no go around and, and . . . you know, you know what I mean."

"Gabe," Harriet retorted, "that was before he took his vows. You never knew that? That was before he became a priest. He has a child with Gloria Nunes, and the boy's name is Jason. That's David Fonseca's real son."

"Who Gloria Nunes? You mean Matilda Nunes."

"Isn't her name Gloria?"

"Matilda," Mary said softly.

"No talk like that about my cousin's grandson," Gabriel said. "David Fonseca? Ha! He never do something like that, even if was before he was one priest."

"Eh, Gabe . . . that's my cousin, too, you know. David Fonseca is my grand-nephew."

"I know. Mine, too."

"But all this is true," Mary offered.

"Then how come I never know that, then?!" Gabriel burst out. "If I never know, then that means is not true."

"Oh . . . don't be such one hard head, Gabe," Harriet said. "But going back to who put all those signs up . . ."

"Harriet, would you like more coffee?" Mary asked.

"Yes. Please. But going back to the main subject, Gabe, you're not the only one doing the sign-making. It's me, too. Plus many others in Kānewai are involved, too. All this business about a ghost putting it all up is shibai. Everyone is doing it, and everybody is hiding from everybody else. But I've known all along who was putting it up and who wasn't. I've been watching the happenings all along. In fact, I know who put the very first sign up. I saw with my very own eyes."

"Then who put up the very first sign?" asked a disbelieving Gabriel Hoʻokano, trying to hide knowledge of the fame that he had readily claimed.

"Was your brother. Jacob."

"You crazy. He wen ma-ke three, four years ago. Cannot be him."

"But he wasn't dead when I saw him."

"You saw him! How?"

"He died three, four years ago?" Harriet stared at Gabriel, waiting for him to give up the lie. "I did see him."

Gabriel chuckled. "Who you saw maybe looked like him, but was—"

"Maybe . . . maybe was his ghost that put it up."

———

FATHER FONSECA KNEW that the time had come to make that move toward apocalypse. Now that Father Rosehill had reprimanded him, there was no other choice left to him. It was urgent that he make that move, that action which he had held in desperate deliberation for the longest time. However full of goodness Father Rosehill was, the old priest was also blind to the evil that was rampant everywhere. It was up to him, then, to do something about it. If he failed, the community would be left to its doom. But if he was successful, every soul in Kānewai would be saved.

After his meeting in Father Rosehill's office, Father Fonseca went to the chapel and prayed for an hour, asking the Lord for His forgiveness. He confessed to all of his sins, listing each with specific details. And when the hour had passed, with a sense of irresolution still lingering in a tight fold of his soul, the Father called the prison hospital, asking the attendant about the status of Kalani's condition. He was told that Kalani's condition had gotten worse. In his room, opening the footlocker in the closet, he took out a shoebox. In the box were a package of blasting caps and an old book he had borrowed from the downtown diocese library. He laid out the objects carefully and orderly on his bed, then opened the book to a marked page. And into the early morning hours of the next day he studied this section of the book, frequently interspersing his study with a Rosary.

Twenty-Four

Ⓣ IT WAS A mild surprise, even a welcoming one at that, for Hiram Ching when the apparition of Claudio Yoon came into full manifestation. And for Claudio, it was the first time in his entire existence, worldly or otherwise, that he was witness to Hiram smiling at him and saying something genuinely nice: "So how come took you so long to visit?"

Claudio was at loss for words, but that was quickly remedied when he remembered the why of his visit. "You one sonavabitch, Ching, for making me look like one fool in everybody's eyes."

A hurt, defensive look came to Hiram's face. He had never heard Claudio in such an angry tone. He knew he had done a lot of bad things in his mortal life, but he didn't remember doing anything especially wrong to Claudio, whom he barely knew. Yet, it was important—very important, he realized—for him to keep his sincerity and honesty if he were to journey to that ultimate state of nonbeing. "I don't know what you mean," Ching said truthfully.

"Don't give me that bullshit, you fat pākē. All the time I was living in Kānewai, you always was giving me one stink eye, like I was dirt. And then you put up that stupid sign, saying that I was one māhū. No make up one sad story, Ching."

"I never in my life said that you was one māhū."

"You fat liar. You was the one that tol' me I was one, right to my face. And you wen paint dat friggin' lie right on yo' frickin'—stinkin'—suckin'—wall!"

"It wasn't me. It was—it was—"

"Who?"

And though a ghost cannot produce tears, Hiram Ching began to cry. Fat globs of ectoplasm rolled off his translucent cheeks, sizzling into air as they fell, like drops of water on a hot griddle. "You right," Hiram sobbed. "I did all that. It was my fault. I'm sorry. I wen paint that sign. But I never mean no harm!"

"I knew it! It was you who made me die! You!" Angrily, Claudio grew grotesquely large, then spun himself into a miniature tornado. The old dusty curtains of the theater snapped off their hooks. Seats buckled from the floor, a couple of them ripping free. When Claudio was finished with his tempest, he settled back to his former size and state, though now a distinctive silvery glow radiated in him. "I knew it," he said with exhaustion.

Hiram said nothing. He had fallen into himself and was sobbing, looking like a large quivering fluff of cotton. Claudio's glowing nature grew steadily, and soon his expanded presence commanded nearly the full interior of the theater. In contrast, Hiram became smaller and smaller, shriveling to the size of a peanut. That was when Claudio stopped the inimical growth of his self-righteousness and began to regard Hiram's diminishing form with the wide-eyed, innocent curiosity that was so characteristic of his former self as a mortal. The glow of his essence deteriorated, until he was his former size and color again. He watched Hiram's quivering, molten mass for a long while, amazed to see the once proud man actually crying and cut down to size. And when Hiram was near equivalent in proportion to a mote of dust, Claudio touched him. The depreciating process reversed itself, and in a short while, Hiram more than increased his mass by a hundred-fold, though still small enough to be held in Claudio's hand and crushed. With a purplish tint to his eyes, Hiram looked fearfully into Claudio's bewildered but softening eyes, then turned away painfully.

"I know I was wrong," Hiram said. "But please don't make me suffer because of this crime for the rest of my . . . my

. . . life. I can't live here anymore. I need to get to that . . . that other place. Whatever it is. Okay? I am really sorry."

It was exactly at this time when the precise positioning of the planets and stars occurred. Claudio tried to say something judiciously to his now new friend Hiram Ching, but already his ability to enunciate in the dimension was being eradicated. His arms and legs were becoming faint. Hiram could see that something was happening to Claudio, and he pleaded for him not to leave. But it was too late. Claudio reached out with his index finger to touch Hiram's head. And then he disappeared.

But the touch, though fleeting and weak, was enough to transmit between them a requited understanding. Hiram soon found himself dissipating, too. At first he was alarmed, but then, gleefully, he realized that Claudio must have forgiven him and that now he was entering the realm of non-being that he so desired. He smiled, then felt himself being sucked into a vortex that seemed to take him everywhere and nowhere at the same time.

Twenty-Five

IT WAS AN event that everyone would have lovingly remembered Father Fonseca by; it happened hours before the most prophetic and most powerful sermon delivered in the history of Kānewai (though unfortunately no one could hear it); it would have been judged as the singular reason in the repulsion of the dark minions of Satan that had settled among the people; it could have served as the monumental catalyst that would have brought together the residents —friends and enemies—of the town at a time of its most desperate need; and—if people would have taken the effort to understand it—it would have made Father Fonseca the real hero of the town—indubitably, its only leader against the evil forces of the unknown—and not a priest gone lōlō as he would be erroneously—and finally—known as.

At the time of the event, however, people would have had difficulty seeing beyond what seemed like the shaken sanity of perhaps some fugitive ward from a state institution. From their first sight of Father Fonseca preaching his three-hour sermon from the peak on the theater's roof, they would have mistakenly identified him as (1) a runaway mental patient, (2) Kalani Humphrey, (3) the Devil himself, (4) the ghost of Hiram Ching, or (5) a composite of all of the above. But there he was, Father Fonseca, on the second highest point in Kānewai (St. Matthew's steeple was over thirty feet higher), urging the masses of Kānewai to repent for their sins, then reopening the yellowed, crusty pages of that archaic book from the diocese library in Honolulu and repeating the Ritual of Exorcism.

It was late morning when the Father ended his sermon, hours after he had performed the ritual. He had been up on the roof since the night before, still questioning himself about the necessity of this holy endeavor. And it was later in the night when he was given a vision, or a go-ahead, that dispersed any ambivalence in his mind and set the foundation for his plan of action.

As he sat on the peak of the roof brooding under the stars and moon, there came a sudden rumbling under him. The theater began to sway, which made him lose his balance and slip to the edge. At the very last moment he grabbed hold of the rusty rain gutter, and when one end of the gutter broke off, Father Fonseca found himself swinging to and fro across the side of the theater, the other end of the gutter attached precariously by a nail. He held on while the building continued to shake, and after a minute, when the rumbling stopped, he carefully pulled himself back up on the roof. But the theater began to shake again, at first with an easy sway, then building to a tremble. The roof broke free and hovered at least a foot above the supporting walls, for what seemed to be a terrifically long time, finally settling back down in a cloud of dust.

At first terrified, his heart running away from him, the Father then became aroused by a sudden recognition of this unequivocal sign from Heaven dictating to him the necessity of the exorcism. And to crown the sanctitude of the experience, Father Fonseca saw a shooting star streak *up* toward the heavens, followed by another a few seconds later. *Those* were wondrous sights. He searched for a third star, which never came, then closed his eyes and recited a most memorable offering of the Lord's Prayer. Under the light of the moon, he opened the leather-bound book, the cover roughened from mold, squinted his eyes, and began to read silently the instructional text that had been reprinted in the original Latin from the feudal manuscript. By the time the first rays of the morning sun struck his worn face, he was near finishing the ritual. And when he did finish, exactly thirteen minutes later, he closed the book and looked into the blinding rising sun, then tottered back and lay himself on the roof's peak, his mind blackened by his body's denial to breathe regularly in that trance with words.

LATE THAT EVENING, as David Fonseca was gripping that medieval manuscript of exorcism and groping for some significance in his life while perched on the theater's roof, as he was gazing at the stars but perhaps more the infinitude of space between for a sign of any magnitude, trivial or not, Harriet, Gabriel, and Mary were doing their business at the theater, right below the Father's position. The wall had become so full with messages and signs rendered by at least two-and-a-half-dozen contributors that Harriet made a suggestion to move on to virgin territory. With Gabriel's nodding approval, they went to the front of the theater, while Mary stood as a watch from across the street. They soon found that the bargain paint they were using applied surprisingly well to the glass doors and windows.

"Where did you buy this paint?" Harriet asked her cousin.

"Das da one on sale," he said. "Was cheap."

"Goes on terrific. Look."

Gabriel regarded the dripping sign Harriet had just slapped on the glass door. "What dis means? And how come you pickin' on David Fonseca?"

Harriet took a step back and regarded the sign. "I don't know, Gabe. It just came to me. When we first came here tonight, I thought we had a plan on what was to go up. Then I couldn't think about what we had planned. But now the idea kind of just came to me without my even thinking of it. I don't know how it came to me. It's like my hand did the thinking."

"Well, yo' hand bettah start thinkin' some mo'. Hurry up befo' somebody catch us."

Harriet agreed. She tried to put her mind, or rather hand, into the next sign, but nothing came out. "I'm sorry, Gabe.

That's all for me tonight. One sign. Not too great of a production, eh? And now . . . *what's that?!*"

The glass doors began shaking crazily.

A nonchalant "What?" was Gabriel's response.

"That! Look at the doors—they're shaking!"

"No get so excited. Das only the wind blowing against." He placed a palm over the space between the two doors and felt a draft of air blowing out. "There . . . you no can feel 'em?"

Harriet followed Gabriel's example, then pressed her hands to her bosom. "Yes . . . I guess you're right. For a minute, I thought that . . . that . . ."

"Thought what?"

"Oh, never mind. Anyway, what was I saying? Oh yes. Anyway, now that you mentioned it, I'm wondering what *does* my sign mean?"

"What yo' sign mean?!" Gabriel shook his head. "You put da sign up and you dunno what it means."

"Gabriel, tell me what it means."

"No time fo' dat. Later on, maybe at the house. We gotta finish our business and then go, befo' da next shift come and catch us red-handed."

Gabriel finished his sign, then the two gathered their utensils and hurried off. Gabriel stopped and called Mary, but Mary didn't respond. She was staring straight at them but didn't seem to see Gabriel waving her to cross. "Mary! Com'n! Le's go!" Gabriel called anxiously.

Mary snapped out of her trance and crossed the street. They started back to the house.

"Whassmattah wit' you?" Gabriel asked Mary when they were a half a block away from the theater. Mary hadn't said a word all that time.

She turned to him, smiled weakly, and said, "Nothing."

"Nothing? Nothing makes nothing. What you saw . . . one ghost?"

Mary was about to nod but stopped herself and shook her head instead. She smiled at Gabriel, who grumbled something unintelligible and then turned to Harriet, criticizing about her wasting too much paint as a result of not wiping clean one side of a dipped paintbrush against the inside rim of the can.

What Mary saw was just too bizarre to describe. She probably had imagined the whole thing, she told herself, it being way past her 8:30 bedtime, which made her drowsy and dream up crazy things like the roof of the theater levitating three feet above the walls and fireballs like that of a Roman candle shooting out from the gap.

––––––––

AT A FEW minutes before noon, Father Fonseca, rubbing the sleep from his eyes, stood on the highest point of the theater's roof, having been stirred to consciousness by the heat and glare of the sun. Shielding his eyes, he scanned the main street, then gave a silent prayer and finished it by crossing himself. Meanwhile, what little traffic that was on the street below came to a standstill. The few pedestrians, too, stopped and looked up at that high perch, wondering who the hell was that person and what the hell was he doing. A small crowd gathered across the street, and among them a rumor was passed around that the crazy man—whoever he was—was about to commit suicide by jumping off. Another murmur conjured him up as a deranged Vietnam vet, recently escaped from the state mental institution, possibly readying himself to snipe some unsuspecting Kānewaian. A few panicky gasps went through the crowd. One keen-eyed observer announced that the figure wasn't carrying an M-16 or any kind of fire-arm, but what looked more like a book, perhaps even a Bible. Then one member of the crowd loudly identified the man as being none other than Kalani Humphrey.

"What the hell Kalani Humphrey doing in Kānewai?" were the words and thoughts circulated in the crowd.

From his seat at the service station, Freddie Tanaka noticed the crowd growing in size and also the lone figure on top of the theater. He went into his office and from the lower drawer of his battered file cabinet took out a pair of high-powered binoculars, something he had bought from a mail-order catalog three years before for the sole purpose of hunting, though he had never once used them in that capacity. He stood on the gas pump island for the best view. "Das . . . Hiram Ching up there," he said to himself, shuddering.

"What you looking at?" asked Richard Pimente, who had just pulled in for some gas.

"Up there . . . das the old man."

"Up where? What old man?" Richard got out of his van. "What you talking about? What you looking at?"

"There," Freddie said, pointing with a shaky finger.

Richard noted the crowd and the dark figure above. "Lemme see that," he said to Freddie, motioning for the binoculars, which Freddie handed to him. Focusing, he viewed the figure, then the crowd. "Look more like da Devil himself with his crowd of believers." He laughed. He panned back to the unidentified figure. "Who dah hell is that?"

The figure on the roof seemed to be reading a book.

Richard Pimente smiled, recognizing the figure. "I wonder what thc hell he doing up there and I wonder what the hell he dressed like that fo'?"

"Who dat?"

"Father Fonseca."

"What?" Freddie Tanaka narrowed his eyes in disbelief. "Let me look at that."

Richard gave him back the binoculars and started to pump gas himself.

"No kidding!" Freddie exclaimed. "Das da priest! But what *he* doing up there?"

"Das my question," Richard said.

"Actually he look more like Kalani Humphrey, come to think of it."

"What?"

"The Humphrey boy. Look like him. Da kine clothes only he would wear."

"Let me see that again."

Freddie gave him the binoculars. He took over the gas pump. "How much you like?"

"All right," answered Richard.

"All right what? How much gas you like? You mean fill 'em up?"

"Yeah, das what I said. Nah," Richard said firmly, "das da priest. You cannot tell?"

Freddie shrugged his shoulders, which Richard couldn't see since his eyes were glued to the binoculars.

"What the hell is he doing?" Richard added. "What the hell he wearing dat kind of clothes fo'? You wen call da cops?"

Freddie topped the tank. "What fo'?" he said. He screwed in the gas cap and returned the nozzle to the pump. Leaning against the van, he studied the crowd. "Why call the cops if das dah priest. And anyway, this town got mo' crazy since they wen put your boy in prison."

Richard Pimente snatched the binoculars from his eyes and glared at Freddie. "What you said?"

"I said this town so crazy since they wen lock up Kalani Humphrey."

"No—no. What you said right befo' that?"

"Das what I said."

"You said something that Kalani Humphrey is my son, right?"

Freddie rubbed his hands together and looked uncomfortably in the direction of the theater, trying to avoid the scorch of Richard's accusing eyes.

"Damn Japanee, das what you said, right?"

Freddie remained silent, continuing to rub his hands.

"Never mind," Richard said, returning the binoculars to its owner. "How much I owe you?"

"Eighteen dollars and forty-three cents."

Richard Pimente paid the bill and left promptly without a word.

With one arm resting on the top of a pump, Freddie

shook his head as the van tore out of the service station. "Cannot even face the truth, dat damn Po'tagee," Freddie said to himself in a soft, quivering voice. "Not even the plain frickin' truth."

———

IN THE CASE of Father Fonseca, truth was being served from a high pulpit. In a sermon that he was composing extemporaneously from the roof, the Father lambasted the community's sinners and demanded that they all kneel for immediate judgment by the Lord, the Father, and the Holy Spirit. He commanded them to repent for their sins by coming forward and publicly denouncing the Evil that was spreading so rapidly and cancerously throughout the community, especially calling on those congregated below him. The Father saw the crowd below increase in size, and he also noticed that with every word uttered their faces changed in expression and showed more and more recognition of the severity of the sins in their lives. His sermon became stronger and more infused with the representative vision of God's damning wrath. Then he spread his arms to Heaven, begging for God's forgiveness, praying to the Lord that His people gathered below were testimonies to the power of His eternal might.

The Father paused in his discourse with the approach of a screaming ambulance. Then a fire engine came to a stop below, parking next to the attentive paramedics. He observed the firemen getting off the truck, recognizing among them Matilda Nunes's son, Jason, and Henry Kila's son, and the driver, Watson Kamei. And Father Fonseca knew them all as unrepentant sinners who never went to church. But the Glory of God was bringing them forward, Father Fonseca thought. He looked above, reaching farther and farther with his vision into the expanding clouds of Heaven, and he felt his soul rise higher and higher into the Realm of Mercy and Forgiveness and Salvation and . . .

———

AFTER THE SCREAMS of the crowd subsided, turning first into loud cries and then into a horrid silence as the ambulance wailed away, taking the life-leaving body of the priest, Freddie Tanaka went back to his desk, returning the binoculars to the bottom of the file cabinet, and sat in his chair for a minute, thinking about absolutely nothing. He picked up the phone and dialed a number, listened patiently to the rings, and then asked for Richard Pimente. Perking up suddenly, he yelled into the speaker, "Damn you! Why you always gotta run away from da truth?!"

Twenty-Six

T HE FIRM OF Barclay, Mannheim, Lee and Tanizawa, the law corporation representing Clarissa Ching, unable to locate her, proceeded in the negotiations with Trinity Corporation. After a long hiatus, demolition of the building was finally rescheduled two months after Clarissa gave her attorneys full power to run her holdings. The demolition was, however, again interrupted by the fatal fall of Father David Fonseca from the roof of Kānewai Theater. Fearing a legal suit by the Catholic Diocese of Hawai'i, the lawyers for Clarissa Ching, in counsel with the attorneys for Trinity Corporation, took the offensive by leveling charges against the diocese for trespassing and criminal property damage.

The trespassing charge was obvious; the property damage was not. Investigators for the attorneys, however, discovered a hole in the upper back wall of the theater that seemed to be compromised with explosives. Researchers for the attorneys opened a file on Father David Fonseca and found, among other things, that he had been actively involved in the antiwar movement of the late sixties and early seventies while matriculating at Pacific Theological College in California. They also dug up information concerning his involvement with Matilda Nunes and his part in the begetting of her son, Jason. And soon a trail of illegitimate sons and daughters and acts of terrorism were unequivocally linked to Father Fonseca, or so were the results of the special investigation.

In all three of the city's major dailies, *the* story of the time was not about the starvation of hundreds of thousands in western Africa; or the race and class riots that had broken out again in England's industrial areas; or the secret war the CIA was waging in Afghanistan; or the bloody crushing of workers and students in Kwangju, South Korea, by joint ROK and U.S. armed forces; but how a sexually obsessive, former all-star high school quarterback became a radical communist seminarian and then quietly assumed the priesthood in one of the state's oldest and most respected churches. Subsequent stories on the feature pages portrayed David Fonseca as a romantic revolutionary, à la Berrigans, who may have learned the rudiments of bomb-making and gun-cleaning from none other than the Black Panthers. (It was discovered that he had done voluntary work at a draft counseling center in Oakland, California.)

Before the end of the first day of this sensational, late-breaking story, the Catholic Church of Hawai'i was on the defensive. In a press conference in the Catholic Church's headquarters in downtown Honolulu, Monsignor Hermann Reese issued a press release stating that Father David Fonseca was one of the most respected priests in the diocese and had served his parish well; that he had received throughout his career numerous praises from both prelates and members of the congregation; and that nothing, not even the fantastic stories of the media, would change the Church's position and feelings about the matter. Two days after the press conference, the Catholic Church filed a defamatory suit against the daily newspapers, as well as countersuits at Barclay, Mannheim, Lee and Tanizawa, and Trinity Corporation.

WHILE THE CHURCH and private sector were trading blows, the people of Kānewai prepared their minds and souls for the wake and burial of one of Kānewai's own favorite sons. The funeral came seven days after the fall. The people lined up outside the church where Father Fonseca's body lay in state to see their beloved young Father one last time.

Among the few who at first refused to pay respects to the Father was Jason Nunes, who had not learned of his consanguineous connection with the Fonseca clan until three days after the Father's death, when he read about it in the obituary. Among the survivors was listed his name. This matter was brought to his attention by one of his best friends and co-worker, Jeremiah Kila. At first Jason took it as a mean typographical error. But intuition told him after reading it for the eleventh time that there was some truth to the matter. But perhaps there was another Jason Nunes?

He woke up his mom the following morning and asked her about his name being listed as the sole surviving son of Father Fonseca. Matilda insisted that the inclusion was an honest mistake, reassuring her son that his father was a good man who had died in Vietnam fighting for his country. But her eyes told him another story. He left the house with an empty feeling, that his life, as he knew it now, had become a terrible lie. Instead of reporting for duty at the fire station, he got into his car and drove to the Falls, where he sat on a wet rock at the edge of the pool for most of the day, sighing heavily and occasionally looking upward at the falling water, but otherwise not moving much at all. Then, when the sun became hidden by the mountains and the mosquitoes had for the most part ceased to bother him, having had their fill of him, he stood up and stretched, looked to the top of the Falls and said something abusive, then dived into the icy water of the pool with all of his clothes on. A full minute later he burst through to the surface with a loud gasp that blew the Falls' mist away. He climbed out of the pool and onto the rock, his clothes heavily soaked but his mind a thousand times lighter. Then he went to his car and drove back home.

For the most part he was taking the matter pretty well, although he still could not forget completely the hurt that came with the realization that the "new" news for him was "old" news for those in the town thirty years or older. He had been fond of the priest even though he hardly knew him since he had never gone to church in his life. He had originally planned to attend the funeral to pay the Father his respects, but now learning that his real father had not died in Vietnam but a few feet from his outstretched arms, he changed his mind. He was finally persuaded at the last minute to attend the funeral by his girlfriend of five years, Laura Pimente, who told him that it was only right that he bid his real father good-bye for the first and last time even though he found the truth difficult to comprehend.

————

It was around the time of the Father's funeral when Flora and Matt Goto decided to do something about the threatening situation of the old Kānewai Theater. Somehow rejuvenated in her positive feelings about the theater as a result of the death of Father Fonseca, whom she now referred to as the Savior of the Theater, as well as somewhat blissful in her sense of life's purpose as a direct result of the rebirth of passion between herself and Matt, Flora became unconditionally the strongest advocate for the preservation of the now historic (in her mind) Kānewai Theater. She began by talking to anyone and everyone: her neighbors, fellow marketgoers, church members. She organized a steering committee of three—herself, Cindy Cordeiro, and Sandy Kim—and the triumvirate came up with a petition that asked in polite language for the preservation of the building since it was next in age to the oldest building in Kānewai (St. Matthew's Church was noted as being more venerable), perhaps the second oldest structure on this side of the island.

They collected a total of thirty-nine-and-a-half signatures (Val Rodrigues helped his baby daughter, Sunshine, to make her chicken scratch). Then the three drove to the downtown office of Barclay, Mannheim, Lee and Tanizawa, where they presented three xeroxed copies of the signed petitions to a cordial and overdressed secretary who advised them to return in a week. "Mr. Barclay and Mr. Mannheim and Mr. Lee and Mr. Tanizawa are all exceedingly busy right now," the secretary affirmed, with a smile.

They returned exactly as instructed and were again

offered another excuse. Another aborted attempt and at least two dozen futile phone calls later, Cindy Cordeiro, already complaining all the way over from Kānewai, stood in front of the thick impervious oak doors of the attorneys' office, refusing to go in.

"Com'on," Sandy persuaded. "They going be in this time."

"You think I one stupid fool?" Cindy said. "I sick and tired coming here and getting one stupid smile, one after da ada, from that damn stupid secretary, telling us that them frickers are busy again. You gotta be outta yo' mind if you going see me go in there and make one ass outta myself. Again."

"But we here already," insisted Flora. "We might as well cross our fingers and go inside."

"Cross our fingers?! I going geev dem all one right cross fo' jerkin' us around so much. Screw dem."

"At least we can go in and find out," said Sandy.

"Den—you—go," Cindy said, emphasizing each word with the weight of an elephant stomping the count of three. She made an about-face, marched to the elevator, and pressed the down button. The elevator doors opened immediately, as if anticipating her hasty return. She went in, pressed the hold button, and said, "Coming?" Then she stabbed "G." Hesitating for a moment, Flora and Sandy scurried toward the closing doors of the elevator.

But either Cindy didn't hear their cries for her to wait or the elevator refused to reopen. The two women watched the flicker of the digits above the elevator doors signal Cindy's descent of thirty-nine stories.

"You know what?" Flora said.

"What?"

"Since we up here anyway, why we no go in and check it out. Maybe the attorneys are going see us today."

"Good idea," said Sandy flatly, while sullenly regarding the falling numbers transform into the finality of G. "Why not? Yeah . . . le's go."

So they went into the office, approached the secretary, who was now addressing them as Mrs. Goto and Mrs. Kim, and received the latest excuse.

"I'm sorry," the secretary offered. "Perhaps we can set an appointment."

The same apology with the same concern, wondered Flora. How can she continue doing this?

"But we have an appointment," Sandy said.

"If you remember the last time you were here," the secretary said in a dry, decorous manner, "I informed you that Mr. Barclay and his partners and associates are booked with appointments for the next six months." A crisp smile. "I informed you also that if it were all possible, we'd try our best to accommodate you by fitting you in-between appointments. But we're just too busy today. Mr. Lee and Mr. Mannheim have just returned from business trips and their calendars are both full with appointments. Mr. Barclay is out of town. And Mr. Tanizawa is at the moment in an important meeting. I'm very sorry. Would you like to try again, perhaps early next week?"

Flora and Sandy looked at each other for guidance.

"All right," Flora said with the air out of her voice. "Maybe next week we can come back, try again. Thank you."

"You're very welcome," said the secretary. The intercom began to buzz. "Please excuse me." She picked up the phone and pressed the flashing button.

The two women left the office and waited for the elevator. Silently they watched the flicker of the lights. Before the elevator doors completely opened, Cindy burst out.

"Cindy?" Sandy said. "Where you going?" Cindy was headed for the law offices, clutching several rolls of pennies.

"Whas all that fo'?" Flora asked, looking at the rolls.

There was no answer. Cindy grappled the door knob as if to lift the door off its hinges, dropping a couple of rolls with the effort. She picked them up and proceeded through the entrance. The two women followed her, worried that Cindy was up to something that might jeopardize their amicable though useless relationship with the secretary, a Miss Forsyth.

Cindy dropped her purse on the secretary's desk and began shouting at her: "OKAY—SO YOU DON'T WANT TO TALK TO US—WHY?—BECAUSE WE DON'T HAVE ANY MONEY?—OKAY DEN—HERE'S ALL THE MONEY YOU CAN HAVE!" She tore open the rolls, dumping the pennies on the desk.

"Cindy! What you doing?" Flora Goto asked nervously. "Com'on. Le's go."

The secretary snapped out of her momentary wide-eyed trance when Cindy tipped over a long-necked glass vase with a single rose, spilling water on some papers. "Look what you've done! Will you please stop this?!" the secretary demanded, dabbing the papers with a wad of facial tissues. "Are you out of your mind?!"

But Cindy continued with her demonstration. "STOP WHAT? DIS? THE HELL NO! I JUS' PAYING YOU POOR FOLKS HERE WITH WHAT WE OWE YOU—"

"Cindy! Com'on—le's go!" insisted Sandy, tugging at her sleeve. Cindy shook her off.

"—FO' ALL THE TIMES WE HAD TO COME HERE, SPENDING OUR TIME AND ENERGY AND GAS, AND BOTHERIN' YOU PEOPLE HERE WHO GET THE MOST PRECIOUS TIME IN THE WORLD—MO' PRECIOUS THAN ANYBODY ELSE'S IN DIS FRICKIN' WORLD! ALL RIGHT?! WE JUS' PAYING YOU FO' ALL THE TIME WE TOOK FROM YOU SONAVABITCHES"—staring at the secretary—"BITCH!"

"That's it!" the secretary said, in a sing-songish tone as if reciting a nursery rhyme. She lifted the phone off the hook and began touch-toning digits. "I'm calling security."

"Le's go!" said Flora.

"Com'on, Cindy," Sandy said. "Enough is enough."

"What's the problem, Miss Forsyth?" said a middle-aged, well-dressed haole, who had come out of an office. "What is the ruckus about? Is there something wrong?"

"Cindy!" Flora said, pulling her away from the desk. "Le's go! That's the attorney!"

"Well, yes, Mr. Mannheim. It so happens that—"

"OH! NOW YOU LIKE SEE US NOW, IS THAT RIGHT?! WELL, THEN! I SUPPOSE YOU LIKE YO' CLIENTS FO' THROW THEIR MONEY AT YOU FIRST BEFO' YOU SEE THEM?! WELL, HERE'S YOUR SURPRISE!" She grabbed handfuls of pennies from the desk and scattered them all over the office. Secretaries, paralegals, and associates were ducking behind desks or running into side rooms for cover, as if a terrorist were spraying them with bullets.

Lee and Tanizawa appeared from their offices. Mannheim was smiling nervously, as if trying to find all of this amusing, while the secretary hid behind him. Cindy fired her pennies at him, and his smile faded. He retreated to his office, as did the other partners, who ordered the secretary—anyone—to call security. Cindy grabbed for more pennies and found that Flora and Sandy had opened the other rolls and were firing away, too. One of the most effective shots occurred when an associate came out of his office and gave an order to a paralegal to physically charge them. But Flora's toss hit him straight in an eye, popping out a contact lens and forcing him back to his office.

With the penny supply depleted, the trio hurried out of the office. Sandy ran to press the down button, and the three waited for an immeasurably long time for the elevator to come up. The door of the office opened cautiously, and several paralegals poked their heads out, giving them bewildering looks.

Cindy shouted at them, "What you panties looking at? What?—you all like yo' 'ōkoles get bruised?"

Undeterred by her comments and the laughter of the trio that followed, the paralegals continued their scrutiny. One of them began scribbling notes on a legal pad.

It was Sandy's turn. "Oh—wow! You can write! What?—you can read, too?"

The elevator doors opened. They got in with four other people. The elevator took them to the ground floor, where they were met by two hefty young men in blue uniforms.

"Excuse me," said one of the security guards who was standing in front of the other. "But did you folks just come from an attorney's office on the thirty-ninth floor?"

"Yes," Flora said timidly.

"Well, we just got a complaint that—"

"Uh . . . howzit, Auntie Cynthia," the other guard said, smiling uncomfortably.

Cindy turned to him, and her smile shot across the lobby and back. "Junior?! Junior boy?!" She wrapped her arms around him. She kissed him. He reciprocated. "And den —what you doing heah?" she asked.

"Working."

"My God! Oh . . . dese are my friends from Kānewai. Dis heah,"—to Flora and Sandy—"is my middle-sister's boy, Robert, but we call him Junior Boy. Look how big him. I never recognized you. You grew *so* big. And so how's the family? How many kids you get now?"

"Three."

"What?"

"One boy, two girls."

"My goodness!" To Flora and Cindy: "Look how big him! He was one lineman on his school's football team. All-star."

The nephew grinned shyly. "Nah. Second team."

"But I thought you was all-star?"

"Yeah, but second team. My younger bruddah, Delbert, was first-team linebacker."

"My goodness!"

The first security guard looked uneasily at Junior Boy.

"Oh, Auntie Cynthia," Junior Boy said, "dis my partner, Solomon."

"What? Simon? Like 'Simon says'?"

Solomon chuckled. "No. *Solo*mon."

"Oh, Solomon. Very nice to meet you."

The other two women introduced themselves.

"So what you guys do over here?"

"Had one call from the thirty-ninth floor. Some kind of disturbance. Got to check on it."

"Well, you know dese damn attorneys," Cindy said, reading their look. "All they like is yo' money. They dry everybody up of their money."

Junior Boy smiled, nodding his head.

"Eh, we bettah go," Solomon said to Junior Boy, his eyes pointing to the elevator.

"Yeah," was the answer. "Okay den, Auntie Cindy, I gotta go back work."

"Yeah," said the other security guard. "Nice meeting you folks."

"Yes, was nice meeting you, too."

"Okay, Auntie. Gotta go back work." Hugs and kisses. Then the two parties separated.

Outside the air-conditioned office building, the afternoon sun warmed them as they made their way to the parking lot.

"Can't believe I saw my kid sister's kid . . . of all places," Cindy said.

"Big," said Flora.

"Yeah, big," Cindy said.

"Good to know people in high places," commented Sandy.

"Yeah," said Cindy, smiling. "Good to know."

Twenty-Seven

SHORTLY AFTER MARY Wahineokaimalino served Harriet O'Casey her second cup of coffee, the rebellion began.

"Where mine?" demanded Gabriel, who had stopped in the middle of a sentence about how the smell of the cow manure was related to what the three women had done at the attorneys' office.

"I want to listen to what you folks talking about," said Mary.

"But I said I wanted some mo' coffee," added an irritated Gabriel. "How come you only brought coffee fo' Harriet?"

"So you think what they doing is good?" Mary asked Harriet.

Harriet nodded her head.

Bothered by Mary's snub, Gabriel stared across the road at the empty lot, in particular the area the old Mustang had once occupied; thriving clumps of grass now were patching the bald spots. "Evah since dey wen take dat junk away," thought aloud a somewhat disconcerted Gabriel, "everything been falling apart. What mo' going happen?"

"Yes. I think those three women are doing a wonderful thing for Kānewai. We ought to join them. It's all right what we're doing, but I think it's better if we all join forces and oppose them monsters who want to take away something we like so much."

"How you think we should go about helping them?" asked Mary.

Gabriel decided to give Mary one more chance. "Where my cup coffee?" he demanded.

"Can you go get it yourself, Gabriel?" said Mary. "The pot on the stove."

"Oh, Gabe. Can't you see Mary is talking with me? Please don't disturb us."

Please don't disturb us? Who da hell she think she is, talking to me like dat in my own house?!

Gabriel rose slowly from his chair, stopping halfway for a moment, glancing at Mary; she showed no intention of lifting her bottom to fill his cup. So he took his empty cup to the kitchen, grumbling about how the weather was always changing on him. He poured himself some coffee, but chose instead to stay in the kitchen. He sighed and looked out the window, though his ears were tuned to what the two women were talking about out on the porch. But what was happening to him, and to the community? Until a few months ago, everything seemed to be all right. Then all kinds of terrible things started happening. More writing on the theater's wall. Dennis Umeda cracking up. Father Fonseca jumping off the theater's roof. The disappearance of Clarissa Ching. The junk car taken away. What else was going to happen?

Maybe I should have listen to my brother, Gabriel mused, *and did something about it when I suppose to do something about it.*

His brother had warned him of evil happenings that would come to Kānewai with the loss of the taro land as well as the other land traditionally used for other agricultural products. "If no mo' 'āina," his brother had told him just before his being shipped off to the war in the South Pacific, "no mo' kaukau fo' da mana'o. Da Hawaiian lose his land, he lose everything. Da Hawaiian separated from his land, the mana going run away from him."

Gabriel now knew what his brother had meant. There was nothing exactly to pinpoint, but the feeling was strong. Gabriel understood it well, for he had had it for a while now. The loss of the junk car had just aggravated the feeling a bit more, to a point of being intolerable. But there was nothing more that could be said or done about that; it was just something to feel and deal with and not to be explicated about like how a haole would do.

Gabriel laughed to himself, remembering the time when his brother had told him—when they were on speaking terms —about a haole professor from the university visiting and persuading Jacob to take him in as a student of the ancient Hawaiian art of healing. Holistic medicine, the haole had called it.

Gabriel laughed to himself, then said loudly, "Like one hole in his head!" The two women stopped their talk, stared through the window screen at Gabriel, then continued with their conversation. Embarrassed, Gabriel stepped back from the sink, sipped his coffee, then joined back with his interrupted thoughts.

Yes, he remembered his brother's story dearly: how the haole had just come out of the blue moon and planted himself under Jacob's swinging tree house with his notebooks and camera. And Jacob came out and gave the haole a hard, curious look, then ignored him. How the haole, like the hen of a hen-pecked husband, began to follow him, asking him all kinds of questions. Said he would like to teach a course in the ancient Hawaiian art of healing since he felt it was important to perpetuate the Hawaiian culture; and that if it were possible, he'd like to live with Jacob to learn all that there was to learn so that he could not only accomplish that goal but perhaps even write a book. All of this, the haole urged, was to be regarded as an important attempt to preserve the old Hawaiian ways.

Gabriel chuckled to himself. Remembering this reminded him about that television program he watched one night about how some scientists were living on the slopes of Mauna Loa trying to locate a rare Hawaiian bird and to study it before the species died out. "Hah!" declared Gabriel. "If they going die, let dem ma-ke in peace, wit' no mo' needles poking deah 'ōkole!" Gabriel peeked from the corner of the window and saw that his small outburst had not bothered the discussion of the two women. "And da nerve," he whispered bitterly, "*they* coming here and screwing up everyt'ing is why all da goddamn birds all ma-ke-ing *anyway!*"

He sipped his coffee. *What they talking about now?* he asked himself. He stole a look at the two women, bothered by their choice to talk only to themselves. Now, it seemed, Mary had moved between him and his cousin. He didn't feel like the Man of the House, the Main Talker, anymore. And he had to get his own coffee. Since when did he ever have to get his own coffee?

He eavesdropped on their conversation. He singled out a few words, like "garrison" and "stonewall" and "sun" and "moon," but that was all. He couldn't make sense of how the words were related to one another, though he knew his hearing had deteriorated of late and perhaps that was why he didn't understand. Funny how so many things had changed in just a few months. In just a few months.

———

"So you think we should join them?" asked a wondering Mary.

Harriet nodded her head. "The pōhaku in that wall not going to speak for themselves. We have to shake some sense in them."

Mary nodded with understanding. "Boy, all this is really getting outta hand. First time we get all dese kine problems. This used to be one real nice, slow town. But now—auwē!"

"You can say that again."

Gabriel Hoʻokano burst out of the kitchen—actually, he hobbled out, real fast—and rushed to the corner post of the patio, grabbing it hard. His eyes were bulging with fear, his body trembling.

"Gabe! Whassamattah?" gasped Mary.

Gabriel was trying to answer and catch his breath at the same time. He couldn't do both, mouthing silent words while hanging on to that post as if he were clinging onto the last threads of his dear life. Actually, he *was* clinging onto the last threads of his life, for in the kitchen his soul had suddenly decided, for no good reason, to leave him. It shot approximately twenty yards away and hovered over that new patch of grass.

It was a frightening experience, to see one's soul escape from one's body. Perhaps it was like watching one's ghost come back to watch you die.

"Gabriel?! What's the matter?" Harriet cried.

"Quick, Harriet! Help me put him in his chair!"

The two women struggled to free from the post a Gabriel that seemed to be setting into beginning rigor mortis. Gabriel's grip was just too much for them to break.

"Whassamattah, Gabe?" Mary cried. "Is it something you saw? Is it—something I did?"

"He's so *cold!*" Harriet howled.

Harriet pulled Mary away from Gabriel, his face petrified with an expression of absolute horror.

"He'll be all right," Harriet comforted, though her voice was shaking. "You might want to get him a blanket, though." She coaxed Mary to sit. "He's all right. He just gotta catch himself."

"Catch—what? Whachu mean?"

"I mean . . ." She didn't know what she meant. It was just something that she had blurted out without any thought. She reasoned about what she had just said for a few seconds, then added, "Well, what I mean is that . . . that he's excited about something. He's just . . . he's just pissed off that you didn't get him his coffee." To Gabriel: "Gabe, can you stop acting this way? After all, Mary has been getting your coffee for a long, long time. If you could excuse her for just this one time." *I do hope longer.* "Gabe, my cousin, if it's not too much for the asking, can you sit down?"

Gabriel wished that he could, but his soul had a mind of its own. In fact, Gabriel's soul began to laugh at him. It came toward him and lit on a patch of grass right below the porch, as if teasing him, and began to talk.

You sonavabitch, the soul began. *You think you can order me around any kine style? Well, you better forget it, bruddah.*

Dis soul is his own soul. You understand? Hah! And to think for a moment that I was in yo' body all dis time, taking all da stinkin', stupid orders from you! My God! You got one nada thing coming!

But wha-whas da problem? thought Gabriel. *My God! Whas da problem?*

"You think we should call da ambulance?" asked Mary.

"I dunno," Harriet said. "Maybe. Maybe. But first, let's watch him for a few minutes. Maybe he's all right. But do get him a blanket."

Mary rushed into the house and came back with a blanket, which she draped caringly over Gabriel.

"He's not all right," Mary said, trying to rub some warmth into his back. "I never, never seen him like this befo'."

"Well, maybe you should call the ambulance, then."

Mary nodded, then slipped back into the house to phone the nearby fire station.

Gabriel's soul shook his head. *My God? My God? Whose yo' 'God', you sonavabitch? Me or you? Or Him?* Pointing to the sky. *I should tell you what I think, but I not going 'cause I going let you make up yo' mind. You understand? Make up yo' mind.*

Wha—what you mean? inquired a fading Gabriel. *But come back here. I not feeling that good. And I know I going die if you no come back.*

You going die?! Hah! You already dead.

But I no like die now. Get too much things I gotta do.

What "too many things"?! All yo' life up to right now is sitting on dis goddamn porch and futtin' around. Das all you do all day.

Den what you like I do?

What I like you do?! Who's 'I'?

You.

No. You.

Like a blast of stars, just as Gabriel felt himself fading out for what he thought would be the last time, his soul shot smack back into himself. The impact sent him stumbling backward into his rocking chair, then falling onto the floor with a forward rock. But he lay unhurt and strangely happy and—perhaps better—memory-less of that temporary separation from his soul.

"Mary! Mary!" cried Harriet. *"Hele mai! Hele mai! Wiki-wiki!"*

Mary hurried out, her hand over her chest, and when she saw Gabriel motionless on the floor, she collapsed next to him.

Gabriel sat up, shook his head, and noticed a motionless Mary next to him. "Mary . . . what—what you doing, sleeping here? What—what I doing . . . here?"

"Gabe!! Mary!!"

Gabriel nudged an unresponding Mary.

"Quick, Gabriel! Go inside—call the ambulance!" ordered Harriet.

Now aware that something was wrong but still in a daze, Gabriel could only babble numbly.

Harriet dashed into the house and called the emergency number. An operator answered and told her that an ambulance had already been dispatched to the said address and that it should be about a minute before it should reach there.

The paramedics arrived two minutes later. They frantically applied CPR on Mary, then transported her in the flashing, silent ambulance to the nearest hospital, her face a darkening shade of impending mortality.

Twenty-Eight

As Gabriel wiped his eyes that were barren of tears after several hours of continuous weeping, and with Harriet comforting him in the hospital waiting room, Mary Wahine-okaimalino lay in a semi-coma in the intensive care unit at St. Anselm's Hospital. Intermittently, throughout the night, the nurse-in-charge would hear Mary say odd but distinct words, like "leaves," "stars," or "newspaper." She'd write down the words, hoping that the information would be helpful for the doctors in their morning prognosis, though it already was a given, as alluded to by the reports of the doctor and nurses of the previous shift, that Mary was uttering her last words. Her pulse was weakening by the hour, despite an odd fluttering now and then, and her bodily fluids were getting more toxic: Both liver and kidneys were failing.

But if Mary were allowed to have her underlying consciousness speak, she might say, in other words, that the scientific measurements of her physical well-being—or, rather, ill-being—were but nonsensical representations of a hypothetical, completely gross condition of her bill of health. First, she'd remark that her body was getting some needed rest, especially those organs that the doctors contended were failing. After all, being in tiptop shape and performing well after all of those many years gave the organs a good excuse to slack off a bit (though not entirely, since that would mean "good-bye" to Gabriel, family, and friends) and take a well-deserved rest. Lying on that hard clean bed that smelled faintly of disinfectant, Mary was also experiencing a wonderful euphoria even with her body strapped down with nylon belts and impaled with needles and tubes.

————————

STARS SPARKLING SPRINKLING through branches moving kamani tree heart soothing warm hands warm touch neck then breasts rustle leaves kamakani cool warm gentle gentle sway limu warm clean ocean flow through living coral breath of life giving water sway water warm night stars warm itchy feeling spread from tippy toes to toppy head skin touch cool wind cool warm kamakani warm night touch more touching more soft back forth back forth back forth tides flow out in out in out whiskers neck on breasts kamani singing now listen 'auhea wale 'oe singing our song oh my love 'auhea wale 'oe yes love I wait forever for this love when ocean spreads far unreachable sky of stars and darkness and the waters lap one on another and surge out in out in where fish dance with limu and limu dance their love and stars blend with leaves and leaves make magic shadows of wind my love oh love 'auhea wale 'oe oh love

————————

"GA-A-A-A-A-A-A-A-A-A-A-A-A-A-BE!!"

Mary jolted from her bed, but the restraining nylon strap snapped her back. The force from the rebound was enough to liberate her from the IV of saline solution as well as the connection to the dialysis machine, both the bottle stand and the machine trundling across the room and smashing into the wall. The electrical power of the entire hospital browned out for one-and-a-half seconds.

Mary's scream shook Gabriel from the middle of a dream (one of the many he had during the day), in which he and Mary were small children playing on a swing set in a deserted school yard. Mary had gone off to drink some water (that's what she told Gabriel she was going to do), and Gabriel waited for her return while swinging higher and higher. He was climbing to the zenith of a swing when he heard her cries of help. Reacting immediately, he let go of the swing and fell in an arc to the ground.

Falling out of his dream, so to speak, a snoring Gabriel slipped down from his seat in the waiting room and landed smack on his ʻōkole. Lucky thing for him that the floor was carpeted or else it would have really hurt. Harriet snapped out of her nap and found Gabriel flat on his back.

"Gabriel?! What's the matter?" she asked, helping him to his feet. "Are you all right?"

Gabriel's eyes were full moons. "Mary—she calling me—my kuʻuipo—she need me right now!"

"Gabe, you were dreaming," Harriet sighed. "She's going to be all right. Don't worry, cousin. I'll be here with you, however long it takes."

"No! She like me right now! I heard her! I can feel she like me right now! I know!"

He was off hobbling toward the double doors of the intensive care unit.

"Gabe, what are you doing? Where're you going? Gabe—you cannot go inside there."

"Who said?!" He glared at Harriet over his shoulders, quickening his pace.

Harriet hurried after him. "The doctors won't allow that, Gabe."

Gabriel turned suddenly, stopping Harriet. "Piss on dem pricks!" he sputtered, then proceeded on. He pushed through the doors, held them open, and looked back at a stone-still Harriet. In a voice so incongruous for the moment, in a monotone as calm as ripples of waves lapping on shore before a storm, he said, "She all right. She calling me. I know. No need tell me somet'ing somebody wen tell you I already know already." Then he entered the restricted area.

He slipped quietly into Mary's room. The nurse was already trying to calm Mary as well as contain her own amazement at the sudden well-being of a supposedly terminal patient. To her shock and dismay, the nurse discovered that

Mary had pulled out the tubes that had been inserted into her nostrils and veins.

"Mrs. Hoʻokano, please lie back," the nurse cautioned. "I must connect you up again."

"I no wanna get connected up," Mary argued. "And dis belt! What dis belt foʻ?"

Gabriel entered the room. "My kuʻuipo!" Gabriel gushed. "I knew was you calling! Oh, my kuʻuipo."

Mary smiled, then ordered him to take off the nylon strap. "Every time you get one belt around me. Get dis doggone belt outta my way, Gabe—RIGHT NOW!"

Gabriel was in shock. Never had his sweetheart spoke to him in such an abusively commanding tone. It was embarrassing for him, especially with another woman watching, listening. Giving the nurse a sheepish grin, he commented to her how Mary must be feeling well.

"Mary! How excellent you look!" With a glorious smile, Harriet wiggled past Gabriel.

"Oh, Harriet," Mary beamed, "so nice to see you."

Why she saying dat to her and not me?! Gabriel thought jealously.

Gabriel turned away from the two embracing women, feeling sorry for himself, and started walking out of the room. But before he could shuffle himself entirely out of the door, he heard Mary beckoning him, this time in a voice that he was better accustomed to, in a tone that had the power to melt him to his toes: "Gabe, sweetheart, please come here and plant one kiss on me."

Gabriel thought that he wasn't hearing right. But when he turned and saw a glowing-faced Mary—the Mary that he missed ever so much—he was relieved, thinking that his fear of Mary changing for the worse was just a passing nightmare. He hurried back to her side and bent low over her—never mind the ache he had in his lower back—and smacked her with a kiss so large, he thought, that she'd never forget it for the rest of her life.

"Now, Mrs. Hoʻokano," the nurse said, resuming her position next to the bed, "please don't move so I can reconnect you to the IV and the dialysis machine."

"No, I no want to be connected to nothing and to nobody. Gabe, tell her no bug me. I'm going home." She tried to sit up, but the belt still was restraining her. "Gabe, I tol' you take dis belt off."

Gabriel nodded his head and took the end of the strap when the nurse stopped him.

"Mr. Hoʻokano, please don't do this. Your wife needs to be hospitalized. She needs the care of a doctor."

Gabriel looked to Mary for further instructions.

"Gabe, you going listen to her or to me?"

"Nurse," Harriet interjected, "I think Mrs. Hoʻokano is feeling a lot better now. She was in a terrible shock, but she has miraculously come out of it very well. Don't you think so? Don't you believe in miracles? I think she's capable of returning home now."

"Yes, she looks very well, and that's good. But the doctor's orders say that she must remain in intensive care for further observation."

"She look all right to me," Gabriel remarked.

"I think it's all right for her to return," said Harriet with a persuasive smile.

"I no belong in here," Mary said. "Dis place only for sick people. I well, I not sick. Gabe, get me out of dis bed."

"Look," the nurse said firmly, looking at Harriet and Gabriel. "If you continue with this, I will have to call security to escort both of you out of the hospital. Can you please leave this room?"

"Gabe, take that belt off. Mary feels good, and I can see this with my very eyes. I can *feel* that her health has come back. Let's take her home."

"Can you please leave before I am forced to call security?"

"No," said Harriet.

Gabriel nodded at her. He thought about that incident with his brother and the university professor. *Jus' because he went haole school and get one big haole degree they think they can push us Hawaiians around! Da hell wit' dat!*

"That's my last warning," the nurse said. She hurried out of the room.

"She only gave us *one* warning," Harriet said calmly to Gabriel. "But if that's her last warning, then be it her last warning."

———

How the trio got out of the labyrinth of corridors and doors and floors without being detected by anyone was truly a mystery. What was more amazing was that they managed to leave in less than the minute that it took the nurse to scurry to the nurses' station (a mere twenty-five feet away) to call hospital security and return to the room. She covered her gasps when she realized that Mary and her two conspirators had vanished, as the cliché goes, into thin air. The window was opened, and a gentle steady breeze had entered the room. Later, in front of her superiors, the nurse could not explain how three senior citizens were able to open a locked window and survive a fall of four floors. It was also an impossibility for the three to have left the room and hobble down the corridor to their escape; with the exception of the moments it took her to touch-tone hospital security's four-digit extension number, her eyes had never left the doorway of the room.

Twenty-Nine

IN A WARD one floor above Mary's room, about the time when she was arguing with the nurse who was desperately trying to get her reconnected to the hospital lifelines, Joyce Hayashida lay in critical condition, having fallen in and out of a coma for the past three weeks. Though this was her first stroke, it was a severe one, and at home she had escaped death by minutes. Nearby in a waiting room, George had established quarters, a scraggly beard like a rampant growth of black and white mold now covering his face. Though urged by his son and daughter to go home, he refused to relinquish his kuleana on a particular couch.

He had gone through the ups-and-downs since Joyce's stroke. First, he reckoned that Joyce's misfortune "was just one of those things." Then, he wept miserably for the longest time when he realized how lost his life was without Joyce as his sounding board or homemaker. A day later he made a brazen resolution, expounding that his life must go on, with or without Joyce, but a few minutes after that declaration, panic set off a wild trembling in his gut, a lightheadedness and an iciness in his feet when he regarded the front door of the hospital as the portal to a world that he had never experienced before without Joyce. So he finally decided that the best situation for himself was to stay as close to Joyce as possible, though he could not bring himself to stay in the same room with her; he knew he'd be embarrassed if she suddenly woke up and saw him in the condition he was.

After his son left for the night, shaking his head in frustration at his father's obstinate ways, George sat squarely on the couch, his eyes devoid of emotion. He was not alone in the waiting room; on the other couch across the room stretched out a softly snoring, elderly Portuguese man. He, too, was waiting on the fate of his wife, who was being observed for a heart ailment. The magazines on the table next to the snoring man were neatly stacked. George had tried to sleep but couldn't; the snoring and an occasional bout of teeth-grinding by his partner-in-wait were too annoying. So he decided to take a stroll down the corridors of the hospital.

The hall lights were dimmed, visiting hours having ended two hours earlier. He passed the nurses' stand, and the nurse-on-duty lifted her eyes from a chart, smiled coolly, then returned to her work. George ambled the length of the ward; took the stairs down to the third floor (although he didn't enter the intensive care unit—where Mary Wahineokaimalino and friends were in the final stages of disappearing— since there was a big red sign painted on the doors that read, "RESTRICTED: AUTHORIZED PERSONNEL ONLY"); followed the path of blue dots on the corridor's floor to the elevator; passed the elevator and continued on to another set of stairs; entered it and came out on the second floor; sipped the frigid, metallic-tasting water from a shiny cooler; found himself at a nursery and watched the newborn babies sleep behind large glass walls, the infants' faces swollen and red and decidedly content; left the nursery when a nurse politely but firmly asked him to leave . . . and on and on.

His meandering took him to the first floor of the hospital, where he found next to an emergency fire exit the hospital's isolated chapel. The door was open, and George stopped at the entrance and looked in. It was a small, dimly lit room containing three small pews, each able to sit three thin people. A warm, musty odor of oiled wood exuded from the interior. Anxiety stirred him, a feeling not unlike what he had experienced when, running out of gas late one night on the dark Pali, he began recalling stories about Hawaiian spirits haunting the area. But there was also something pleasant and alluring about the chapel, and this paradox attracted him in. He took a few steps inside, his eyes focusing on the thin metallic cross that glowed in a dull, golden haze. Dark red curtains were draped behind it.

George was a Christian, or so he claimed whenever filling out forms that required him to declare his religious inclination. Actually, he was born a Buddhist. Coming home one night stoned drunk after returning from serving his country in the Korean War, he had a big fight with his father, who hated everything American, the argument erupting from a disagreement with—of all things—religion. His father had falsely accused him of becoming a Christian because he had failed to pay his respects to the local Buddhist temple immediately after his return from the war. The squabble was so blown out of proportion—his father was also drunk, having just finished his weekly bottle of sake—that George, right there and then, gave justification for his father's accusation by declaring, "Yeah, Papa, I one Christian! And I damn proud of it!" George had gotten fed up of being constantly accused of being this or that, especially when his father was drunk, and though the other times he had silently swallowed the imprecations like, "You pilau son of mine—born undah da dark sun! You going have children with two heads and four toes!" and false generalizations like, "Every time I turn my back you taking something from me!", this time he wasn't going to take any crap, for now in addition to being older and wiser, he was also stronger, more Americanized, and drunker than his father. He shouted at his father, "Yeah! I one Christian! And to prove it I going show you my cross I left in dah car!" (It was a lie; he had no cross.) He ran out of the house threatening to bring the crucifix in, though, of course, he never could go back in as he had no cross. Instead, he drove off in his recently purchased, secondhand Plymouth and spent the night on a couch at a friend's house. But it was a good excuse for him to leave the house, for if there was one thing that he still could not deal with—even with two years on the war's frontlines—it was his father's mean "samurai" glare.

And though he was past the age of getting a strapping from his father's belt, he still shuddered at the thought of it.

George left the chapel. He scanned the empty corridor that he had come down, then looked the other way, at the emergency fire exit. Through the narrow, vertical window in the door, George saw a light shining brightly outside. He looked back into the chapel, at the cross, then, with a grievous sigh, entered it again, this time sitting in the back pew. He bowed his head. He sighed again. Settling clenched fists on his lap, he raised his eyes to the cross and took in a deep breath of the scented air.

Then he snorted.

A cynical contortion came to his face. He squared his shoulders. And in a voice loud enough to chase away the venerable smell of the room, he said, "Bullshit."

He took the elevator back to the fifth-floor waiting room and sat quietly for a few minutes. The Portuguese man was changeless in his position and volume. Then George, too, lay down to rest. He remembered the last time when Joyce had made her intoxicating oxtail soup with peanuts (his stomach growled). A few minutes later, his mind between the real and unreal, he was being served (by Joyce, of course) a large steaming bowl of the soup that was filled with globs of fatty meat fallen from the bone.

Thirty

O N PAGE 5 of the daily morning newspaper was a small article in the "Police Beat" column, reporting a break-out from the Central Oʻahu Correctional Facility.

COCF Prisoner Escapes

Prison authorities are puzzling over the unusual circum-stances surrounding the escape by an inmate from the Central Oʻahu Correctional Facility last night.

According to prison warden Delbert Dias, Kalani Humphrey, 38, was last seen in his locked cell at an early evening head count, but was reported missing at 10:21 P.M. by prison guards.

Dried blood was found on the wall by the cell's barred window, though prison authorities have dis-missed the possibility of its connection to the escape.

Humphrey, of Hoʻomakani Road, Kānewai, was serving a ten-year sentence for a series of burglaries in Kānewai and the armed robbery of a savings and loan in Honolulu.

He is reportedly to be potentially armed and dan-gerous. He is a Hawaiian-Caucasian male, six feet one inches tall and weighing 195 pounds. He has short brown hair and was last seen wearing faded blue jeans and a blue prison work shirt. He has a self-made tat-too—the word "mom" with an "X" over it—on his left upper arm.

In an apparent sighting of the escapee, prison offi-cials released a report that a young boy, who was waiting at a bus stop near the prison, said he was approached by a shirtless man bearing Humphrey's description. The man left without further incident and was last seen running in a mauka, Diamond Head–direction.

If anyone has any information regarding the above mentioned escapee, please call the Honolulu Police Department's Confidential Hot-Line at XXX-XXXX.

"E BOY, WHAT time you get?"

"Hah?"

"Da time."

"I dunno. I no mo' watch."

"Da last wind wen come already?"

"Da bus?"

"No. Da wind. Wen come already?"

"Hah?"

———

THE PAGE 5 blurb began to stir the Kānewai air approximately one hour and forty-seven minutes after the first newspaper was off the press. Richard Pimente, who was also the Kānewai district manager of the morning paper, picked up his supply at the delivery truck's drop-off point, distributed the bundles to his delivery people, then drove to Breezy's Drive-in for his usual breakfast. He gave his order to the counterperson, Matilda Nunes; filled the newspaper stand with fifty copies of the morning paper; then waited for his breakfast while scanning the front page. Paying for his food, he went to the covered eating area at the side of the building and seated himself at his customary seat in the back row. He spread the newspaper on the table and began eating. (Twenty-six years ago, when he first got the job as district manager, he savored the honor that he was the first person in all of Kānewai to read the morning newspaper, a selfish enjoyment that had gradually lost its pleasurable effect over the years. Now, reading the paper in the morning had become just part of his daily routine.) Eventually he came to the "Police Beat" section.

His mouth stopped moving halfway into the second slice of mildly spiced Portuguese sausage. He continued his chewing, but took an extra long sip of coffee. He read the short article again. Then again. Then he rose shakily from his seat —the food ingested so far now disturbing rather than soothing his gut—and lumbered to the pay phone. Dropping a quarter into the slot, he dialed a long-distance number but cancelled the call after the first ring. A few moments later, the edge of the shock having subsided a bit, he reinserted the coin and dialed the number again, followed the instructions of the operator to drop in more coins, then listened while the other end rang four times before hearing an answer.

"This is Richard . . . Richard . . . Yeah, me . . . Look, I gotta tell you something. He's out . . . Kalani . . . Hello? You still there? . . . Yeah—yeah—yeah. Kalani jus' escaped from prison. Was in da morning pepah. I jus' wen read about it right now . . . Hey, you heard what I said? . . . All right, den . . . So what *I* going do?! Com'on now. I jus' calling you let you know what's what. That's all. But maybe you should come back . . . Yeah-yeah. Come back. You heard me right da first time . . . No—no—no. Nobody knows. Not yet . . . What I mean by that is—. . . Look, if you no like come back now, I think we going get mo' trouble den what we asking fo'. You know what I mean? . . . Yes—yes—yes. I really mean that. That's da feeling I get right now . . . Of course, I am. Why you think I calling you fo', so I can get my jollies getting you all worried? . . . Bullshit! Com'on! Geev me one break! [whispering] You think after all these years all these feeling I have fo' you is all gone? You know where I stand wit' you. Com' on. Jus' da fact I calling you means something . . . [long break] . . . Look, all these things, is like water under—["Please deposit $1.35 for the next three minutes. Thank you."] [click click click click click click]—What I was saying now? . . . Oh yeah. Like I was saying all this stuff is like a lot of water under da bridge already. Right? . . . Okay. So we gotta start from scratch, if you know what I mean. Kalani is out right now. We gotta talk to him. Is his right to know what he suppose to know . . . I know what he knows already, but he don't know the entire picture. Right? . . . I know what you doing. I seen da stuff . . . Yeah, I seen da stuff. I don't like what I see. In fact, it really tears my heart. But my feelings fo' you is still da same . . . Yes, even after all these years wen pass . . . Yes . . . Yes . . . No . . . Yes . . . All right then. Geev me a call. You know where I stay, what time to call . . . Okay, but geev me one call. Soon. We have to do it . . . Yes—yes . . . All right. Bye."

Before Richard would turn his head to see if anyone had been listening, Matilda Nunes retreated from her silent puttering about at the counter window that was closest to the pay phone. She hid from Richard's sight behind the shelves of paper goods and dried and canned food. Feverishly, she fished out a tiny crucifix from inside her blouse, holding it in the palm of her hand and rubbing the shiny warm metal. Whispering the late Father's name, she closed her eyes and prayed silently. When she finished, she wiped away her tears and returned to the main window.

———

Matilda did not hear anything that was said in that conversation between Richard Pimente and Clarissa Ching. She didn't have to. She knew exactly whom Richard Pimente was talking to and what was being said. She also knew that Kalani had escaped from prison. She didn't know it as a fact à la media—she obviously could not have gotten the information from the papers—but several days ago she had a dream that gave her a frightening look into the future. The dream was about a time when she was younger, watching her small son Jason play on a sandy beach.

A huge wave had suddenly roared on the shore, sweeping Jason out to sea. She could do nothing but cry for help because she did not know how to swim. Out of nowhere came Kalani Humphrey, diving into the surf and grabbing the boy and pushing him to the shallows. Matilda pulled Jason out of the water and dragged him to higher land. Then she searched for Kalani and found him fighting the powerful currents that were pulling him farther out. A large wave broke over him, and he disappeared from sight.

Waking in mid-afternoon with her hair damp from the humidity and trauma of the dream, she went to the bathroom and washed her face. She gazed at herself in the mirror and remembered the submissive smile on Kalani's face before the wave had broken over him and pulled him under for good.

She never knew Kalani; that is, she never talked to him or was formally acquainted with him, though she knew who he was and the identities of his natural father and mother. She also knew him as a classmate from high school (and elementary and intermediate school). She knew that David Fonseca and he were good friends, especially since they both played on Wilson's football team, but even when she was clandestinely carrying David's baby, she still did not meet him formally. She also knew him from his frequent visits in the early morning hours before school to the Kānewai Bakery (where Matilda held a job until a couple years back when she quit, after working there since her senior year of high school, a year after Jason was born, since she didn't have to struggle to make ends meet anymore with Jason out in the workforce and helping her financially). She learned that Kalani had a sweet tooth for long johns and especially for Kānewai Bakery's own original, glazed sweet potato rolls (the sweet potatoes from the famous soil of nearby Waiola Valley). All the times Kalani went into the bakery he never said a word to Matilda, indicating to her what he wanted by pointing with an index finger into the glass display, not even once looking at her directly in the eyes. Soon, Matilda could tell by the day and the weather what exactly he'd choose, though it was rather simple guesswork since Kalani liked only one other thing besides the items mentioned above; after a while, it became unnecessary for Kalani to indicate what he wanted. And he always had the exact change, placing it on top of the display case and waiting patiently for Matilda to choose his pastry of the day. Even with the price of everything in the store rising almost every other month—or every other week—she'd still charge him the same price that he was accustomed to paying. After taking the pastry wrapped in waxed paper, he'd walk out of the store and attack it as if he were having a sugar withdrawal; she sometimes wondered if he had ever accidentally eaten the waxed paper. Once in a while, when she'd feel sorry for him (stories of his childhood abuse by Mr. and Mrs. Humphrey were widely known), she'd give him two for the price of one.

When Kalani was in prison, Matilda often thought of taking to him a box of his favorite pastries. She felt a sincere sadness for him since she truly believed that whatever notoriety was bestowed on him was really not of his own doing. She was one of three people in Kānewai who would be considered to have sympathy toward him, the other two being David Fonseca and Clarissa Ching. At times she felt badly that this genuine son of Kānewai was ostracized by his own community.

But it was not for her to stand up for Kalani, at least not in public. For she herself was banned from taking any active part in the goings-on of Kānewai, she being the mother of an illegitimate child. It did not help that her father was the town drunk who was found dead one morning on his wife's grave. She had an older brother whom she or anyone else in Kānewai really didn't know, he being a quiet, reserved kid who had received nothing but Cs and Ds at Wilson High, barely graduating, but who had become a fierce combat soldier in the Vietnam conflict and was now a decorated Master Sergeant based somewhere in South Korea.

When she finally did get around later that afternoon to reading the newspaper, Richard Pimente's newspaper that he habitually left on the eating benches after finishing his breakfast, the news of Kalani's breakout was then, for her, really old news.

———

AT A LITTLE past two that afternoon, while napping and dreaming about playing with her future grandchildren in Harriet O'Casey's pasture, Matilda was rudely awakened by three knocks on the bedroom wall next to her head. The memory of her dream was immediately erased. She bolted up, gasping for the air of reality, finally realizing the familiar smells and shapes of her own bedroom that was semi-darkened by drawn curtains lifting and falling with a gentle breeze. She heard another series of knocks.

"Jason?" she called, thinking that her son had forgotten his house key again.

"Matilda." A deep, whispered voice.

"Who's that?"

"It's me. Kalani. Please let me in."

Thirty-One

HE ASKED FOR a cup of coffee, which Matilda willingly, though anxiously, prepared for him. She offered him something to eat, wishing that she had his favorite pastry. He shook his head after deliberating for fifteen or so seconds, during which time Matilda became drunk with suspense. She set the cup of black coffee on the table and sat across from him. He stared at the steaming cup with eyes brooding in relief and suspicion. Since entering the cottage, he had kept his eyes under her gaze, never once looking her straight in the eye, just as he had always done at the bakery. Matilda noted how drawn his face was, how lean it had become since she last saw him munching on a sweet potato roll, at least twenty years ago.

He sipped his coffee, then set the cup halfway across the table between them. "I heard David died," he said.

Matilda nodded.

"How you took him dying?"

Matilda rolled her shoulders languidly. A solemn look was on her face, though not intended for her former lover. "A lot of people went to his funeral," she said. "They liked him in Kānewai."

"You, too? You liked him?"

Matilda lowered her eyes to the steam rising from the coffee. "Yeah . . . he was okay. I liked him. Everybody liked him."

"But did you *like* him?"

She couldn't answer him. She didn't know the answer. She had seen so many changes in David Fonseca. As a young boy. As a strapping young man. As a long-haired student talking like a haole after coming back from a mainland college. Then, the most abrupt change, his entrance into the priesthood. Whatever David Fonseca did, bizarre as it was, was not a surprise, however, for Matilda. His death was not a surprise. His death could only be a redemption after a life of changes.

"Yes," she said finally. "I really liked him."

"You lie, Matilda. But I know he really liked you."

Matilda was at once fired by his accusation and pleased at the latter comment. Her eyes bore into his *(he's got the nerve to come to my house and tell me these things)*, but he still wasn't looking at her; his eyes were now directed to something under the table. She glanced beneath *(what is he looking at? I don't see anything)*, looked up and now noticed that he was wearing a prison workshirt. A chill entered her, for here in front of her was Kalani Humphrey, Kānewai's best con artist and an escaped convict to boot *(should I call the police?)*. Nervously she looked toward the living room and the telephone *(how can I phone the police without Kalani knowing?)*.

But there was something sobering in his eyes that lowered her guard.

"I need some help," he said.

"What kind of help?"

"Kamakani began talking to me in prison. Kamakani been talking to me in my cell. Kamakani been telling me about things no one else knows. Kamakani told me what to do."

"Who . . . who's Kamakani?"

"My friend," he said. Then he looked her in the eye.

Frightened by the boldness of his swollen red eyes, she nodded her head.

"I going fix this town, but I need your help."

Her soul was collapsing into itself, then expanding quickly. Her eyes were thin membranes ready to burst from the pressure within. She rambled something to him, not knowing what she was saying. And funny how she now had the sudden urge to look at herself in a mirror, the need to see her physical self to prove that she was not in a dream or nightmare. A terrifying sensation came over her that she might be floating away.

The kitchen clock became her savior, her anchor. Two thirty-seven, it said. Her mind gripped on the time; then she searched for the day's date. And when she remembered the day—the date and time now securing her to her chair—she heard his request. She nodded *(what was it for?)* . . . and now he's getting up from the chair and going out the kitchen and into the living room, laying on the couch, closing his eyes . . . and now she sees his mouth opening slightly and a buzz escaping, his eyes twitching, then his feet twitching . . . and soon she's covering him with a thin blue blanket because she thinks he's cold, his arms folded across his chest and his face pale like the bluish gray color of a gravid sky before a storm.

Thirty-Two

HARRIET O'CASEY COMMENTED how everything was so nice now that Mary was home. Mary nodded her head, smiling pleasantly, knowing exactly what Harriet was referring to. Since coming home from the hospital, Gabriel had gone out of his way to do everything in the house—everything—the housekeeping, the cooking, the marketing, the laundry.

They were sitting on the front porch, waiting patiently for Gabriel to return from the market. Mary straightened up. She sniffed the air, then looked over at the vacant lot, the bare area where the abandoned car once was, now overgrown with buffalo grass and melding indistinguishable with the rest of the wild growth. She got up slowly, went to the edge of the porch, and leaned lightly against the simple balustrade that was still a bit tacky from a painting the other day by an industrious Gabriel.

"The wind stay strange," she said to Harriet.

"What is it, my dear?"

"The wind. Try smell the wind. Funny kine smell. But one good smell. I never smell dis kine smell fo' one long time. I no remember when the last time I smelled dis kine, salt-kine smell."

―――――――

IT WAS A long hike, a hike that Gabriel had not taken for a long time, the last time being when he had delivered that invitation about their niece's wedding. He rested several times on the side of the steep trail, catching his breath and slapping the mosquitoes that had probably not tasted human blood for a while. "They probably think we the same person," said Gabriel on one occasion, smirking, thinking about Jacob and smearing his blood and the crushed mosquito on his arm. He noticed broken branches and dead grass along the trail. Though he had died several years ago, Jacob still had many visitors coming up to see him. "Damn university professors," Gabriel cursed. Finally, puffing and wheezing, he reached the top of the climb.

He rested just to the side of Jacob's old hanging house, studying the fine turnings of the rope that held the box house ten feet above the ground and noting the general tidiness of the area. But in one corner of the clearing Gabriel discovered a shiny gum wrapper. "Damn outsiders!" he cried. Yet for the most part, the area was nicely kept. *Funny,* he thought, *how everything so well-kept like my brother was still taking care of the place.* But he shook his head, for the near immaculate condition of the place shouldn't have been a real surprise to him, and he spouted with satisfaction, "Da Akua wit' you, my brother, and I hope He mālama you good!" Then he sighed as grievously as he could, with his body slouched in a position that, if Jacob just happened to be around reading him, would suggest his unfathomable gloom.

Gabriel was silent for about a half an hour, intermittently interrupting his moping with exaggerated sighing, when a cluster of noisy birds (sparrows? cardinals? mejiros?) in the tree above caught his attention (they had been there all along). He turned to the box house, regarded it for a long moment, then cleared his throat and said, "Jacob, my brother, I need your help. You know, I no have too much long in dis world." Gabriel continued, telling his brother about the dream he had three nights before, the night before Mary was to come home from the hospital.

He had wakened with the dream's culmination, his eyes absorbing the darkness of the cold early morning. Though the newspaper had been delivered for three minutes already, the ghostly echoes of John Kim's car trundling down the road were still lingering outside, the sounds splintering as they slowly reverberated down the road in the morning's dead air. It was a startled awakening for Gabriel, for it was the first time in a very long time that he woke up remembering what he had dreamed. Like time-lapse photography, his dream was about anthuriums growing out the windows of the abandoned Ford Mustang. The flowers were colored in a spectrum of pastels. And with his eyes wide and unblinking and his ears drawing the fracturing, thinning rumblings of John Kim's car, the dream began to unfold itself again before him like a movie. He shuddered, drew his thin blanket to his chin, but otherwise remained quiet and motionless.

He understood that the dream was about his death.

At first he was terrified, but with the end of the dream, he turned to his side, looked out the open window, his eyes moistening, and, as calmly as he could, rattled off, "So whas new 'bout dis?"

Still he needed comforting, someone to help him understand the unknown to come. He could not talk to Mary even if she was home—the subject of dying was a forbidden topic with her. There was no other person to turn to but his brother, and Gabriel knew that Jacob was obviously experienced in the matter. His brother would listen and respond, Gabriel thought, even though they had ceased to be brotherly in the last decade or so; in death, all human beings became brothers and sisters, and even his obstinate brother Jacob, Gabriel knew, would have to defer to that principle set forth by the Great Akua.

Under Jacob's hanging house, Gabriel told his brother of the dream, how the anthuriums had bloomed and how they had grown enormous and grotesque like elephant ears, and they began to droop, then pale and wither, and metamorphose to ash, then flake apart and fall into an untidy heap. The heap began to smoke, then redden with heat, then burn into the ground. The land quivered, then tremored. The ground surrounding the smoking hole collapsed, and the hole widened, taking in trees and plants and the abandoned car.

Gabriel had woken up before the dream itself was sucked into the subterranean void.

"And so you see," Gabriel said to his brother, "I know my time is coming. And I like you help me get ready fo' what gotta be done, what I gotta do befo'—" He stopped himself. Though he was comfortable with the fact of his future demise, he was still a bit superstitious about stating it aloud.

Gabriel waited for a response, anything that he could interpret as a sign. He looked at the branches of the kukui tree, waiting for a bird to fly down and talk story with him. He squinted his eyes at the several large moss rocks nearby to see if they would come alive and fill him with a "funny kine feeling inside." He scrutinized Jacob's old house for any movement, but the movement never happened. He rubbed his hands for warmth, rolled his shoulders, and readied himself to sense a strange, perhaps a crawling feeling up his back. But nothing happened.

Nothing happened.

For that entire hour of anxiety.

"I thought you was my brother!" Gabriel finally raged. He was exasperated and stared hard at the hanging house, the bush, finally the dilapidated, abandoned chicken coops. He pounded the ground like a spoiled child. "And to think I thought you would kōkua yo' own flesh and blood!"

Gabriel got up slowly, his joints creaking, and stretched himself real fine, ending his upward reach with a loud and disgusted yawn. He took a step down the trail without a good-bye when laughter broke out. He turned and saw the house shaking as if the box itself was laughing. A smile came to Gabriel's face, but after a minute of continuous laughter, Gabriel began to suspect something was wrong.

"What you laughing at anyway?" he demanded. "I never come here be one laughing stock."

The laughter continued and grew louder, so loud that Gabriel had to cover his ears. The laughter entered through the chinks between his thick-knuckled fingers, and his ears began to ache.

"You—! Stop laughing!"

But the formidable outburst went on.

He gotta take at least one breath of air, thought an upset Gabriel.

As quickly as he could, Gabriel ambled down the trail, leaving the rollicking madness behind. At the bottom, where the trail joined the broken asphalt road, Gabriel paused, his breathing hard and rhythmic, and turned in the direction of Jacob's house. The laughter was hardly audible now; it could have been mistaken for a rustling of leaves.

Gabriel shook his head and sighed. "If das yo' way of telling me I not invited, das one hell of a way to do it." He shook his head again. "But you know something, my brother," he added with a sardonic smile, "no matter how hard you try, you nevah going get me in da place you staying at right now. And das dat!"

With that, he turned, vowing never to return.

After returning to his car and settling in the driver's seat, he surprisingly remembered the task he was supposed to have done instead of visiting Jacob: Mary had instructed him to go to the market and pick up three small, fresh red fish ("aweo-weo," she had suggested, "or get me one big kūmū") for dinner. With a relaxed chortle, and delighted that he had remembered what he should have remembered, he started the car, gassed the engine for a couple of short blasts, then drove over the potholes while whistling the tune to one of his favorite songs, "Blue Moon."

Thirty-Three

T HE FLIGHT FROM LAX to HNL was delayed. There was a mechanical problem in a hydraulic pump of one of the wing flaps, grounding the plane for two hours. And two-and-a-half hours out of the airport the "Fasten Your Seat Belts" sign was prompted; on the intercom, the captain announced that unexpected air turbulence was forcing the flight crew to detour slightly from the original flight plan. At Honolulu International Airport, the arrival time of Flight 177 was changed six times.

Richard Pimente was waiting anxiously for Clarissa Ching's flight to come in. It had been scheduled to arrive at 2:54 P.M., but now with the hour hand on the 5 and the minute hand just past the 12, Richard was hoping that the plane would just arrive. He had exhausted his excuses to his wife why he would be late coming home. For a moment—just for a fleeting but quickly dispersing moment—he wished the plane would vanish. But that would mean a crash into the sweet Pacific or on the hot concrete runway, and it wasn't in Richard's heart to really wish something tragic to occur.

Waiting was not one of Richard Pimente's favorite pastimes. He spent a few minutes in one of the hard, plastic-molded seats in the waiting area, then went to the airport lounge and ordered a beer. He drank it quickly, ordered another, and sipped this one for twenty or so minutes, then left the lounge and relieved himself in the bathroom. Then he paced the length of the terminal six times, studying with frustration the information on departures and arrivals on whatever video screen he was passing. Finally, he found a quiet, solitary area along an open walkway at the end of the terminal. There he lit a cigarette, leaned forward on the railing, and watched an interminable number of takeoffs and landings, which strangely kept his attention and glued him to the spot. Wouldn't it be right-on, he thought, after viewing the ups and downs of dozens of planes, if life was simple like the coming and going of an airplane? He took an extra-long drag to emphasize the insight, then blew the smoke through his nostrils, à la Steve McQueen. A rugged, individualistic gesture always complemented common sense.

CLARISSA CHING NEVER liked traveling on airplanes. She had often heard the adage that being in an airplane was much safer than driving down an LA freeway, but she never wholeheartedly believed it as truth, especially when she was over 30,000 feet above the Pacific. It helped little that she was in first-class, though at least she was able to grip both armrests without interfering with the territoriality of the next passenger. She could not eat, for her stomach was like, at the moment, a churning cement mixer, ready at any time to spew out its contents. She was able to drink a couple of cans of 7-Up. At least the lime taste was pacifying her reactive stomach.

But there was something else on her mind besides her fear of flying, a crisis more desperate and immediate. Simply put, it was the apprehension of returning home to face the truth, something that had been pestering her since jumping in that taxi to leave Kānewai. It was a kind of specter that had increasingly haunted her since Richard Pimente's last long-distance telephone call. *Yes, it's about time I sit down and spell out the truth-of-the-matter,* she had reminded herself over and over again for the three days before her departure. At first she had doubts about returning, though she courageously called the airlines to reserve the next available, first-class seat to

Hawai'i. She knew that reserving the seat would force her to override her doubts and make her take the necessary action, which was to return home and bring the matter—though so painful—out to the public.

Now with the jetliner in its cruising level at exactly 33,749 feet above sea level, Clarissa started to have her doubts again. Could she go back to Kānewai and expose her true nature to the others? She was concerned especially with the fact of her complicity with the signs, in particular, those signs that had proclaimed the sexual perversions and inadequacies of certain individuals. (She, however, never fabricated the signs about her husband, Hiram. At first she thought the culprit might have been Dennis Umeda, though later she found out his complete innocence.) And would she be able to accept the responsibility—and the likely backlash—if she exposed herself as the party responsible for turning Kalani Humphrey, her biological son with Richard Pimente, into the terror of Kānewai? If she loved her only son so, why *did* she direct public opinion, this way and that way, against him?

She began to cry. Turning her face toward the bright window so as not to attract the attending stewardess, she took a wad of tissue paper from her handbag and dabbed her eyes dry. Then she plugged the earphones into a music channel and listened, trying to deafen her thoughts with Mantovani ("King of the Road"). Tilting back her seat, she closed her eyes and tried to sleep.

She was still clouded in her doubts when ("Somewhere My Love") the plane began its descent. Looking out into the late afternoon sunshine, Clarissa was able to see a part of an island (perhaps the Big Island? Maui?). It was another twenty-seven minutes before Diamond Head, Waikīkī beach and the hotels, and the dirty harbor waters of Honolulu came under the long shadow of the plane. The plane dipped to the right, making a wide turn to approach the reef runway. It dropped quickly, giving Clarissa that tumbling feeling in her stomach again. She gripped the armrests, her heart palpitating, lips trembling, and temples perspiring freely. And when a strong shudder shook the plane just before it touched down, Clarissa gasped, then blacked out, choking on the truth that was emptying from her stomach.

Thirty-Four

A T FIRST SHE was terribly afraid of his presence in the house. She even had considered the thought that he had become a ghost or vampire because during the day he lay motionless on the couch, sleeping without a sound, and at night he was gone until dawn. She remembered how frightening it was when, returning home one early evening, her usual night off, she was about to insert the house key into the lock when she heard and felt a tremendous stirring in the air. The air churned with a hurricane-like force, as if by the flapping of large wings, and then it became icily still and quiet. Running in, she called her son at the firehouse, but hung up after the first ring, afraid that she would be disturbing him needlessly. She shook terribly, then quickly took refuge in her bedroom, closing and locking the door, waiting up for Kalani's dreadful return. But she fell asleep. Wakening in the now sun-dashed room, she peeked out into the living room and was relieved to see that he had not come back. Later that afternoon, however, returning from the market, she found him curled on the couch, his back facing her, his usual position.

She never saw him leave the house, and only once did she see him awake. Perhaps her working the late-night shift at Breezy's, she rationalized, was the probable reason she missed seeing the active part of his life. Still, she felt that eerie feeling that he was not human, that prison had changed him into something terrible. He seemed not to need food since she kept tabs on the supply in the pantry and refrigerator. Perhaps he ate elsewhere? But he had no money, that she knew: How could he have money when he had just escaped from prison? But perhaps he was starting where he had left off, robbing the innocent people of Kānewai. Would that make her an accessory to his crimes?

And then there was that time when she got up late one morning to use the bathroom and found him looking into the mirror, making bizarre faces, and mumbling strange words that she had never heard before. *Latin. He was speaking Latin. That's what Cindy Cordeiro would have remarked if she was listening to him mumble those words in that trance-like manner. She also might have speculated that they were the exact words Father Fonseca had said immediately following the prayer for them* (she and Sandy Kim) *at the theater's wall, after stumbling back and falling on his 'ōkole, his eyes widening with an insurmountable fear as if he had seen a horrendous vision of the last day of the world, or perhaps the last day of Kānewai.* (And yes, he indeed had seen a vision of the last day of Kānewai, and in the vision Kānewai was engulfed in hellish flames, the entire town having fallen into a gargantuan crater of molten lava. Yes . . . and then he saw the blood oozing from the walls, the blood of Jesus Christ—Yes, Jesus Christ!) *But, of course, Cindy Cordeiro or Sandy Kim never knew what he saw—though how they used their imaginations to describe what they thought the Father had seen!—and their story multiplied into several variations, as in any honest attempt to reconstruct the truth, as it was told and retold and re-retold in those crosslinked conversations so characteristic of good old Kānewai!* But she also remembered the first afternoon when he came to her for sanctuary *from* the wind (that was what he said, those were his exact words, Matilda reminded herself) and how the next day he was mumbling to himself most of the time in that same strange way, then speaking to her in utterly soft, humble tones for three or four decipherable words, then back to mumbling to himself for a string of twenty or thirty of those strange words (he definitely was talking in that same strange language—was it a language? was it a language of pictures? did he learn it in prison?—yes, he was using those same words in front of the mirror, Matilda remembered) before saying something again to her in that monotone voice, devoid of any inflection or color, for another three or four or, at the most, five words.

She did not know where he went during the night, nor what time he came back to sleep, for when she came home in the morning he was never home; but when she woke in mid-afternoon, she'd find him in his customary curled, sleeping position. Once she was bold enough to venture close to him and study the slow and steady rise and fall of his rib cage. She peeked over his wide shoulders at his face, but when his arms twitched, she leaped away, telling herself that she'd never do that again. *Strange,* she thought, *how once both back and front doors were locked* (it wasn't done intentionally; she just forgot —oh, she was so tired from work—that he was coming back *does he sleep?* to sleep on the couch), *and yet he had managed to get into the house* (how did he get in? did he pry open the windows? *yeah, that's how he did it! everyone knows that he's an expert in breaking and entering!* flow in with the wind? float through the walls like a ghost? does he have a spare house key that I don't know about? and why is it that whenever he's here, most of the time sleeping, there's always that ocean smell, that limu smell? *does he go to the beach at nights? what does he do there?* and why are there so many geckos running all over the outside of the house when I leave for work? where do they all come from? why are they here?).

Thirty-Five

T HE GECKOS WERE all over Gabriel Ho'okano's house, but the situation didn't bother him for the simple reason that they had always been there. Generations and generations of geckos had populated the Ho'okano property, even before the house (which Gabriel had built himself) existed. Gabriel knew the genealogy of the geckos, or the mo'o as he would correctly call them, since he regarded their lineage and his to be one and the same. He would call a particular gecko Uncle or Auntie; and with the death of his wayward brother, the newest gecko to appear on Gabriel's nightly screen was given the name Kopa, Jacob's childhood nickname.

It was amazing that even with a failing memory Gabriel never forgot any of the names of the hundreds—perhaps thousands—of geckos that surrounded him. What was even more astonishing was his ability to communicate—rather, talk story—with the mo'o, with the exception of the new one, Kopa, who had never once kah-kah-kahed since his advent at the Ho'okano house (though he had taken a royal share of termites, flies, mosquitoes, and other resident arthropods).

Even if Kopa never talked to him, Gabriel made it a habit to talk with him anyway, for he knew Kopa was hiding in some nook of the porch and listening. In the early evenings, after finishing the supper that he now often cooked and while Mary and Harriet were washing the dishes and talking story (Harriet had taken the habit, as requested adamantly by Mary and not-so-enthusiastically by Gabriel, of having her meals at the Ho'okano residence; for the most part, she had moved in, taking quarters in the back bedroom of the house, which was ideal for her since the room gave her a near-panoramic view of her pasture [with the old, rickety, termite-ravished, one-car garage partly blocking her right-side view of her lot] and it was but a one-minute stroll to her beloved cows), Gabriel would talk stories to Kopa. He'd relate the day's events, and if he could not remember what had happened, then he would make them up. This was done with an understanding of his brother's situation: Kopa, frolicking in the spiritual world that made him know almost everything, would know how to interpret Gabriel's stories and turn them into truths.

Gabriel noticed how boisterous the geckos had become over the past few days (with the exception of Kopa, though Gabriel did note how his brother had become a bit edgy at times, skittering back and forth across the dusty screen faster than usual, as if anticipating a big storm), with the geckos on the mauka side of the house being contentious with the geckos of the front porch. They'd meet at the intersecting corner of the house, usually near the eves, and have it out. Most of the time Gabriel heard them argue about how many more termites the other side was getting, though once there was a savage fight that involved two geckos locked in each other's jaws. Gabriel, who couldn't stand the sight of a family fighting (there had just been too much of that in his immediate, human family), shooed them off with a bulldog look and a loud kah-kaht! But the next evening Gabriel heard more racket, this time coming from the makai Diamond Head corner of the house. And this continued for the next three days. Or was it four? Something was definitely bugging the moʻo, and Gabriel found no rest when the moʻo were in such a troubled state.

And then it rained hard for five days and nights, which gave some peace to the residents of the house. The heavy, wet air seemed to pacify the geckos and, correspondingly, Gabriel too. The rain had come in from the ocean, and at first the showers were intermittent. When there was a break in the rain, Gabriel would look toward Waiola Valley, which was lost in low-lying clouds. "Kopa, I know you behind all of dis," Gabriel would say deliberately and repeatedly throughout the day, but with a smile, since Gabriel knew that Jacob, even after years and years of indifference and down-right mistrust, really had a soft spot in his soul. Once, after gazing at the rainy clouds by Waiola and making his comment, Gabriel was sure that he heard a subdued kah-kahing somewhere above him.

But on the second day, the rains came down hard, and it got harder as the day progressed. By the third day, a small lake began forming in the front yard of the Hoʻokano house. Gabriel called John Kim, the newspaper district manager, to terminate temporarily the delivery of the morning daily. Now Gabriel would look up at the always cloudy sky and the rain and begin cursing his brother: "And den! You going float my house away or what?!"

STRANGE THINGS BEGAN to float in the growing lake. At first, Gabriel took no notice until Mary peeled off a scrap of newspaper that had washed up on the second porch step from the bottom.

"Look, Gabe, how old dis newspaper is."

Gabriel continued rocking in his chair, wrapped in that moldy mood of his that was getting moldier by the moment.

"August 19, 1956," Mary announced, as if the date had a special significance.

It didn't, but the uttered month and last digit echoed through those mossy arches in Gabriel's mind. Funny that with all his forgetfulness he was able to remember the exact date of his induction into the United States armed services: August 6, 1944.

"Mo' bettah I should have quit when I was ahead," he said.

"What was that?" inquired a half-listening Harriet, who was sitting across on the other end of the patio.

Turning to his cousin, Gabriel repeated his comment and added, "Das what history is all about, I think, about having to do things not yo' own way but den you da one gotta face da truth or consequences."

And strange how Gabriel's words triggered a recurrence of a bitter memory in Harriet, of the day when she received the telegram declaring her husband's death on the *U.S.S. Indianapolis,* one week after its sinking. Harriet didn't cry, but she had a sudden desire to visit her cows.

"I'm going," she said to no one and everyone.

"Where you going?" Mary asked with alarm, looking up from her self-appointed work of piecing together the soggy bits of the old newspaper. "How you going out of dis house wit' all of dis rain . . . and dat?" She pointed to the lake. Though it had lightened up, the rain was still drizzling miserably. "And where you going?"

"I . . . I have to go," was Harriet's answer. And then she rose from her seat and entered the house.

"Dis funny kine weather making everybody funny kine, everybody jumpy," Gabriel quipped. He sat pensively, his face as solemn as a doorknob of an old church. Nodding his head, he said, "Dat damn war . . . if it wasn't fo' it, I would be da one making all dis rain instead of suffering from it."

———————

THE BIT OF old-time newspaper that Mary discovered washed upon her shore was the first of many other vintage newspapers. Other newspapers appeared, all soggy and in pieces, yet not failing to denote the approximate date or style of a time gone-by. Even newspapers that were printed in Hawaiian were discovered. The residents of the Ho'okano house were alarmed by the ominous regularity of the news from the past turning up on their porch steps, despite the fact that they could not read them since the newspapers were broken in fragments or the ink was bled too weak to be readable. The Ho'okano household was also getting more and more isolated from everyone else since the lake was growing like an epidemic and was becoming more or less a lake of dislocation, cutting them off from the rest of Kānewai.

Come the fifth day and with the rains stopping, the residents of Kanakawai Lane began to resist the admonishing touches of despair; they became rejuvenated with the expectation that the lake would recede; and they rose in the morning with the hope that it would take but a short time before life would swing back to normal: driving casually down Kānewai's streets and shopping for specials at Leong's Market.

But the lake did not recede, and the objects they fished out of the lake were more old newspapers that were concocting in them a strange sense of time past and time lost. Their conversations were now tempered with nostalgia, at first reminiscing about happy times but moving invariably toward dark memories that Gabriel, Mary, and Harriet thought were vanquished by over-remembering. They also were running out of food, though the condition did not alarm them since, as they found with the days moving lugubriously on, they were requiring less and less of sustenance. (A pot of rice, for example, would last them four to five days.)

But when Kopa began making his first, undecipherable sounds (like anyone introduced to a strange, new kind of existence, part of this incipient experience is to learn the requisite language, if applicable; in Kopa's case, facility in the moʻo language came quickly since he was a fast learner, but more important he was already familiar with the basic tenets of the language, having learned them necessarily when as a mortal he needed to communicate with his ancestors, though he did need practice [he had refused to talk to anyone or any of the other moʻo when he first arrived on the scene] to be able to manipulate the complexities of this, his only means of communication), Gabriel was all ears. Gabriel and Kopa rekindled a relationship that was marked with the openness and aloha that had distinguished their uncompetitive, unjealous, uncontrived, and timeless boyhood years. In the span of one human day, they compressed the love and understanding that should have been theirs during that long period when both held animosity to one another. (Though Gabriel would deny that he had a feud with his brother, everyone, including Gabriel's inner soul, knew he was a damn liar.)

Gabriel and Kopa at long last were united in blood and soul; their hearts now understood how to weep and rejoice as one. And Gabriel did not stop the relationship from spreading. In fact, he actively shared this new experience with Mary and Harriet, for he believed—and Kopa did, too—in the importance of sharing the love of loved ones with other loved ones.

Their isolation, then, became a blessing, since they were not distracted by diversions of the community. Even the cows were included: They'd eat their fill (the pasture was on higher ground and not affected by encroachment of the lake), then leave through the now unfastened gate and wade through the belly-deep water to the front of the house, where they'd spend their time learning, too, this language of isolation.

Thirty-Six

THE BODIES OF Gabriel Hoʻokano, Mary Wahineokaimalino, and Harriet O'Casey were discovered in the Hoʻokano house seven days after the heavy rains had cut them off
from the rest of the community. Six days after the heavy
rains began—on a Tuesday morning, a day before Harrison
Kila (who was Gabriel's grand-nephew and Harriet's third
cousin, though Harry always called her Auntie Harriet, out
of respect) had waded through the lake and broke through a
dam of newspaper pulp and found Gabriel, Mary, and Harriet sitting stonestill out on the front porch, looking at one
another with their faces frozen in laughter, Patrick O'Sulli-
van, Harriet's oldest son, called from his downtown office to
inquire about her well-being. (Later the next day, Harry to
Henry Kila over beers at Rusty's: "I tell you, cuz, already
when I started wading in that water I was feeling kind of
funny kine. Dah watah was so still . . . too still. Was heavy,
dah watah. And nevah had one small breeze or nothing. But
funny, yeah, dis funny kine smell I wen smell. Yeah, cuz, I
going tell you dis 'cause you my cousin and we close. You
know, had dis funny kine smell all ovah da damn place. You
going think I crazy telling you dis, but wen smell like one
Kona wind. I no shit you . . .What? What dat smell like? Eh,
no ask me. I dunno. But das all I could think about when I
wen smell dat strange smell . . . Yeah, one Kona wind. Was dis
warm, heavy, kinda touchy smell, one smell that come right
up to you and cling on you and no let go. Was real *freaky*. I no
shit you. Den I wen come up to the front porch, I wen call for
Uncle Gabe and Auntie Malia and Auntie Harriet 'cause I seen

dem far kine, but was strange 'cause I could see dem laughing but couldn't hear dem laugh . . . No, was quiet like one grave-yard. But still I never think anything was wrong 'til I started climbing up da porch steps and I saw Uncle Gabe. My heart wen stop. Ho—my skin was crawling. He was laughing like hell, jus' like somebody wen throw out one good joke. Only thing, his face was frozen . . . Yeah, I no shit you. And I seen Auntie Malia, she was sitting on the rattan couch and laugh-ing up too, but her face was frozen too. Ho—dah skin on dah back of my neck was crawling. My eyes was popping. Ho . . . I was never so spooked in my life! Worse den da time I had to check out da Humphrey house . . . Yeah, da Humphrey house. You remember, eh? . . . At least dem guys' faces was all regu-lar, dey wasn't laughing or anything like that, dey was jus' staring at da frickin' TV. But Uncle dem—ho!—I was spooked. Plus dat, das our uncle and aunties. Was jus' like dey laugh-ing up, like dey was in one wax museum or something like dat . . . But at least I can say one thing about all dis. At least dey looked like dey was having one good time wen dey all-of-a-sudden . . . went. At least dey wen get one good last laugh. Whatevah was about.") Patrick was leaning back in his chair, looking out the large window that looked over a section of downtown Honolulu. The sun was shining brightly, which had been the norm for most of the week. As the phone on the other side rang (there was a lot of static on the line, he knew it had to do with the heavy rains that Kānewai was having) and as he watched men and women in their colorful aloha apparel (is it a Friday?) walk up and down the sidewalks below, it dawned on him that he was immensely fortunate to be living in Hawai'i and to be able to consider the islands as his roots. It was such a unique and unusual place, where it could be pouring on one side of the island and just a few miles away it'd be as sunny as an average summer's day, a place where the peoples of the Pacific lived in harmony with one another as reflected by the symbol of a rainbow.

Gabriel answered the phone.

"Hi, Uncle Gabe. This is Patrick."

"Who?"

"Patrick. Harriet's son. Her oldest son."

"Who dat? Who you talking about?"

"Harriet. Your cousin. My mom . . . isn't she staying with you?"

"Mary? Harriet? Oh . . . Harriet. Patrick?"

"Yes, I'm Patrick." Patrick laughed to himself. "And so, how are you, Uncle Gabe?"

"Oh, I fine."

"How's the weather in Kānewai?"

"You wanna speak to yo' mother?"

"Yes, if I can. How's the weather like?"

"What you rather do? You no wanna speak to her?"

"No—no. I want to speak to her. But I'm just asking about the weather. Is it still raining?"

"Yeah—yeah. Wet. Plenny rain. Jus' like the Akua trying flood us out, house, stock, and marrow." Laughter.

Patrick laughed to himself at his uncle's bungling of the idiom. "Can I speak to my mother, please."

"Yeah—yeah. Wait a minute."

"Thanks, Uncle Gabe."

The receiver on the other end dropped on a hard surface. In the background Patrick heard Gabriel calling for Harriet, then an answer from Mary in a language he could not understand. They're speaking in Hawaiian, Patrick thought. He smiled, guardedly. And when he heard Harriet's voice surface from Gabriel's and Mary's and from the humdrumming of the heavy rains outside, Patrick had a sudden urge to see his mother.

Earlier in the morning, before coming to work, he had studied his thinning scalp in the bathroom mirror, parting his hair in several places and noting the many hairs that had turned white. And now, listening to his mother's distant voice, he realized her mortality. He needed to see her, immediately. When she answered the phone, he asked to visit her but was promptly turned down, Harriet stating that it was too wet out and that it would be better to wait until the rains stopped. Patrick argued that he had to see her that night.

Touched by her son's fondness, Harriet laughed and repeated her reason. "But I tell you what," she added, "why don't you come by and take me and Uncle Gabe and Auntie Malia out somewhere eat, after we pau talking our stories." Patrick asked what time that would be. "After the stories are all told out," she added, "after our blood has gotten thicker together."

Now, more than anything, he found it necessary to see her. "I'm not taking a 'no' for an answer," he said.

Harriet laughed. "Then how about Wednesday, after the rains have finished their work. I'll be ready. We'll all be ready."

It was Harriet's compromising tone that made Patrick accept her proposal, though he had an inscrutable feeling of uncertainty.

After hanging up, Patrick stared out his window, his eyes filmed with a glossy gloom. Then he touch-toned another number. His ex-wife answered, and he asked her about their eleven-year-old daughter, who was at school. After talking about her grades and the scope of her extracurricular activities (she was involved in the Chess Club, soccer, and the Future Physicists of America), he asked his ex-wife to remarry him. Surprised, Monica turned down his proposal. Then he asked her if it would be all right to spend the night over, and he was again refused, this time in a voice as flat as missionary history.

"I need to talk to someone," he pleaded. "I need to talk to you."

There was a silence on the line that stretched for a mile. Then followed a dry "All right." A whispered "Goodbye." A click.

Slowly, Patrick set the receiver on the base. He gazed out the window, the adjacent sunlit buildings now a mixing of blurred colors and forms.

Thirty-Seven

AT 3:17 A.M., a workday morning, an earthquake tremored through Kānewai. It wasn't an unusually large quake—3.9 on the Richter scale—but it was enough to waken half of the residents of Kānewai. For most of the residents, the tremor itself was not the cause of disruption; those who could never be shaken from sleep short of a *major* natural calamity were awakened by a flooding of calls originating from no one. The jolt had knocked down a termite-ridden utility pole that had collapsed on a telephone substation, knocking out the lone technician for approximately thirteen minutes while short-circuiting the computer, which began randomly calling nearly every other household in the area.

One resident who was stirred by the quake was George Hayashida. In fact, anything moving in the night air would have done so, including a lethargic mosquito. Since Joyce's stroke, which had atrophied the left side of her body, George had become attentive to all of her needs and whims to a point that Joyce became bothered by this excessive vigilance. Even Joyce had recently made a mental comment that she didn't think it was possible for her to feel this way, given the fact that George had never given her any attention whatsoever before the stroke.

Another resident who was shaken by the quake was Val Rodriguez. He had just gotten out of the shower after coming home from his night job as a bouncer at a Waikīkī night club when he felt the beginning hints of the tremor. Stumbling into the bedroom while struggling to put on a pair of shorts, he aroused his wife, gathered baby Sunshine in the unbreakable cage of his gigantic arms, then plowed through the house, his thick shoulder crunching the door jamb that joined the short hallway to the living room (as a result, getting bumped on the head by a collapsing transverse) and bursting through the front door into the cool early morning air, with Laverne close behind. Then he turned to his wife and apologized, "Babes, I think I forgot Sunshine's blanket." Sunshine slept on, blanket or no blanket, not missing a beat of rhythmic deep sleep.

Despite the damages to the community, which were mostly induced not by the earthquake itself (except for the impairment of the telephone substation) but by the reaction of the residents, the earthquake was considered but a minor, passing subject of morning breakfast talk before the town went on about its usual business. An earthquake was just not a rare phenomenon in Kānewai. Like the one just experienced, the earthquakes were usually small and thus seldom felt; to solicit any sustaining amount of interest, an earthquake needed to be one of a large scale.

What were on the minds of the people of Kānewai, however, were the bizarre deaths of Gabriel Hoʻokano, Mary Wahineokaimalino, and Harriet O'Casey, the newest additions to the plague of deaths haunting Kānewai.

Some people were now talking about leaving the town for good, pulling up stakes when the stakes were actually intransigent roots of centuries standing. Some people were coming up with hard questions, like "Why is the town all of a sudden being destroyed?" and "What's causing all of this?" and "Who started all of this?" and "Who was the one who made the Akua angry at us?" Everyone had questions, and no one had answers.

Except one person.

———————

KALANI HUMPHREY WAS the only person who had some idea about what the hell was going on and was aware that it was his destiny to prevent Kānewai from degenerating into a modern ghost town. The only problem was that he didn't know what exactly he needed to do to save Kānewai, though what he was doing every night while Matilda Nunes was working at Breezy's—he was guided by instinct and profused with energy by the spirit of his genes—was actually working toward solving the problem.

For months while in prison, Kalani Humphrey had a recurring dream that, in the wee hours of the early morning, would wake him up mouthing a string of Hawaiian words. He never knew ka ʻōlelo Hawaiʻi, so when he'd completely waken to consciousness, his discourse would stop; he'd stare into the darkness of his cell in bewilderment, wondering what the hell had he been talking about. One day, when his cellblock was being fumigated, he was temporarily placed with another inmate, an older Hawaiian man who never talked to anyone. The first night in the old man's cell he dreamed that dream again and woke up speaking the words of a warrior. The old man, sensing that Kalani was awake, cozied up to him and whispered in his ear. Kalani shoved the old man to the floor, thinking that the old man was making a homosexual advance: "Get the fuck away from me, you fricking māhū!"

"Eh boy, take it easy. I not like dat. I jus' like know how you know."

"What? Get dah fuck away from me, you fuckin' queer."

The old man went back to his bunk, lay back on his pillow, and rubbed the soreness of his shoulder from the fall.

"Eh boy, you know. I like know how you know."

"I dunno what the fuck you talking about, old man. Shaddup already."

The old man began speaking to him in Hawaiian. Kalani told him to shut up again.

Swinging his legs to the side of the bed, the old man stomped the hard concrete floor. "No shit wit' me, boy! I heard you talking right now! Talk!"

"Ah shaddup, you old fut, befo' I smack yo' fuckin' head!"

They didn't talk to one another for the rest of the day. But that night, after the eight o'clock head count, the old man spoke to him again.

"Eh boy, you know something? You was talking to da spirits of my dead family last night."

Kalani belched loudly and turned his back to him.

The old man continued. "What you talking about when you moe, what you saying when you moe . . . means you know."

Crazy old man. "Leave me alone, you fucking old fut."

"Eh, I know," the old man said, sitting up. "*You* know. And dis makes me happy. Dat you know. You wait. When kamakani come right in dis cell, you going know what I mean. You wait. You going find out when kamakani come inside here, talk to you."

The old man reached across the cell and placed his hand on Kalani's head.

Kalani sprang up, shoving the old man back. "Fuckin' old man! Get yo' fuckin' hand off me! Fuckin' faggot! Fuckin' māhū!"

The old man lay back on his bed. Kalani stooped over him, ready to pounce on him. Tears were flowing from the old man's eyes.

"Boy, I going tell you som't'ing . . . and only you going unnerstand. Kamakani stay talking to me, say fire going come fo' take som't'ing. Might be long time befo' fire ask dis, but when fire ask, fire gotta take som't'ing."

"What dah fuck you talkin' 'bout, old man?"

The old man continued, "I say wen fire gotta take som't'ing, gotta take. If you unnerstand dis, you geev yo'self up, can save plenny people. Dah fire like yo' fuel."

"What? Eh . . . go fuck off, old man." Kalani returned to his mattress, turning his back to him but strangely glad that he didn't hurt him. "Fuckin' old man, no bothah me."

The old man released a long breath, then said two words that grabbed Kalani's throat, paralyzing him for a long moment: "Pono keʻahi." (Translation: "Fire makes clean."

They were the exact words of the warrior in Kalani's recurring dream.)

The old man turned toward the wall and in a few minutes was softly snoring.

————

AT THE 6:00 A.M. wakeup, the guards discovered that the old man had died in his sleep. The medical examiner would later declare his death by natural causes. Kalani would never forget the old man's face before they covered the body and wheeled him out of the cell. On it was captured the most serene human expression that he had ever seen.

Thirty-Eight

IT WAS NOW or never.

Kalani Humphrey sat on the edge of the couch in Matilda's living room. He could hear the music from her clock-radio. Mantovani? Mancini? Kalani couldn't figure out who was playing. But it was the kind of music that he hated, the kind of music he associated with his stepparents. Every morning in his childhood he had wakened to the serenading strings of the FM mood music channel played in the bathroom where his stepfather was shaving. And in the kitchen, too, while his stepmother prepared breakfast. The same station. He had asked his mother a number of times if she could change the station (he'd never ask his father), but always the answer was "No." Then one morning, he said something wild about the music. His mother made an ugly face and scolded him. His father poked his head into the kitchen and, thinking that Kalani had swore at her, struck him on the side of the face. Kalani flew off the chair, striking his head on the oven door. Mother Humphrey pleaded with Father Humphrey not to take the belt from his pants. "But that's too bad, isn't it?" Father Humphrey answered. "Perhaps next time he should watch what he says in this house." Father Humphrey withdrew the belt deliberately, absorbing with a warped excitement the fear showing in Kalani's eyes, and despite the cries of mercy and apology from his son, proceeded to lash at the cowering eleven-year-old. Alas! Father Humphrey would not waste any of his strokes. Always methodical, the good father used the buckle-end to strike his son for the first three times to make him really feel the wrath of discipline. Of course, as Kalani grew older and even with the count of three buckled strikes rising to five, then seven, Mr. Humphrey was incapable of inflicting any pain on Kalani. That was around the time when Kalani used to skip breakfasts at home and went instead to the bakery where he began his strange but amicable relationship with Matilda Nunes. Funny how the person whom he now trusted the most listened to the same kind of music enjoyed by the people he most detested.

Kalani rubbed his hands in the darkness, stopped when he felt the warmth absorbed by his fingers. Tossing his head back as if to rid the ghostly dust of memory of his many-times forgotten parents, he rose quietly from the otherwise squeaky couch and went to Matilda's bedroom, stopping at the door. He breathed the sweet, warm air of the room, then padded toward her bed and stopped a few feet from her, watching her sleep with her mouth open, noting the rhythmic discord between the music and her deep breathing. (Despite the darkness, he saw her face clearly, an ability of his that had evolved while in prison.) He reached over to the clock-radio, pressed the buttons until he got the right one that turned the music off. At once, Matilda's breathing was interrupted. She stirred, squirming one way, then another, finally turning to her side and facing Kalani while slipping a hand under the pillow to give it more support. Then she entered another phase of deep sleep.

He left the room. He washed his face, then went into the kitchen and finished what was left of a carton of milk.

Outside, he listened until there was a change in the wind's sound and direction (the rustling of mango leaves, the smell of a stagnant sea). And while the new wind gave him another portent, another vision of the catastrophe that was about to erupt and take with it all the living of Kānewai, Kalani took in a deep breath, as if readying himself to enter a crucial moment of a ball game. He ran up the zipper of his sweat jacket, its nylon teeth lubricated with the steam off his fingers, until it touched the tip of his throat. Then he ran off into the dark night, fighting off false pleasantries promised by demons who were now oozing out in droves from dark hiding places of the trees.

———————

THE HIGHEST NATURAL point in Kānewai and vicinity was Wailana Falls, where mountain waters rushed over a jagged stone lip and crashed down a 457-foot drop to a mist-covered pool.

It was the first time Kalani had ever been to the top of the Falls. He had swum in the pool at the bottom or hung out in the parking lot where often he had taken Kānewai's maidens smitten by his quiet masculinity. (At last count, though nobody was counting—or rather, no one wanted to count—Kalani was responsible for approximately 2.37 percent of the live births in Kānewai over the past three years, or the equivalent of seven babies: three boys and four girls.)

At the top of the Falls he carefully waded across a small basin of water to the edge where a cold wind blowing up the Falls was forcing up a fine mist, while another wind from behind him was pushing it down. They were like two disparate spirits locked in battle, and the symbolism was not beyond him: The contentious winds were like his contentious parents, always at odds with him or with each other, always at odds with the world of Kānewai, which they thought as a locale rather low in social status for their inherited airs (after all, Father Humphrey was a Williams graduate, and Mother Humphrey had been an adjunct professor in English literature at Mills College). And though they thought they had done a civil good deed that was beneath them by adopting the half-breed newborn, they were instead snubbed by almost every citizen of the community who described them as "think-they-know-it-all" and "think-they-bettah den-us." With the exception of Claudio Yoon who, from afar and without formally being introduced to the Humphrey couple, admired the Mr. and Mrs. for what he truly believed to be their sincerity and generosity. Kalani nodded his head, thinking that it was good that they had died at the same time and in the way they had died, locked together in a biting embrace that would take them an eternity to unravel. Good for them, those suckers, he thought. Then aloud, though drowned by the roar of the falls: "Good fo' dem, dose motherfucking suckers!"

————————

To reach the state of vision beyond plain seeing, when one can be best suited to encounter a life-death situation (like the one shortly to face Kānewai), one must eat the stomach of the red ʻōpae. This was told to Kalani in the dream by the smallest warrior who, if traced cosmically, was the old prisoner's long-lost kin, though, of course, Kalani didn't know about that. And he also wasn't sure whether he was to eat the *stomach* of the ʻōpaeʻula or a stomach*ful* of them. So to cover himself, he did both. He found the ʻōpae in the brackish stream under the bridge that connected Kānewai and Waiola. When he was about ten, the stream used to be thriving with red shrimp (in fact, the beach nearby was called Waiʻula since in the old days the river used to be filled with so much of this ʻōpae that the water was red like blood); now, he had to go halfway up the mountain before he could catch enough to fill two inches of his five-gallon Wesson Oil can. Having eaten the shrimp, he was told in a subsequent dream of the necessity to test his soul in a life-threatening situation, a situation that, once entered, offered no chance of turning back; and survival from it could only be had by luck. "And make sure you know the time the thing occurs," he reminded himself, translating into English what the warrior in his dream had told him. Why he needed to know the time he could not comprehend, but it was something, he felt deeply, that was beyond questioning.

That he feared heights was a determining factor why he chose to climb the Falls. Perhaps it stemmed from the time when his parents had taken him on an outing to the ten-story Aloha Tower—at the time, the tallest building in Honolulu— that overlooked the city's busy harbor. (Yes, that could have been it. He was about six years old. It was neat climbing those stairs all the way to the top. But at the top, his father frightened him. Grabbing him around the chest. Holding him against the guard rail. Looking at the harbor. Saying, "You can see the whole city from here." Saying, "I wanna go down!" Saying, "Don't you like it up here? Isn't this exciting?" Saying, "No! I wanna go down! Mama!" Saying, "Goddamn mixed-blood kid! We come all the way up here and he tells us this." Saying, "I wanna go down! Mama!" Saying, "Put him down, dear. The child's terrified." Saying, "Oh, so you're terrified, huh? Well, why didn't you tell us that before we came up here, goddamn kid!" Crying, "I wanna go home! Mama!" Saying, "Please, Perry! Put the child down!" Saying, "You're going to make our climb up here worthwhile. You hear? Let's have a better look at the city." Lifting him higher. Sitting him on the top of the guard rail. Legs dangling in the air. Body shaking. Crying. Dying. Flying.)

"Goddamn asses! I kill you!" Kalani swung at the two wind spirits.

There was a rumbling, and the surface of the stream began to shatter like disintegrating glass.

Then slipping. Splashing. Scrambling. Arms flailing. Falling.

Despite the panic and a scream that was held lingering at the top, Kalani remembered the importance of knowing what the exact time was. But the tumbling motion confused his equilibrium, preventing him from looking at his watch.

About a hundred feet from the bottom, his fall stabilized. Face up, through the mist he saw the vague glow of the moon (there was no moon that night). Then, a few feet before landing in shallow water that hid a clump of rocks, time came to him, emblazoned above him in bold DeVille lettering.

12:37.

He was turning a smile when he hit bottom.

Thirty-Nine

AT I 2:37 A.M. on September 14, 198_, the North Pacific Center of Seismology and Tsunami Warning, based at ————, Hawaiʻi, recorded an earthquake with a magnitude of 5.9 on the Richter scale. The epicenter of the quake was located sixteen miles due east of the Center, in Kānewai. Though the magnitude was not severe, personnel at the Center were concerned since Kānewai was a moderately populated area, and that secondary repercussions of the earthquake—power outages, broken water mains, and corresponding anxiety and fear among the population—would be possible agents of detrimental effects.

What the earthquake did was to sever the power and communication lines into Kānewai for approximately forty-eight hours. The water main was also damaged, and the people of Kānewai had to get their water from nearby streams and boil it for sanitary reasons. A few homes were partly destroyed, such as the Kahalewai's car port, which had collapsed completely (it was fortuitous that their 1979 Chevy pickup was, at the time, being borrowed by their son-in-law), and also the picture window of the Goto's home was cracked, and so on for about a dozen houses in the town. But most notable was the damage done to the theater. The entire building was destroyed, leveled to the ground—with the exception of a large triangular-shaped section of the celebrated wall, which stood defiantly as if it were a crumbling memorial to the destruction.

But another funny thing happened. Overnight, two names appeared on the wall: David Fonseca and Kalani Humphrey. And though this raised eyebrows throughout the community, no one was concerned, probably for the reason that everyone was helping each other sort out the mess that the earthquake had created, there being no time and energy for anyone to be bothered by another action of a sick prankster. People were cooking outdoors on charcoal or propane grills, and cooking more than their family could eat; sharing food and other amenities was becoming more and more the rule in those days of discomfort.

And something else happened. More names began to appear on the wall. At first there were three names, then ten more were mysteriously added, until, finally, fifty-seven names glistened in white enamel paint, the names of all those who had contributed, at one time or another, to the making of this wall of slander. But no one seemed to care, for no one wanted to spend another minute thinking—or being bothered—by any sign, slanderous, juicy, or whatever.

One week after the earthquake, a small tremor rolled through Kānewai. With the exception of raised heartbeats, no real damage was done, though it was enough movement to shift the foundation of the remnant wall and thus bringing the theater now completely to the ground. But by this time, though everyone knew about this final falling, not much attention was paid to the theater and its circumstances. The residents of the community were too involved in the process of healing the community from the after effects of the earthquakes. (Although the first earthquake had created a minimum of damage to Kānewai, the situation became a needed focal point for the energies of the residents.) But it was also incumbent in the minds of all that the deepest sense of appreciation and thanksgiving was felt—and done very silently so —for David Fonseca, as his actions at the theater were interpreted as proceedings of a true savior. (In addition, we in-the-know might also interpret Kalani Humphrey's contribution as heroically saving of Kānewai from falling into a cosmic or perhaps criminal demise.)

And so it was in Kānewai . . . at least for this moment's snapshot in time. And so it was.

Forty

GABRIEL BEGAN THE morning with his revised daily routine: picking up the newspaper, tossing it on the old rattan chair for Mary, packaging the daily dog shit in the folds of yesterday's newspaper, washing his hands at the side of the house, sitting in his chair and rocking, then starting his daily list of complaints to himself interspersed, as always, with his good observations of the weather, the air, the surroundings (like, "The grass so green 'cause last night's rain"), though now pausing after the fourth complaint and making a slight adjustment in the next grievance: "I wonder when dose buggahs going bring back dat piece of ugly junk they wen dump befo' ovah here."

Gabriel perked up in his chair, his neck stretched like that of a curious turtle, then returned to his deliberate, steady rocking, the chair and the termite-eaten floor boards creaking in a kind of discordant unity, though now there was—given by Gabriel's perceptive hearing—another discolored note added to the disharmony, from a loose joint in the chair. For the next fifteen minutes, he stared straight ahead at that patch of growth-enraged grass, which seemed to be rebelling against its brother and sister clumps for being so color-deficient those long months turned to years.

Mary joined him, having finished her morning chores in the kitchen, and sat with her usual pleasant air on her chair, giving her customary thanks to Gabriel for getting her the newspaper. She took the rubber band off the newspaper, dropped it in the collection of other rubber bands in the mayonnaise jar at the foot of her chair, then unfolded the newspaper and began reading. Gabriel studied her face to see if there was an expression of discomfort or anguish. He found none. Everything was the usual, it seemed, for Mary.

Gabriel's eyes returned to the boisterously colored patch of grass. He belched without excusing himself and said, "Dis weather no like change. Going be one nada hot day."

Lowering the newspaper, Mary said, "Oh my, Gabriel Hoʻokano. Must we make excuses for ourselves someday?"

"Huh?"

Mary returned to her perusal of the newspaper.

"And since when you start talking like my cousin? Ho . . . I dunno 'bout dat Harriet."

"Gabe, we gonna make some change sometime, no?"

"You . . . what?"

Mary didn't answer him.

"You . . . what?" There was a noted drop in the authority of his question.

Gabriel returned to the patch of grass.

"Kuʻuipo, what kind sales get today?"

"What was that again?"

"Sales. You like I take you and Georgette to dah market today?"

"No, not today. But how 'bout you take us—Georgette, Harriet, and me—to dah movies?"

"Dah what?"

"Dah movies. Isn't dis one good idea? We go holoholo town and catch one movie."

Gabriel confusedly scratched his head. "Wen rain last night," he offered. "I heard. About three, four o'clock dis morning."

"Yeah, but das last night. But speaking of heard, you know what I heard?"

"What you heard?"

"I heard get one good movie at dah Princess. Harriet tol' me. You can geev us one ride there? Get one matinee at 12 noon."

No answer.

Mary lowered the newspaper. "You know what I heard? I heard Joyce Hayashida doing good. She still no can talk too good. Georgette tol' me on the phone dis morning. And she so young. But I heard she doing good. But we go holoholo today. Okay? I go call Georgette and Harriet. If you get ready now, we get plenny time fo' make dah matinee."

Mary got up and entered the house.

"I not talking about that," Gabriel said. "I talking about wen dat somebody going bring back dah car."

"Gabe, com'on," Mary said sweetly from inside the house. "We go get ready now so get plenny time pick up dah girls and get to town."

Gabriel lowered his eyes, his face showing exhaustion, as if he were blowing up an enormous balloon and had run out of wind halfway there. He looked up, his eyes focusing somewhere above and beyond the fuzzy tips of the buffalo grass across the way. "Why they nevah at least tell me they was going move 'em," he lamented.

Then he rose from his chair and entered the house.

"Ku'uipo," he said, "wait fo' me. I coming."

And from deep within the house, "I always waiting fo' you, Gabe. Always. But hurry up. 'Cause we no like keep Harriet and Georgette waiting . . . not fo' dah rest of our lives."

THE END

About the Author

GARY PAK teaches creative writing at the University of Hawaiʻi at Mānoa. He is the author of two books, *The Watcher of Waipuna* and *A Ricepaper Airplane*. He is also the author of *Beyond the Falls,* a children's play that was produced by the Honolulu Theatre for Youth in 2001. In 2002, he was a Fulbright Senior Scholar at Korea University, Seoul.

Production Notes for *Pak / Children of a Fireland*

Cover and interior designed by Trina Stahl
in New Aster with display type in Trixie

Composition by Josie Herr

Printing by Versa Press

Printed on 60# Glat. Writer's Book, 360 ppi